DRAGON'S ROSE

A GRYM HOLLOW NOVEL

TATI B. ALVAREZ

ISBN:

E-book: 979-8-9893168-1-6

Paperback: 979-8-9893168-2-3

Edited By: Shelby Goodwin and On the Same Page Editing

Cover Designer: Coffin Print Designs

For those who aren't sick of fairy tales yet.

AUTHOR'S NOTE

This book contains elements of:

- Death of a loved one (off page)
- Explicit sexual scenes
- Cheating (off page and not by the MCs)
- Violence
- Strained sibling relationship
- Difficult childbirth (off page)
- Torture against FMC
- Magical induced comas
- Fantasy war

Please make sure you are protecting your mental health. If you need more information send me a message on any of my socials. Otherwise, happy reading!

Kraken
Lagoon
Nephilim
Land
Dragon's
Keep

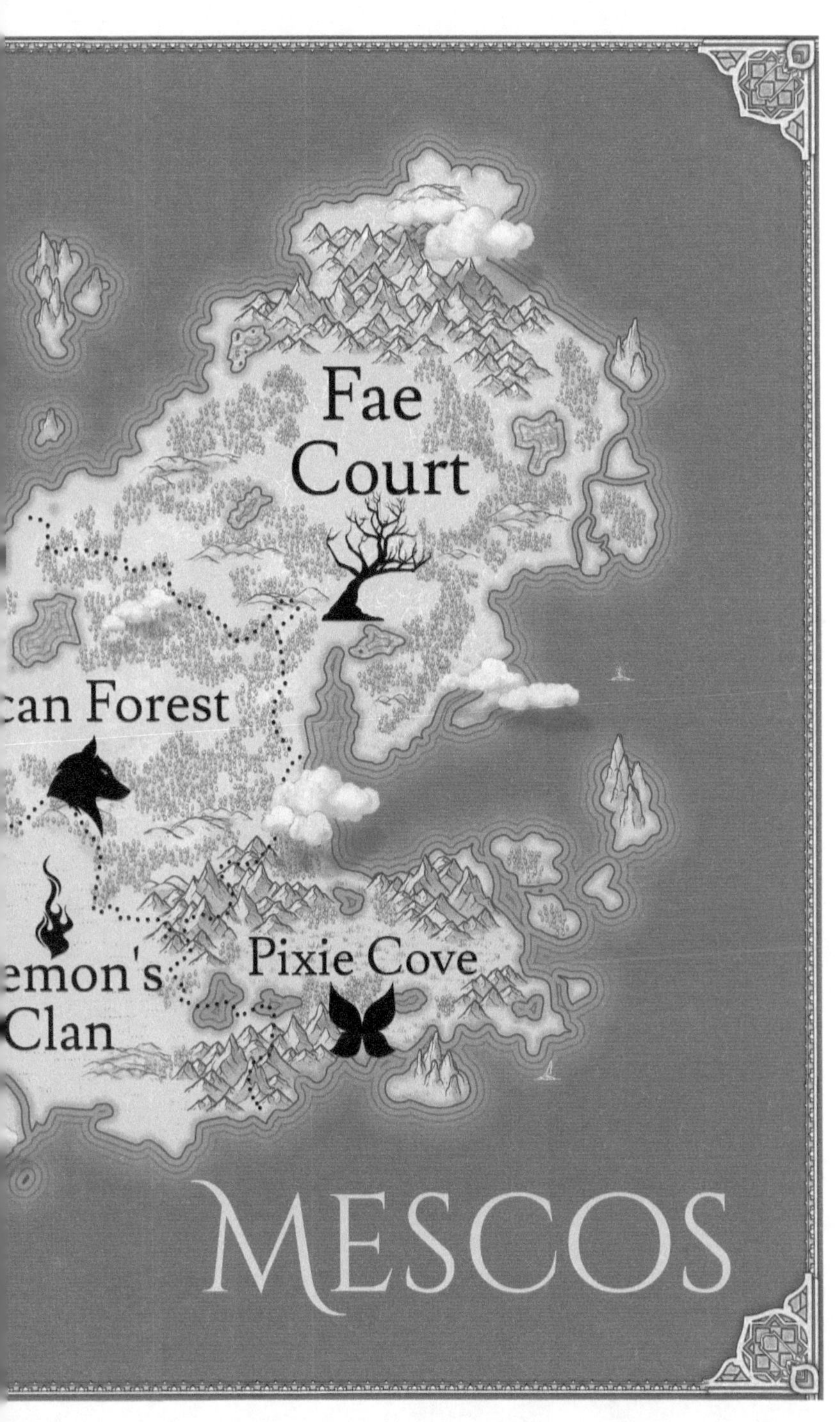

Fae
Court
...can Forest
...emon's
Clan
Pixie Cove
MESCOS

CHAPTER 1
ROSE

I've never held a baby before.

Actually, I guess that's not entirely true. I probably held my sister when she was born, with the help of my parents, but that was a lifetime ago. Now, I'm holding a swaddled little human, with the biggest brown eyes I've ever seen.

The same beautiful eyes as her father.

I once loved them. They brought me peace after my parents died and looked upon me with empathy as I told him my fears of being my sister's only living relative. I swore I could look into his eyes and see a future.

Now, all I see is pain.

The baby—she hasn't been named yet, and I'm not going to come up with one—begins to cry. A nurse rushes to my side, taking her from me. I don't put up a fight. She needs to be with someone nurturing, and that's not me. It's the woman in the hospital bed next to us.

Or it would be, if she were conscious.

"Ms. Briar, your sister..." The nurse calls after me, but I'm already heading out the front door.

"Will be fine. I'll see to it," I call over my shoulder, digging through my purse to locate my phone. It's all the way at the bottom. Typical.

There's no taxi service or fancy rideshares in Grym Hollow. No, instead, we have Sister Tammy, our resident nun by day and driving service by night. Don't ask me if that's allowed or proper in her religion; I don't fucking know. All I know is that I need a ride, and Sister Tammy is the fastest old lady in town.

I quickly type out a short text.

> Need ride stat. At Hollow Hospital.

Hospital is a stretch. Really, it's the size of a single-family home and houses the only doctor in town. He's a curmudgeon, but he's damn good at what he does.

Except, not even Dr. Stein can help my sister. No one can. No one but me.

"Rose, where the hell are you going?" a familiar voice shouts behind me.

I hold back the groan threatening to leave my lips as I turn to face him. The man I once loved.

Stefan isn't looking great these days. He's still as handsome as ever, with his perfectly sculpted jawline and symmetrical square-shaped face. But now there are dark circles under his eyes that were never there before. I also don't know when he last washed his hair. It's lying flat and lifeless against his head, begging for someone to run shampoo-covered fingers through it.

I would have once. Until he betrayed me.

To be fair, he didn't act alone. But my anger for him is easier to manage than the mixed feelings of betrayal, anger, and helplessness I feel toward my sister.

"Amelia is dying, and you're just standing out here on your phone?"

"And you're standing out here talking to me." Since we are apparently just stating observations now.

I see anger flash in his eyes, but it's misplaced. He should feel angry, just not at me.

"So what? You're just going to let her die alone? Leave me alone with a baby to raise by myself? A child needs their mother!"

If he wanted me to be the mother of his child, he wouldn't have slept with my sister, but here we are.

He's so close to me now, and I do everything I can to not punch him right in that perfectly straight nose of his. A broken nose would probably only make him more attractive, and I definitely don't want to help him in any way.

With the patience of a saint, I say, "If you would let me go, I can help."

"Help by running away? Yeah, fuck that. You always run when things get too hard. You ran away when your parents died; you ran away when our relationship got tough—"

"When you cheated on me with my sister, you mean?" I ask, deadpan.

"—and you're leaving now." He speaks over me, too self-absorbed in his own spiel. "Listen, I know things didn't end well with us, but if you've ever loved your sis—"

And that's where I stop him. I don't know what comes over me, but all I see is red. One moment, I'm a few feet away from him, and then next—on its own volition—my fist is colliding with his stupid face.

He staggers back, hitting the door. If I wasn't so angry, I might actually find satisfaction in the look of pure shock on his face.

Yeah, hurts to be kicked while you're down, doesn't it, buddy?

"Rose..."

Flashing headlights behind me, illuminating the scene, tell me Sister Tammy is here. We're out of time.

I'm out of time.

"I hope your daughter never realizes how much of a dick her father is," I say to Stefan, the last words I'll ever speak to him. Part of me wants to run back in and see Amelia once more, but another part of me knows I'll change my mind if I do.

I guess she'll know that, even after all the shit she's put me through in the last year, I'm still her big sister, and I'll take care of her.

With that sobering thought, I hike my purse up and head to the car.

"Honey, are you sure you won't reconsider? I know you want to save your sister, but this is a one-and-done deal. With the power of prayer—"

"I'm sure. Thank you, Sister Tammy, for driving me here," I interrupt her before she can dive into a lecture about the power of prayer and why I'm making a big mistake. But my mind is made up. It has been for a long time, even before my sister's complications from the birth of my niece.

I want out of this hell hole. Too many memories. None of them good.

I guess, in a way, I'm running away from my problems, like Stefan claims I do, but at least something good will come from it.

"Okay, fine. But we are sure going to miss you around here. Grym Hollow won't be the same without you." Sister Tammy offers me a sad smile, but doesn't attempt to argue with me. I see the way her eyes shift from left to right, waiting for something to jump out from the trees or shadows.

I'm barely out of the car before Sister Tammy is peeling out and heading back toward town. Her tires screech down the winding road, and she's out of sight within seconds, off to do whatever nuns do on a Thursday evening.

I pull my purse closer, using it like a personal shield between me and the man I know very little about. They call him The Guardian. He's unofficially in charge of our town, determining who comes in and who leaves. I've lived in Grym Hollow my entire life, and the only new residents are the ones born here.

People leave, not many, and those who do, never come back.

I signed the contract. My fate is already sealed. I'll be a story the people in town talk about, embellished with whatever lies will gain the gossiper the most listeners. Rose Briar: the brokenhearted woman who was betrayed by her sister and boyfriend of four years. Poor Rose. She just couldn't stand to see their happiness.

I take a minute to gather myself and to take in the house before me. On the outside, nothing appears out of the ordinary. It's a small cottage with a low-pitched gable roof. A covered patio surrounds the front of the house, decorated with plants and a comfortable-looking seating area.

The house looks like it jumped right out of a storybook. Like it belongs to someone's grandma they visit for cookies and milk before reminiscing about the joyful times of their childhood.

I doubt The Guardian has made me baked goods to welcome me to his home.

His oddly normal-looking home.

I make it two steps up the sidewalk before the door to The Guardian's home bursts open. A man—and I use that term very loosely—surveys his surroundings before walking out. He looks so strangely out of place, having to duck his head to leave his own home.

The Guardian doesn't try to pretend he's human, neither in his appearance nor mannerisms. His skin is an ashy-gray color, reminding me of a skipping stone you'd find near a lake. His eyes are golden, and he's wearing loose-fitting jeans and a shirt that does little to hide the muscles underneath.

He also has horns. Like two large, prominent horns on the top of his head, ending in sharp points that look like they could cause serious damage to anyone unfortunate enough to piss him off. And yet I have the urge to reach out and touch them.

"Ms. Briar, you're early. I wasn't expecting you until tomorrow." His tone is curious rather than annoyed. I take that as a good sign.

"Yeah, that was the plan. Unfortunately, my sister took a turn for the worse tonight, and I feared waiting another day would kill her." Despite the anger and resentment I have toward Amelia, she is still my sister. I don't want her dead, and I don't want my niece to grow up without a mother.

The Guardian nods like he understands the problems of mortals, but I doubt he does. "I see. And the contract?"

Of course, the contract. He won't do shit until he sees

my name at the bottom. I quickly rummage through my purse, pulling out a wrinkled packet before handing it to him. "You know, this would have been a lot easier to go through and sign if you sent me an editable PDF."

He ignores my remark, invested in the mound of papers in his hand. I watch his eyes scan them rapidly, searching for something in particular. After a few minutes, The Guardian nods, clearly satisfied.

"Do you understand what it means by signing these papers?" he asks.

"Seems a little late for that," I murmur.

"Ms. Briar—"

"Rose. Just Rose," I interrupt, but he ignores me.

"—do you understand what you just agreed to? I will not take a human who is ignorant to their role in this deal."

I sigh. I'm not an ignorant human like he thinks. Perhaps if I didn't grow up in Grym Hollow, I would be, but I learned long ago that our world is not the only one in existence. It used to scare me as a child, but it just became a fact everyone knew growing up.

"I understand. You will make sure my sister makes a full recovery so she and Stefan can live their fairytale life. And, in exchange, I willingly accept to live in and help my new realm in whatever capacity I can." How I could help is still a mystery, but if The Guardian isn't concerned about that detail, then I'm not going to stress about it either. At least, not right now.

"Failure to uphold your end of the bargain will end in your demise," he says, and I wince.

"You'll pull me from the realm and kill me?" My voice rises an octave.

"I won't need to," he replies cryptically. "The realm will do that for me. And for your sake, as well as the benefit to those you'll live with, I hope that never comes to fruition."

With that fucking depressing thought, I shift awkwardly from foot to foot before he motions me forward. I follow wordlessly, knowing I'm no longer in a position to argue. I'm his, technically.

"Would you like to know where your new home will be?" He leads me past his house.

I frown as I jog to keep up with his long strides. "Yeah, that would be helpful."

"The realm is called Mescos, but you'll specifically be living in Dragon's Keep."

I all but stumble, having to thrust out my arms to catch myself before I face-plant.

I knew I would be living as a human in a supernatural world, but I was thinking of fairies or mermaids. Or something not scary. Not fucking dragons. Because, surely, with a name like Dragon's Keep, the occupants are none other than giant flying lizards.

"I'm going to get eaten alive! Literally." The panic sets in now. My heart beats faster and faster the more I think about it.

Dragons. Deadly, fire-breathing dragons.

"You won't. Dragons don't eat humans," he says like that's common knowledge. "Most of them can take on human bodies. No harm will come to you. You have my word."

"No offense, but I don't know you. Your word means shit to me."

"And yet, you sought me out." He sighs. He has me there. I approached him. Not the other way around.

"Besides," he continues, "you will be under the dragon

king's protection. No one will dare cross him if they know what's best."

We stop abruptly in his backyard, void of trees and grass. Instead, small rocks crunch under our feet, laid out in a large circle. In the center is an archway made of stone; moss and vines cover it in its entirety.

The Guardian steps up and runs a long, sharp nail—talon?—down the edge of the arch. A shimmery white light appears, expanding the entire archway. He steps back and gestures to the white film. "Are you ready?" he asks with more patience than I thought him capable of.

"For what?" I delay the inevitable a little longer.

"To go to your new home." He dusts off a leaf that had floated onto his shoulder. And then, casually, he adds, "And to meet your husband."

My what?!

CHAPTER 2

MALIX

The large wooden table occupying my meeting hall once sat the head of households for ten of the most prestigious families of dragonkind. Today, that number has dwindled to five, including myself. The others remain in a death-like sleep, hidden beneath the castle for their own protection.

More will follow and soon I will be the only one at this table.

A hot gust of air hits my left side. I'm not one to be summoned at will and take my time turning my attention to the dragon nearest me. Aeron is temperamental on a good day, and today isn't a good day. He's outright deadly, but tiptoeing the line the best he can.

I'm the only one who didn't show up to the meeting as my dragon. I walk in my human skin, not because I prefer this version of me, but because it's a power play. Everything I do is a power play. Calculated to ensure the best outcome possible.

The dragons around the table need to know I possess

power in both forms. That I do not fear them and can handle the table without using my dragon.

"If you have something to say, Aeron, say it. I don't wish to be here all day." I have matters to attend to because today *she* arrives.

No one but me knows that yet.

Aeron's voice is gruff, booming inside my head. As a member of my council, we are linked in ways other dragons aren't. *"King Malix, the Nephilim are gaining power at an alarming speed. Without the full council, our very livelihoods are threatened. More and more fall to the curse each day, strengthening the Nephilim. We must—"*

"And what do you propose we do, hmm? What plan do you have to save our people from the sleeping curse? Enlighten us."

I know he has no solution. No one at the tables does, but they certainly like to complain as if they do. If the past year has taught me anything, it is that "prestigious" is a relative term. Most of these dragons have done nothing to earn their spot at my table. Nothing, other than being born into a noble family.

If things ever go back to normal, that is the first change I will enact.

Aeron doesn't like to be interrupted or put on the spot. The anger rolls off of him in waves, but I don't so much as flinch. I wait, ever patiently for his response.

His yellow eyes narrow to slits and he gnashes his teeth at me. *"We need to be actively seeking a solution and not sitting on our asses, letting the curse pick us off one by one."*

"Our people are nervous, sire," a new voice adds to the mix. Vivia is a petite, purple, almost black dragon, extremely swift and cunning. She's one of the only ones at

the table whom I'd want to keep as an advisor. Her feelings toward Aeron mirror my own.

"There has been talk of potentially moving our people to the Demon's Clan. A few have already started to pack their belongings, ready to leave at a moment's notice," Vivia continues.

Demon's Clan. Our closest allies. From what I've heard through my contacts in the demon territory, the Nephilim problem has reached their lands as well. It's still in the early stages, but picking up and moving would put my people in the same precarious situation they are in now.

The council begins to all talk at once. Some favor a mass exodus, while others believe it is best to stay and fight. It's all a pissing contest now. Who can growl the loudest and intimidate the other with their size and teeth.

I let this go on for another few moments before I say, "I have already found a solution to our problem."

The entire room goes silent. Each yellow, cat-like set of eyes stares directly at me, waiting for me to explain myself. I will, but they aren't going to like it. I decide that's not my fucking problem.

"I've spoken with Ender and agreed to his deal."

My proclamation is greeted by more silence. Even Vivia, who typically backs me, is silent, her body tense, as if waiting for a fight. Though I'm not sure if she intends to defend me or sink her claws into my back.

Dragons are private by nature. Asking for outside help does not come easy for us. Even the demons, our closest allies, rarely hear from us because we prefer to stay within our walls. Going to Ender was not an easy decision, but desperation crept in and I'm not as prideful to think I can single-handedly defend my people.

I can't. I need another option.

"You went to The Guardian...why?" Vivia asked, echoing the question on everyone's mind.

Last week, after losing two entire families to the sleeping curse—a total of twelve people—I swallowed my pride and summoned him. He came almost immediately, taking one look at me, surrounded by dozens of sleeping dragons, and nodded.

"I will help you," he said without even hearing what I had to say. Without knowing what my problem was or what he would get out of the exchange.

But that's the thing about Ender—or The Guardian, as he's more commonly referred to—he has this ability to know what is going on everywhere. The guy's old as fuck and I'm sure he's seen it all, but damn, it's intimidating.

My gaze drifts around the room, to the dragons staring back at me. This room is equipped to handle ten fully-grown dragons. The few of us left is a stark reminder of the severity of our problem.

And how it will only get worse.

"I went because there is no other option for us," I say, pushing my chair back so I can stand and walk the large expanse of the room. "I will not stand to see anymore of my people fall. Which one of you is next? Each time we meet, fewer and fewer of you are here to participate."

"But allowing a human here—"

"Has been done in the past," I snap. "For years, dragons with royal blood hunted for their human mates. Finding their human mates made their kingdom stronger, made *us* stronger. When we defeated the Nephilim during the first Great War, we knew we were surviving on borrowed time."

I don't need to rehash the history lesson. Everyone at this table knows it and falls silent. Even Aeron looks somber, which isn't natural for him.

Nearly one hundred years ago, my father, along with the help of the rulers of Mescos, fought the Nephilim, tricking the giant monsters and trapping them within the mountains. The Nephilim leader, Gadreel, made one final curse before my father and the other could seal them away.

With his last bit of magic, Gadreel not only cursed all their bloodlines, but vowed that the Nephilim would return with a vengeance in one hundred years. That our powers wouldn't be enough to hold them back a second time unless we found our mates.

Our human mates.

However, Gadreel's final rebellious act before being entombed in the mountain prison was destroying the portal between our world and the human one. No one has been able to go through since. No one other than Ender.

He remains a mystery to us all.

"Can we trust him?" one of the council members asks, breaking the heavy silence of the room.

"Do we have an option at this point?" I counter, and he remains silent. They all remain silent, because they know I'm right. We have no other option. Our hundred years are coming to an end and if we don't want to be casualties in the upcoming war, then we have no other choice.

"So that's it then. The Guardian will bring over a human for our king to marry and we simply hope they mate? And Ender asks for nothing in return? You can see why I'm skeptical, my king," Aeron says, tone belligerent.

He has a right to be skeptical. *I'm* fucking skeptical and questioning my sanity. But as their king, I can't allow Aeron to speak to me that way in front of the most powerful people in my kingdom.

The stone room heats up, my dragon fire coming to the surface. My eyes flash from green to gold, narrowing at

Aeron. When I speak, my voice is full of command which makes his head dip in subservience.

"The decision has been made. The human is on their way here now. If anyone wants to challenge my decision, do so now. Be warned, I won't be holding back." My dragon nearly breaks through the surface, I feel scales cover my skin, ready to change at a moment's notice.

No one but Aeron and Vivia meet my gaze. Aeron looks ready to rip my throat out, but does nothing except simmer in his own volatile emotions.

"We trust you know what you are doing, sire," Vivia says at last. It's not an agreement, but it's something. I'll take it.

Just then, the door to my meeting room opens and a small dragon the size of a cow flies in. He's still a hatchling and the poor boy looks like he would rather be anywhere other than this room.

"My...King. I..." he stammers, darting his eyes around the room but never meeting anyone's gaze. I can be a patient man when needed, so I wait for the hatchling to continue.

"I was sent to tell you, erm...that the, uh, human *is here."* With his message complete, the hatchling spins around and flies out the way he came.

"Meeting adjourned. I have my mate to meet," I say to the room and leave without looking back.

Mate. What an odd concept. Mate implies love, but in order to fall in love, you need a heart, and mine turned to stone so long ago. She'll simply be my wife.

I brought the human here to save us. But I fear she'll be another casualty of the biggest threat to our kind. And it will be all my fault.

CHAPTER 3
ROSE

I imagine being stretched in every direction and then rolled into a ball feels like this. Crossing through the veil is an experience I don't ever want to repeat. According to The Guardian, I won't have to. Grym Hollow is no longer my home. He's made it abundantly clear that signing the contract would take me out of my world and there would be no undoing it. It hadn't scared me then, but now I'm questioning my sanity.

Especially when I gather my wits and take a look around my new home for the first time. "Holy shit. We're not in Kansas anymore, Toto."

"My name is Ender," The Guardian—Ender, apparently —says from behind me. "And I've been to Kansas. This doesn't remotely resemble that state."

I blink, wondering if he is messing with me, but Ender seems quite serious. So, he's a literal guy. Got it.

But he is right about something. This place doesn't resemble Kansas in the slightest. It doesn't even look like anything in my modern world. I feel like I stepped through my TV into an episode of *Game of Thrones*.

We are standing in the middle of a large hallway with stone walls. Carved into the stone are intricate designs, some resemble a window, while others are simply decorative. The windows look as if they were taken from a cathedral, the beautiful stained glass adorned with images of dragons. The sun hits the glass just right to reflect the reds and blues throughout the room.

I hear movement around the corner and turn just in time to see a shadow approaching. "Stay behind me, Rose." Ender pushes me behind him. The move feels less protective and more out of obligation. I don't question it though. With a nickname like The Guardian, I feel relatively safe he won't let me get hurt.

Probably.

My body stills as the shadow rounds the corner, reaching us. An undignified squeak leaves my lips, alerting the scaly creature in front of me. It's the size of a large farm animal, scales covering its whole body. There are two black horns on top of its head, matching the spikes going down its tail.

"Is that a—"

"Dragon, yes. A child," Ender says and my eyes grow wide. A *child?* The child in question looks like they could use me as an ottoman. If this is a child then...how big are the adults?

"Rayn, it's a pleasure to see you again. You've grown since I've last seen you," Ender says and I can hear the smile in his voice as he speaks. The warmth in his tone contradicts the imposing man standing in front of me. I have a feeling Ender could overpower anyone with the snap of his fingers, but instead, he's fondly...petting the dragon?

If dragons could purr, I'm sure the one in front of us would be doing just that as Ender scratches behind their ear. The way the two look at each other seems like they are sharing a private conversation.

A few moments go by and Ender finally steps away from the young dragon. "He is going to get King Malix." As he says this, the young dragon stretches his wings. Using his back legs, he pushes off the ground, immediately taking flight. The air from his wings sends me stumbling back.

Before I can fall on my ass, Ender's hand shoots out to steady me. "Thanks," I murmur. But then remember I'm mad at him. "Don't think I forgot about this whole husband thing. What the hell? That wasn't part of our deal."

He sighs like he's dealing with a petulant child rather than a full grown adult. "It was, actually. Section 2, fourth bullet point. I thought you said you read it thoroughly?"

"I did...pretty thoroughly," I say indignantly, getting caught in my lie.

"*Pretty* thoroughly is not thoroughly, Ms. Briar. I suggest if you bargain for the life of a loved one again, then you might want to consider reading the entire contract. In exchange for saving your sister, you will marry the dragon king and help him win his war against the Nephilim."

"The what?"

"Nephilim," he repeats as if I should already know what that means.

"Ignoring that for now"—because I fully intended to figure out what a Nephilim is—"how is being married supposed to help win a war?" It made no sense. It was like Ender was purposefully being obtuse.

"Have you ever heard the expression love is the most powerful force in the world? I suspect there lies your answer, Ms. Briar," Ender says dismissively.

There's so much to unload in that statement, so much I want to say, especially about love being the most powerful force. Ender is sadly mistaken if he believes love isn't a fragile thing that can be broken the moment someone's mind changes. But I don't get a chance. New footsteps—decidedly human—echo against the stone flooring. The hairs on the back of my neck stand up as, presumably, my husband-to-be rounds the corner.

I don't know what I was expecting, but it isn't this pussy-tingling man. If he's a dragon, he certainly doesn't look like one now. This man is built like a Viking, with the tattoos to match. He's shirtless, because of course he is, and it gives me a good glimpse of the markings covering his body—intricate patterns and symbols laid out as if telling a story.

I force my gaze away from his chest and peer into those soft olive-green eyes. He's studying me as hard as I'm studying him, but he makes no attempts to greet me. Instead he pulls his attention away from me—with something akin to reluctance in his expression?—to greet Ender.

The men exchange pleasantries and I use this time to take in more of my dragon husband-to-be. I'm a sucker for a man with facial hair, so his closely-cropped beard is doing things to me. Things I most certainly don't want to feel because I've all but sworn off men with pretty faces. From my experience, they tend to hurt you the hardest.

"Malix, this is Rose Briar. I assume you will protect your new wife while she is in your care. I don't need to remind you what will happen if you don't." Ender raises a brow, awaiting his answer.

Malix's eyes narrow slightly. He doesn't seem to be one who appreciates being questioned. "Ms. Briar will be safe." His answer is curt and dismissive. I get the sense that there might be a history between the two, but that's information I'm obviously not privy to.

"What happens if I'm not protected?" I ask because these men aren't going to talk about me as if I'm not in the room—not as long as I can help it. I hate being out of the loop and I feel way out of my depth here.

"You will be," Ender says cryptically, providing no further explanation as to how he knows this. He's doing that shit a lot and the verbal whiplash is getting out of hand.

"Excuse me, but I don't belong to anyone. Contract or no contract." I scowl, not caring that I'm the only human among two powerful and probably ancient supernatural beings.

"Of course, Ms. Briar," Ender says, but in a way that feels like he didn't truly acknowledge what I said. He's infuriatingly confusing.

"I believe that is everything, then—"

"Hardly," Malix interrupts Ender. "You still haven't told me how this marriage will help strengthen our defenses and keep the Nephilim at bay."

"I have though, Your Highness. It's not my fault if you didn't like my answer."

"It's not a matter of *liking*, it's a matter of it not *making any damn sense*." Malix's lips curl back, exposing the shiny white teeth underneath. I'm glad to know I'm not the only one annoyed by Ender. I have at least one thing in common with my husband-to-be.

"I'm afraid I can't say any more." For a second, it almost feels like there's regret in Ender's voice, but then it's gone when he speaks again. "I'll be watching. For what it's worth, I'm rooting for you both."

With those ominous parting words, the same sheer white light appears and Ender steps through. Before he crosses to the other side, he turns back to me and says, "Your sister is in recovery as we speak."

And then he's gone. Leaving me alone with Malix and the knowledge that the last thing I did with my time at Grym Hollow was save my sister.

CHAPTER 4

MALIX

Ender leaves and I'm alone with my human wife for the first time. He called her Rose Briar. A pretty name for a pretty girl. It's clear that she's out of her element, even though she attempts to keep a brave face. Still, I can see through the cracks of her facade.

The way her body is coiled tightly, ready to spring into action the moment the situation calls for it, proves her discomfort.

Her flitting eyes scan the room for any signs of a threat.

I think I like her. She at least has some sense of self-preservation, and that will get her far in this realm. Not that anyone would dare touch her. Touching her is a direct violation against me—nobody dares risk my wrath. Especially now. No, my human wife will be safe, as long as she remains by my side.

Now that she's here, I don't know what to do with her. I've had many romantic partners in the past, but never a wife. I'm not deluding myself that this marriage is anything other than a necessity to save my kingdom, but it will still be a marriage—once the proper paperwork is signed.

Nothing screams romance like legal documents and political bargains.

It's a good reminder for us, though. Neither of us can afford to delude ourselves into something more, not when my kingdom and people are on the line. Rose has no reason to care for my dragons, which is why I need to make her fall in love with my kingdom. To *want* to save it.

"Rose." Her name rolls off my tongue, conjuring up pictures of the dilapidated garden I have neglected since the start of this war. "I'll show you to our room. You must be tired from your journey."

"Our room?" She eyes me warily.

"Yes." I don't remind her that she is my wife and married couples share rooms. She'll grow accustomed to my presence in time. She has to. "Follow me."

I don't wait for her to respond as I turn my back and leave the hallway. A few moments later, I hear the soft footfalls of her behind me. I sense her reluctance, but she also seems like an intelligent human. She doesn't want to be left alone in a realm of dragons and I'm her new protector whether she likes it or not.

The castle is far too large and flaunts wealth in every corner. Murals of former dragon kings line the stone wall, sharing glimpses of our history. The footsteps behind me stop and I turn to see Rose staring at a large portrait of my grandfather.

"These are all men," she says without looking at me.

I study her inquisitive face before I answer, "That's because the queens have their own hallway. Closer to the gardens."

She seems to accept my answer and we continue through the castle until we reach the north wing. My quarters alone occupy this part of the castle and it is forbidden for anyone to enter besides a few housekeepers that I have handpicked for the job.

My life is in the public's eyes. As king, you forfeit any sense of privacy in exchange for power and leadership. When I was a hatchling, I thought it was an easy trade. I didn't care about privacy. I wanted everyone to know who I was. I wanted control.

Those were the notions of a foolish boy. Privacy is what I hoard in abundance here. Which is why I'm very selective of who is allowed in my quarters. Rose is the first woman I have brought back because this will be her bedroom now too. I'm not used to sharing my space, but I can't have my wife sleeping anywhere else. We have an image to uphold.

My wife walks in, looking around the darkened room. I have a full wall of arched windows, but the crimson-colored velvet drapes are currently blocking the light from the sun. The fire from the hearth is the only light illuminating this room. For a moment, my wife just pauses and then turns to me with wide eyes, a horrified expression on her face.

"Wait, is there no electricity here?" Rose eyes the room again, probably hoping she missed signs of modern-day technology.

She hasn't. Technology is rare here and many of the territories don't have the ability or magic to support mortal modernity. My mom used to speak highly of the advancements of humans, but dragons have always preferred fire and the blazing qualities it provides us. Safety, food, and warmth, just to name a few.

"You won't find any modern technology here. I trust that won't be a problem." Not that she has a choice in the manner.

Rose sucks her bottom lip into her mouth and I get the

strange urge to haul her closer, tasting that very lip for myself.

No, I can't get distracted. I have a battle to win and I need Rose to accomplish that. I can't get distracted by her too-tight shirt that shows off her pebbled nipples, or the way I imagine her reddish-brown hair wrapped around my fist as she—

"What about indoor plumbing? Please tell me I don't have to pee on a rock." Her questions distract me from my wayward thoughts.

"Why would you pee on a rock?"

"I don't know!" She throws her hands up in frustration. "I don't know the correct bathroom etiquette here."

Despite the silly nature of the conversation and her blatant annoyance, I can't help but smirk. "No, wife, you will not have to pee on a rock. Unless you choose to." She mutters obscenities at me and I shrug them off. "We do not have indoor plumbing in the same sense the mortal world has it. Or at least from what I'm told, but we do have chamber pots when the need should call."

Everything I know from the human world came from two people, one of which is no longer with me, the other being Ender. Ender is our eyes and ears in the human world, though I still don't know why he took that job upon himself.

Rose nods once before walking farther into the room. She stops by my—our—bed, looking down at the untouched sheets. I have the bed as a necessity, but usually prefer to sleep in my dragon skin. Even though the bed is equipped to handle two large bodies in it, more than enough room for Rose, it isn't substantial enough to accommodate my dragon. No, that's on the other side of the room.

I notice the exact moment Rose sees the large pallet on

the floor. It's tucked off into a spacious nook, filled with cushions and pillows of various sizes. There is a sizable indent in the center from where I had slept last night.

"This will be your room now. You are safe here. No one is allowed in without my permission," I say, not sure if I want to keep her safe or simply keep her to myself.

"So I'm your prisoner, not your wife." The fierceness from earlier is back. I'm not naive enough to think I hear hurt in her voice, especially when the look she gives me rivals an angry dragoness.

"This isn't your prison. It's for your—"

"Safety, yes," she interrupts me. Anyone else and I would have their tongue. I'm tempted to do just that. "A cage is still a cage, no matter how prettily decorated."

"Need I remind you that you agreed to this arrangement as well." I will not be the recipient of her ire. I have enough shit to figure out and dealing with an angry wife doesn't even make my to-do list.

Rose doesn't speak, but I feel the anger wafting off her. She doesn't want to be here any more than I want her to be here. Neither of us is getting what we want, but this is our reality. A part of me wonders what made her make the deal in the first place, sacrificing her own life to save my home.

What was she running from?

I don't get to ask this because a moment later there is a knock on the door. I curse silently, forgetting that I had invited him over today. Instead of meeting him in our ballroom, I opted for the privacy of my own chambers. Too many wondering eyes eager to get a glimpse at their new queen. And they would. Just not yet.

"Who is that?" There's a slight tremor in Rose's voice that makes my dragon want to wrap my tail around her and placate her fears. With the strength of a monk, I keep to myself.

"That would be our spiritual advisor. He's come to marry us." With that, I answer the door, allowing another person into my sanctuary.

CHAPTER 5

ROSE

I half expect a dragon to walk through the door, but instead a short, gray-haired man enters the room. He's in vermillion-red robes, the cuffs dyed in a midnight black. He's a far cry from Sister Tammy, but his presence is still oddly comforting. Maybe because I'm no longer alone with my husband-to-be.

The door shuts behind him with a resounding thud. Even though the room is large enough to probably fit a full grown dragon, with high ceilings to match, I feel suffocated.

This isn't real. You're here out of necessity and for no other reason.

Except, that isn't entirely true. This is *very* real and whatever happens to me in this realm will pave the path for this new chapter in my life. I wait for the regret to sink in, but it doesn't. I don't regret what I did. Yes, I primarily did it to save my sister, but there were selfish reasons for seeking out Ender too. In the end, I got what I signed up for.

"My King, I came as fast as I could. There are many dragons at the temple seeking spiritual guidance and we lost another spiritual advisor." The man's words come out all at once and I don't miss the pain in Malix's expression.

What did he mean by lost? It was another question I would ask Malix as soon as we were left alone. Not exactly how I pictured my wedding day to be, but I suppose there have been worse ceremonies.

Honestly, who am I kidding? I really can't complain. Not when my husband looks like the star on the show *Vikings*.

"Then I won't keep you long. Perform the ceremony, and then you can go." Malix gestures for the spiritual advisor to come farther into the room. "Thank you for coming, Solaris," he adds, almost like an afterthought.

Solaris enters the room, moving toward a small table by the hearth. He places a bag down that I hadn't seen him carry, opens it, and takes out two vials and a golden chalice.

My curiosity gets the better of me and I reach out for the small vial to inspect it, but before I can grab it a hand wraps around my wrist. I jerk away, but Malix's grip on my wrist tightens. I hadn't even heard him move close to me.

"Don't touch that." His voice goes all growly and I think it's meant to intimidate me, but it does the exact opposite. My traitorous body leans closer, heat rushing to my core.

"Or what?" I can't help it—I lick my lips.

His eyes drop to my lips, burning with something other than desire. I shudder and he leans closer, his hot breath on my ear. "Or I might have to restrain you, little dragon. And I'd rather not have my wife-to-be tied up during our ceremony."

My breathing grows heavy as I picture being tied up. I have dabbled in BDSM before, but I can't say I'm well-versed in that area. I suddenly want to know exactly what it would feel like to be completely tied up and at his will. I nearly moan at the thought.

Judging from his dark expression, I imagine Malix is thinking similarly.

Solaris clears his throat and it serves as a bucket of cold water dousing us. Malix drops my wrist as if my touch burns him and takes a step back. I try to convince myself his actions don't hurt because we are strangers, but my stupid heart isn't buying it.

Solaris reaches for the vial I tried to grab. "This is just honey, albeit a rare kind meant for bonding ceremonies, so it's hard to come by," he explains for my benefit. His curious eyes stay on me a beat longer than necessary and I hear Malix's growl behind me.

Solaris has the decency to look contrite. "Sorry, Your Highness. It has just been decades since I have last seen a human. They're magnificent."

I try not to feel like a prized pig at an auction, but it's a weird feeling to be talked about in such an otherworldly sense.

"Let's get on with this." Malix beckons, and Solaris quickly obeys. He adds in another white liquid that he says purifies the heart, whatever that means, and finishes up by crushing dried rose petals into the mix. He stirs the ingredients together within the chalice and places it aside once he finishes.

"If you two would grab hands," Solaris instructs, and before I can act, Malix takes my hands in his. His touch is warm, warmer than anyone I have ever touched before. I wonder if that's because dragon fire runs through his veins, but I don't give voice to my thoughts.

The reality of the situation sinks in and I barely register what Solaris says about eternal bonds and everlasting joy. I'm about to be married to a dragon king in a different realm. A delirious giggle almost leaves my lips from the absurdity of the situation, but I clamp my mouth shut.

My behavior doesn't go unnoticed because Malix squeezes my hands tighter. Not painfully so, but enough to say *'quit fucking around.'* If Malix is freaking out, he's not showing it. That bastard.

He remains calm and collected, his face void of all emotion. If anything, he appears bored, and I'm half tempted to stomp on his foot to get a reaction out of him. Probably not the best way to start off a marriage, though.

"It is time for the bonding drink. This mixture symbolizes your union and commitment to one another. For love to blossom, even in the shadows of doubt and uncertainty. It is to give you strength when you have no more to give yourself or each other." Solaris reaches for the chalice on the table and holds it out to Malix first.

Malix grabs the chalice and looks down at the liquid like it personally offends him. He hesitates for only a moment before he brings the cup to his lips and drinks heavily from it. After a few seconds, the chalice gets passed to me.

The scent of honey hits me first since that's the main ingredient in the drink. I didn't particularly like honey in my world, so I'm not excited to drink it in its raw form. Hopefully the smashed-up rose petals and the white liquid Solaris added make it palatable.

I feel the eyes of both men on me, their expectations hanging heavily between us. A part of me wonders what Malix would do if I refuse to marry him. Would he call Ender back and demand a new human to provide aid for the battle?

The thought of another person in my place sends something akin to jealousy through me. Without further hesitation, I drink down the bonding serum.

The liquid is sweet on my tongue, but not overly so. It reminds me of a fresh mango smoothie on a hot summer day. My body instantly warms and my head spins. It suddenly feels like I'm a stranger in my own mind.

"Can you hear me?"

The voice comes so suddenly and I gasp, nearly dropping the chalice. The voice sounds like Malix but he hadn't spoken out loud. No, it had come from within my own mind.

"I'll take that as a yes." Again the voice comes.

"What the hell is that?" And what the fuck was that white substance Solaris put in the drink to make me hear Malix's voice in my head?

When Malix speaks, it's out loud this time. "Dragons can communicate through links. You've been given the ability to communicate with us now. Our link should be the strongest, which means I'll be able to sense your thoughts even if you aren't projecting them to me. And you'll be able to do the same."

I'm mortified by this invasion of privacy, but it's too damn late to do anything about it now. It's just going to be a day of doing things I don't really want to do.

"With the bonding drink fresh on your lips, it is time to solidify the union between dragon and mortal with a kiss," Solaris says.

A kiss? Fuck no! I open my mouth to say as much, but Malix beats me to it. "I don't think that is necessary."

I should feel relieved he said exactly what I was feeling, but I don't. It makes absolutely no sense that I'm this pissed. I know it's not rational, but I've never claimed to be. My current situation can attest to that.

"My King, it is necessary to complete the bond." Solaris sounds like he'd rather be anywhere but in this room with us. I don't blame the man. My almost-husband is an intimidating figure. I can't imagine what his dragon looks like if his human appearance can cause a grown man to tremble.

"It's not—"

"If you don't kiss me, I bet I can find someone here willing to do so." The words leave my lips, cutting Malix off, and the entire room freezes. Solaris sucks in a breath, eyes comically darting back and forth between the two of us. If he had the chance to fly away, I bet he'd take it.

"What did you say?" Malix's voice is formidably low, full of possession he's not entitled to.

My false bravado is failing fast, but I refuse to back down. He made this choice too and he's going to see it through.

"I said, I'll walk right out of this room and find another man to kiss—"

I don't get to finish my sentence before he brackets my neck and pulls me against his hard body. His lips claim mine in a domineering way, stealing an unexpected moan from my lips. Malix uses this as an opportunity to deepen the kiss, his tongue clashing with mine. He drinks me like a fine wine, savoring every last drop.

This close I can feel his hard muscles against me. His hips press into my belly, eliciting another groan. I feel his hardening cock and I smirk against his lips. He's not as immune to me as he pretends to be.

Granted, I'm not immune to him either.

Something snaps into place with this kiss. It feels a lot like inevitability, but I'm not quite sure how to describe it. I don't want the kiss to end and I'm tempted to climb into his arms and demand more. However, we have an audience.

As if sensing it at the same time I do, Malix pulls away, looking as flushed as I feel. He's panting and staring at me like he wants to eat me up. I'm both terrified and turned on, which is a strange combination.

A beat of silence passes between us, and then it's broken by Solaris. "It is done, My King. You're married in the eyes of the gods and rulers before us."

"Then leave us," Malix says, his voice still gruff.

Solaris looks surprised by the command, but makes haste as he packs up his things. When he's ready to go, he turns to Malix to say one last thing, but the look on my husband's face has the poor man nearly tripping over himself as he leaves the room.

My body doesn't know whether to flee or offer myself up to him, so I do nothing, waiting for him to make the first move. He brings his hand to my cheek, his thumb running over my bottom lip in the process. I fight the urge to suck it into my mouth because I don't make a habit of sucking men's fingers. Even if it suddenly feels like the exact right thing to do at the moment.

"Wife," he all but purrs. His hand stays on my neck and I gasp. His fingers nearly wrap all the way around me, but he doesn't add any pressure to his hold. He makes no attempt to let me go either.

"If you threaten to kiss another male in my kingdom, you will watch as I rip him limb from limb. I'll make you watch his undoing so it never happens again. Do you understand, little dragon?"

My mouth suddenly goes dry. Any snappy retort dies on my tongue and all I can do is nod. "Good girl," he says and drops his hand from around my neck. "Now if you'll excuse me, I have business matters to attend to." He pushes past me without another word.

I whirl around to face his retreating back. "Wait, you're leaving?"

Malix stops when he reaches the door and manages a glance back. "Yes. What did you expect we'd do, wife?"

"I..." I don't have an answer for that. I didn't expect him to sweep me off my feet and romance me for the remainder of the day, but I also didn't expect him to immediately leave me postnuptial. It's like he doesn't even want to try to get to know me.

"What am I supposed to do?" I finally say, blinking back the tears that threaten to fall. I fucking hate crying and I don't know why I'm on the verge of tears right now. I won't let Malix see the power he has over my emotions.

"I expect you'll find something to keep yourself entertained." He gestures around the room vaguely. "There is a whole kingdom for you to explore."

I scoff. "Right. Like you'd let me leave."

"I already told you that you aren't my prisoner. You are free to come and go as you please."

"And if I get lost?"

A smirk dances across his lips. "Trying to escape already, wife?" I want to say that I'm not the one running out of the room the moment we get married, but he continues on before I can. "Then I will find you. I will always find you, Rose. Remember that."

And for the second time that day, a man leaves me completely alone and defenseless in a strange, new world.

The moment the door closes behind him, I can no longer keep the tears at bay. I sink to the hard floor and cry until I have no more tears left.

CHAPTER 6
MALIX

The instant the door closes behind me, I regret it. I'm a proud man, to my own detriment, because a better man wouldn't leave his new bride alone in their bedroom. Rose's entire life and purpose changed in less than twenty-four hours, and yet I keep this door between us as a barrier.

That's when I hear the cries begin. She probably thinks I'm already far away from her, unable to hear her pain. Through our bond I feel the grief and fear from here and it feels like talons ripping me in two. I shouldn't feel this strongly for a woman I hardly know, but every part of me is screaming to get to her.

Mate. Yours. Protect.

A growl leaves my throat, low and foreboding. I've never been uncertain about a woman and her needs before. Did Rose want her stranger of a husband to comfort her? Am I even capable of comforting her? Do I *want* to?

"Malix?" A familiar voice calls for me. I'd been so focused on whether or not I should storm back into my bedroom that I didn't hear Vivia approach.

"What is it?" My voice comes out sharper than I intended it to, but Vivia takes it in stride. She's used to my temper.

"I saw Solaris leaving the castle. I presume you are a married man now?" Vivia asks, crossing her arms over her chest. She's in human skin now. Her raven-black hair is cut shorter than normal, cropped close to her face, highlighting her striking features. Resembling a shadow, she has opted for black leather pants and a billowy black shirt. Mina, Vivia's mate, has tried for years to introduce color into Vivia's wardrobe, but to no avail.

"Yes. Dragon's Keep has her queen." I sigh.

"And yet you don't seem happy about that." Vivia peers over my shoulder as if she can stare straight through my door. Dragons have excellent hearing, so I know she hears the woeful cries of Rose. I feel my face heat in shame.

"The situation is complicated."

"Yes, I would say it is," she agrees. "That happens to be why I'm here. Do you have a minute?"

I hardly have a minute to breathe these days, and my work load only ever expands. There's only one thing occupying my head today though: the woman I left back in my room. Vivia must see me eyeing the door because she says, "I know you want to go to your mate, but I think it's best if you give her some time. She has a lot to come to terms with."

"She's not my mate, she's my wife," I say reflexively, even as my dragon growls in protest.

"Right, of course—wife," she says as if she doesn't quite believe me, a poorly concealed smile on her lips.

I go against every one of my instincts and turn away from the door. Perhaps Vivia is right and Rose just needs time to get accustomed to her new life. I sure as hell do, and I'm not even a stranger to Dragon's Keep.

Wordlessly, the two of us walk toward the library which is full of our history and stories passed down from generation to generation. Admittedly, it's not used as often as it once was, but there's still a sense of tranquility when you step between the wooden built-in bookcases, holding pages upon pages of knowledge and entertainment.

The library also has a great view of the rose garden, located directly below us. It once was a sight to behold, but all of the maintenance and upkeep went to the wayside as soon as our kind started falling victim to the curse. If my mother were here to see this, she would be disgusted with how I'm honoring her memory, how I'm neglecting her most favorite part of the castle.

"The goal is to get your wife to fall in love with Dragon's Keep, correct?" Vivia perches on a desk that's at least five centuries old.

I nod. "Yes. The more she likes it here, the stronger her connection to the wards will be. As long as the wards are in place, the Nephilim shouldn't be able to breach our borders."

"So we buy ourselves time, but what about the cursed dragons lying asleep underneath the castle? More fall daily."

Her question is the same one I have been asking myself since Ender offered me a way to win this war. Rose is the answer, I just don't understand how. Ender isn't a talkative bastard, but he has also never been wrong before. I have to believe I'll find the answer. There's no other choice.

"I'm still figuring that out," I admit, and unlike my other council members, Vivia doesn't ask any follow-up questions. She trusts I'll figure it out and I hope that trust is warranted.

"I've talked with Mina after the meeting—"

"Is she pissed at me for not mentioning I'm taking a wife?"

"She only made a few remarks about severing your balls from your body. I think she's calming down."

I smirk. Mina can be the friendliest dragoness in the kingdom, but the moment she is angered, Mina is a force to be reckoned with.

"But she is interested in meeting your wife and I think she would be the perfect person to help the human—"

"Rose," I interrupt.

"Rose," Vivia corrected herself. "I think Mina would be the perfect person to tour Dragon's Keep with. Let's be honest, Malix, you aren't exactly a gentle or nurturing figure. If you attempt to play nice and send Mina in your stead, Rose is less likely to burn our kingdom to the ground.

"She can serve as her maid. Help her learn our customs and provide companionship. Your chambermaids all have the personality of a tea kettle and I doubt they would take much interest in anything other than changing her sheets."

I see the logic in her plan, even though I selfishly—and inexplicably—want to be the one to do that. But between my busy schedule and my inability to be around Rose without wanting to kill her or fuck her, maybe both, I can't be the welcoming reception she needs. Not yet, anyway.

I would have to wait. My wife needed to fall in love with my kingdom. We could define our relationship later.

Mina is not only a good fit because of her kind and welcoming nature, she also has the somewhat rare ability to shift between dragon and human skin. Not everyone in my kingdom is lucky enough to have that ability.

The choice is an easy one.

"Give it a day or two and send Mina to my chambers. I'll make sure the dragons on duty know she has permission to enter. Oh, and Vivia?"

"Yes?"

"Make sure she takes care of Rose. Her safety is the most important thing to me."

"To you, Malix, or to this kingdom?" Vivia tilts her head to the side, assessing me.

"As far as I'm concerned, they are one and the same." I deflect, "Is there anything else you wanted to speak about?"

She knows I'm shutting her out, but she doesn't try to stop me. Instead, she pushes herself off the desk and nods. "That's all I had. Enjoy your day, My King." She walks off and I watch her until she's no longer visible.

And soon I'm left alone to weave through the ever-tangling thoughts, hoping that we aren't at the end of our days.

CHAPTER 7
ROSE

The late morning sun trickles in through the gaps in the embroidered curtains. I normally don't sleep well in unfamiliar places, but the events of the last few days and my hours-long crying sessions took everything out of me. And Malix's bed is surprisingly comfortable. I slept in the middle of the large bed, out of spite, so no matter where Malix decided to sleep, he'd only have a small edge to perch on.

Except, Malix didn't show up the night or any night after. I haven't quite worked up the courage to leave my room yet, except for a quick trip to my private bathing chambers, and I was growing restless.

Which is why when I woke up, I told myself today would be the day I explored my new home. Malix had mentioned I wasn't a prisoner here and I've been treating myself as exactly that, but no longer. If Malix doesn't want to show me around, then I'm going to explore every nook and cranny of this extravagant castle. And hopefully, in the meantime, I'll be able to figure out a little more about the brewing war.

While I was alone in our oversized chambers, I found something resembling a walk-in closet. It wasn't exactly the same as the ones back in my world—this one was built into the stone with various trunks and boxes full of jewelry. It was all very extravagant and I almost expected a fairy godmother to pop out and dress me for a ball.

The one thing I notice immediately is that my attire is sorely out-of-fashion here. There isn't a pair of jeans in sight. My closet consists of dresses varying in styles and colors and somehow are all magically my size. I try not to think about how they managed to guess my size as I pick out a dress with the least amount of fluff and frills.

After a struggle with the corset, I emerge from the closet and stop dead in my tracks. I'm no longer alone.

A young woman, around my age, stands in my room, looking over Malix's pallet of cushions and blankets, which I've started calling a nest. I actually don't know what it's called, but "nest" seems to describe it well enough. She— thankfully—appears human. I don't know what I would do if I walked out to a full-blown dragon in my room.

As if sensing me, the woman turns around. She doesn't seem at all embarrassed that I caught her in my room. Instead, she smiles and rushes over to me, taking my hands. "Let me look at you. Oh goddess, Malix said you were human, but I couldn't believe it. A real human in our land! It's been so long." She laugh like that was the funniest joke she's heard all day. "How long have you been human?"

"Uhm...all my life?"

"Fascinating," she murmurs. The way her eyes drift over my body, though not in a sexual way, makes me feel like a specimen under a microscope. As mythical as I saw the dragons, I never considered they may view me the same way.

"Not to be rude, but who are you?" I ask, pulling my hands away from her.

"Oh, how terribly rude of me." Her eyes widen as if she hadn't even thought about introducing herself. Maybe she hadn't. "My name is Mina. Malix asked me to show you around the kingdom today. I see you are already dressed—does that mean you are ready to go? I have so many questions and I'm sure you do too. It'll be fun to learn from each other!"

If I could find a way to bottle up Mina's energy and sell it as energy shots, I would be bathing in money. The woman is sunshine personified and I can't help but feel like my energy embodies the gray storm clouds hovering nearby.

"I suppose my husband is too busy to show me around himself." I try to leave the bitterness out of my tone, but it slithers out anyway.

Mina crosses her arms over her chest, pushing her tits nearly up to her chin. "Trust me, you wouldn't want Mr. Doomsday to be your guide." I like her already. At least we can agree my husband is a dick. "He may be a good king, but his focus is elsewhere. It has been for months now."

"Because of the war?" Mina looks surprised that I know about that and I answer her unasked question. "Part of the marriage deal was helping with the upcoming war. Except no one told me I would have to be *married* to do that or what exactly I need to do."

The more I think about it, the more the anxiety and panic threaten to take me down. I can't fight what I don't know and no one seems to have any more answers than I do.

"Well, I'm sure the answer will present itself in due time." Her voice is gentle, almost friendly in a way that is too familiar for two people who have just met. Still, I warm to Mina instantly. If Malix's plan was to get me comfortable with someone, it's definitely working.

I had already made up my mind to leave this room today and make the most of it. Now I have my own personal tour guide who seems as eager to get to know me as I want to get to know about this world. "You said something about exploring the kingdom?"

A dazzling smile crosses her lips, showing off her perly-white teeth. "I did. Let's go, My Queen."

My Queen.

I'm not sure if I'll ever get used to that title. Granted, it's only been a day, but I was a nobody in Grym Hollow. Just the girl whose parents died and boyfriend cheated on with her sister. Queens are from storybooks, an anointed title belonging to fair maidens who dream of love and adventure.

I'm certainly no maiden and I've been burned too badly by love to ever want it again. I've never been particularly adventurous, not until I made the deal with Ender. As far as I'm concerned, I make a pretty shitty queen.

"Are you hungry, My Queen?" Mina asks. I follow her blindly out the door, content to have her lead.

"Please call me Rose, and not really. My stomach's still in knots from crossing the portal," I admit.

She nods like she understands. "I've been told it's a nasty feeling the first time. Did you feel like you were being unwound and put back together?"

"That's exactly how it felt. Ender says it gets better, but..." I won't ever know. I'm stuck here and won't ever return home. I wait for a sense of dread or longing to come over me, but nothing does. I'm really at peace with my choice, even though I'm uncomfortable with my new role... and husband.

"What can you tell me about Malix?" I ask, surprising both Mina and myself. I don't mean for her to get caught up in my problems, but since Malix is the master of mystery, I can't deny that I'm eager to learn something about him. Anything.

"Well, he's a private man."

"Yeah, I figured that much out for myself," I mumble.

"I suppose you would, yes. I don't spend much time with him, admittedly. That's my mate, Vivia's, job. I think Vivia might be his only close friend, and I use the term close very loosely. He doesn't open up to her, but he lets her in more than most people.

"From my infrequent interactions and things I've gathered from Vivia, he seems to truly love his kingdom and the people in it," she says, taking an abrupt right. We pass a door slightly cracked and I peer inside to see shelves of books. I've never been much of a reader, but with the free time I'm certain I'll have here, it might be a hobby I'm willing to take up.

"He likes taking flight at night. Vivia says he's a bit of an astronomer, always wanting to find new stars and constellations. He's been doing that since he was a boy." She laughs at the memory we don't share.

Something in her words stands out among the rest. "When you say 'take flight' you mean as a...?"

"Dragon, of course. He's handsome in his human skin, but the fiercest-looking beast in his true form. Has he not shown you his beast yet?" she asks with something akin to concern in her voice.

"No, he hasn't." The concern only grows and I feel the

need to justify his actions. "But we haven't been together long. We aren't exactly a love match, so he can show me or not show me anything he pleases. I don't care what he does."

"Love matches don't always happen instantly," she says gently after a moment of silence. "Dragons are stubborn, especially mated ones. Just give it time."

I open my mouth to argue and then abruptly close it again. I don't have the energy for rebuttal. People want to believe in happy endings where everyone falls in love, but I know the reality. Love is a weapon to carve out the heart. We give it freely to another person and hope they don't stomp on it. It rarely ever ends well.

Eventually I stop prying and allow her to show me around the castle. It is far larger than I anticipate and she promises she'll draw me a map in case I ever get lost. I'm going to need way more than a map to get around here, but I appreciate it all the same.

The castle appears to come out of a fairytale. The wall seems to be carved directly from the rock, with gray stones making up the extra height. Chandeliers with lit candles hang every few feet. The castle holds its own kind of magic, feeling both strong and comforting.

We shy away from any further talk about my marriage, for which I'm thankful, and I listen as Mina speaks of her family. She has a mate, Vivia, and a young son named Bastian. Occasionally we speak about Malix, but she's careful with the information she gives me though, I can't blame her. We're strangers.

Through her idle chatter, I attempt to gain any information about the war ahead, but Mina is careful to side step most of those questions, claiming she doesn't know much and that Malix is a better person to talk to in that regard.

My feet are throbbing by the time we end the tour and head to the dining hall. My stomach growls at the chance for food, and I realize I haven't eaten a proper meal since arriving, only bits of meals someone—probably a maid—leaves in Malix's chambers.

On the way to the dining hall, we pass a courtyard which once might have been a beautiful garden. Now it was little more than a whisper of what it once was.

"What happened here?"

Mina stops walking once she realizes I'm not keeping up with her. "Oh." The smile on her face is melancholic. "This was once the most beautiful garden on the property. It was special to Queen Alegra and she would often spend her evenings here with her ladies or King Broynen. It hasn't been kept since their death."

"Were those Malix's parents?" I ask, feeling Mina tense beside me.

"They were. We don't talk about them much though. I'm sure Malix will tell you more about them when he's ready."

I highly doubt that but don't say as much. "Can we come back tomorrow? I would like to tend to it, if that's okay."

"I don't see why not." Mina shrugs. "Are you sure you want to take that on? I don't know if we can even do much for it at this point."

I nod my head enthusiastically, more sure than I've been about anything in a long time. I like having a task and this will be the perfect distraction. Exactly what I need. "I'm sure."

"Then I'll clear it with Malix tonight and we can start working on it in the morning," Mina agrees and then takes my arm. "But it's time to eat. You're withering away as we speak."

I get my legs moving, following her to the dining hall. I feel a little bit lighter on my feet, finally having a tangible task I can complete here. Despite everything, I feel content.

CHAPTER 8

MALIX

"Another Nephilim has escaped their prison and was spotted east of Kraken's Lagoon. The ocean people have been informed and plan to stay vigilant." A heavy silence hangs in the air at the harrowing—though not entirely unexpected—news. This is the second case this week and more will come. It's not a question of if but when.

"The wards to the north are our weakest points," Aeron continues, pointing at the replica of our kingdom on the table. Another reason Aeron is an asset to me, despite his ability to toe the line between dutiful advisor and potential problem, is that besides me, he knows our borders, weak points, and land better than anyone else.

"And you believe the Nephilim can enter through these weakened wards?" I try to hide the annoyance in my tone, but it leaks out all the same. It wasn't even a fortnight ago when I strengthened those very wards. It had been exhausting then and would be even more so now.

"Yes. Perhaps not all, but some. Especially the more

powerful of the lot," he says, marking the north side with a red flag to indicate a risk for potential danger.

We can't keep their magic out, but I refuse to let the Nephilim in.

"If the wards start to crumble, we will need every abled dragon to fight for Dragon's Keep." The other few council members nod, knowing that the likely outcome will be one final fight for our kingdom. Normally, I would feel confident about our ability to defend our lands, but most of my people lie in a death-like sleep under the castle.

"What are our options?" A council member by the name of Otis asks.

Vivia's eyes flick over to me, a silent question in her gaze. She's letting me decide how much information I wish to divulge about Rose. They knew of my plan to marry her, but I haven't given them any updates since then.

"If what Ender says is true, and we have no reason to doubt The Guardian, then my wife will be the answer we seek. She's currently getting acquainted with the kingdom." It's a fact I have not been able to forget all day. My wife, the queen, is exploring her new home and I'm not with her.

Echoing my thoughts, Aeron picks up on my displeasure. "And you aren't the one showing her."

If I hadn't been trained my entire life to play the role of king and school my features into something that vaguely resembles disinterest, I would have shown Aeron my teeth in anger. I don't need to give him any leverage over me.

"I suggested my wife be the one that shows our queen around," Vivia speaks up quickly. Everyone's attention is off me now, exactly what she wanted. I make a mental note to thank her later. "We thought she would feel most comfortable with another woman. A friend she could feel safe around."

"Shouldn't a mate be able to supply the same comfort?" Otis asks, and I have never wanted to reach out and strangle anyone more than I do at this moment. I don't know where this new violent streak has come from, but it burns inside of me, begging to be released at the mention of my wife.

Mate. Yours. Protect.

The same damn mantra plays on repeat and grows louder with each passing hour.

"She needs time. We will give her that," I say, hoping my hard tone would be deterrent enough for them not to pry anymore.

Except it isn't. Because of course fucking Aeron had to remind me of things I already know. "With all due respect, Your Highness, we have no time. You married her to save our kingdom, not to make her comfortable."

Every fiber of my being wants to punch Aeron in his arrogant face. But another conflicting part of me realizes that he's right. We have no time, and the situation is only going to get worse. My marriage is nothing more than a final act to save my kingdom, but I'm not yet ready to share the burden of the kingdom with her. She deserves a day or two to get adjusted first.

"We can spare a day, Aeron. The queen is getting settled." I see he's about to say something else and I cut him off before he can. "Enough. My decision is final. Soon, we will use her to our advantage."

I hate saying the words, even as they come out of my mouth. They taste like vinegar on my tongue. I shouldn't care about Rose. I have no reason to. She's here because she made a deal and I needed a human to help me keep my kingdom safe and break the sleeping curse.

I would do well to remember that.

The topic of my wife drops, thankfully, as Vivia discusses our borders and gives us updates about the other five kingdoms. I'm not listening. Instead, I search through the fragile bond I have with my wife. There's warmth there, so I know she's enjoying her time. But there's a deep sadness there too and not just from her decision to come here. No, this sadness is years in the making.

What is my little dragon hiding?

I vaguely hear Vivia ask if there is anything else we need to discuss. I think I shake my head no because the council begins to shuffle out of the dining hall, leaving me alone with Vivia. "Are you okay, My King?" she asks, reading me in a way very few people can.

"I'm fine." It's not a complete lie, but it's not the truth either. I don't know how to feel.

Vivia's face softens. "You should go to her."

I shake my head vehemently, not sure why I'm so opposed to the idea. I just don't want to see her right now, not when my brain is a dark cloud of confusion. "Later. She still needs time."

I can tell that she wants to argue with me, but decides against it. She knows I need time to think and that when I'm ready, I'll act.

"Tomorrow, we can meet to strengthen the northern wards. I'll see if Mina will tend to Rose again. I'm sure she won't mind," Vivia says and I nod noncommittally. "Tomorrow then." Vivia touches my shoulder on her way out, leaving me alone with my thoughts.

I will not go to my wife tonight, but knowing I'll remain

in her head gives me some semblance of peace with my decision. This is the only mercy I can allow her because soon enough, I will pull her in the darkness as my queen.

CHAPTER 9
ROSE

My dear husband is avoiding me. If I wasn't so pissed, I might be impressed with his ability to make himself scarce. I haven't seen him since the first night, after our pathetic marriage ceremony. I have a feeling he is trying to give me space—or had heard me crying that night and wants nothing to do with me.

It would be easy enough to wake up in a bad mood, but I refuse because today I'm working in the garden. A sense of tranquility settles inside me just at the thought. It's mindless work, but rewarding. I like being able to see that my work has a beautiful outcome.

When Mina comes to the door this time, I'm ready for her. Dressed in a deep purple dress that's lightweight and easy to move in, with my hair braided back out of my face, I answer the door when she knocks.

"Oh, well, good morning." She laughs as I all but run into her. "I take it you are excited to work in the garden today?"

"You don't even know," I smile, taking a look down the hall.

Mina understands what I'm looking for instantly because she says, "Malix and Vivia went to strengthen our north border today."

I try to hide my disappointment, but I guess I do a piss-poor job at it, judging by the sympathy on Mina's face. "It doesn't matter," I finally say. "He can do what he wants. Let's go."

Mina snakes her arm through mine and I like that it feels so natural. I know I just met her, but I already like being around Mina. She's sweet and has a wealth of knowledge. She's just as curious about my life as I am about hers.

My feet still ache from yesterday's tour when we make it to the rose garden, but since this is the one place I was most interested in, I ignore the throbbing pain. "It's so beautiful out here," I whisper to no one in particular, hands running over rose petals that appear to wilt under my touch and fall to the ground.

"I mean, I suppose it could be beautiful." Mina scrunches up her nose as she takes in the scene.

Sure, it looks like a flower graveyard now, but I can picture it in its prime. The garden has the potential of returning to that state again and I want to be the one to restore the garden back to its former beauty.

One look at the ground tells me the soil is in good condition, but it's dry. "Is there a watering can somewhere?" I ask Mina.

"Oh, yes, one second." She scurries away to a vine-covered outhouse. In her hands are two medium-size cans. "The well is behind you."

I thank her for the can and fill it with water. A hose would be so much more convenient, but there is none to be found and I doubt this place has one.

I start with the small section by the courtyard's

entrance. Mina follows wordlessly behind me, following my lead as I start to water the dehydrated bushes. We work in silence for a while, moving from bush to bush, and filling up our cans when the water runs out.

"Is gardening a hobby for you?" Mina asks after we make it halfway through the courtyard.

I smile at her, nodding. "It was. Back home, I had a greenhouse." Judging by the confused look on her face, I can tell she is picturing an actual house that was green. "It's something we use to grow and nurture plants inside of. It helps stabilize the growing environment. I grew flowers of course, but I also liked growing my own vegetables." A habit I picked up in the wake of my parents death to cope.

"Ah, I see. The human world seems interesting."

"Some of it, yes. Some things aren't as great or wonderful though."

We fall into another silence after that, but all the while I feel Mina's burning question she is unsure if she should ask. She makes up her mind by the time we walk back to the well to fill our cans though. "Is that why you left? Because of the less-than-great and wonderful things?"

"I..." A heaviness settles over my chest, the same one that always appears when I think about the past year of my life. The choices that led me to this very minute. "Yes, I suppose you could say that."

"Was it bad?" The inquisitive nature I learn she has gets the best of her. "Oh goddess, that was so rude of me. You don't have to—"

"No, it's okay," I say, surprising us both. "I've just never talked about it before. Actually, no one has ever asked me about it. Back in Grym Hollow, people tend to avoid difficult subjects so they don't disturb the peaceful nature of the town."

"That doesn't seem like a healthy thing to do."

"It's not," I agree, plunging my can into the water. "It could be quite suffocating at times."

"Did you at least have family to talk to?"

The tightness in my chest increases, threatening tears. I blink rapidly to keep them at bay. "My parents died in a freak car accident when I was eighteen." Mina's look of confusion quickly prompts an explanation from me. "A car is something that transports us to different places. Like a carriage."

Mina nods, understanding coloring her expression. "I see. So, you didn't have any other family?"

I shake my head. "It was just my sister and I for the past ten years. She's the reason I'm here, actually."

"But why—"

"Ladies." At the arrival of the new voice I jump, but Mina whirls around, ready to spring into action if needed. Gone is the smiling, sunshiny woman. Her eyes narrow into slits and she moves in front of me, shielding me with her body.

"Aeron. Is there something you need?" The steel in her voice is unmistakable but does little to deter the stranger.

Aeron—as Mina supplied—is a large man, towering over the both of us. He's built sturdy and appears to be in his forties or fifties. The muscles on his body could rival Malix's, but that's where the similarities end. I feel unease creep in that I hadn't experienced with Malix.

"I heard the new queen was out. I want to introduce myself." Aeron looks past Mina and stares directly at me. His eyes are black and unsettling. He smiles, but it's far from friendly. "Rose, is it?"

"It is." I surprise myself with how steady my voice comes out.

"Beautiful name for a beautiful mortal." He says the last word as a reminder. As if I don't understand my own mortality, especially in the face of a dragon. "My name is Aeron. I'm part of the king's council."

I look at Mina for confirmation and she gives me a shallow nod. She hasn't moved from her stance in front of me and I make no attempt to move around her and offer my hand to Aeron.

"I see. Well, it's nice to meet you Aeron—"

"I'm surprised you aren't with your husband. Newly-weds rarely leave their chambers, far too consumed with each other. I hope there isn't trouble in paradise already."

The fake concern in his tone has me on edge. I don't even know the man and I already don't like him. Perhaps it is simply being a woman in my world and having to know when a guy is bad news. It is literally life and death. Right now, Aeron is setting alarm bells off.

"Aeron, must you always be so insufferable?" Mina hisses.

"Insufferable?" Aeron feigns innocence. "I'm simply concerned for our kingdom. I have every right to feel this way, especially if the key to saving our kind is this mortal."

"Malix has it all handled. Stay out of it." Mina grabs my wrist and turns toward me. "We should go."

I didn't particularly want to leave. We still have an entire section of the garden to finish watering, but I also don't want to spend another minute with Aeron if I don't have to. "Yes, I guess we should."

We turn to leave but Aeron shoots his hand out. Something digs into my skin and I gasp. Looking down, I see his hand has half transformed into a claw and his hold on me tightens. "I'm sure you have a minute to spare. A queen should be available to her people."

"Aeron, drop your fucking hand." Mina is at my side in an instant, trying to pry off Aeron's hand but his hold doesn't loosen. I can feel his strength in this one touch alone and know this dragon is ancient and powerful. More powerful than he is showing us.

"No, I don't think I will. Not until we get to know each other. I'm not a scary man, Ms. Briar. I care for Dragon's Keep and the dragons in it. I would like to get to you, to understand why our king believes you are our best bet."

I hear the tear of fabric next to me and I look at the spot Mina was in moments ago. No longer do I see the curvy woman with deep brown skin. Instead, a large green dragon, roughly the size of a house, takes her place.

"Mina?" I gasp, equal parts scared and interested as the dragoness growls deeply from the back of her throat, sending shivers down my spine.

"Really, Mina? Must we resort to violence?" Aeron sighs as if he is actually let down by her behavior. He opens his mouth to say more, when a dark figure appears behind him.

Anger rolls off of him in waves, his eyes dark, nearly black. It is a face I recognize, but not one I have seen since our wedding.

"Remove your hands from my wife or I'll remove your hands from your body."

CHAPTER 10

MALIX

I'm in a foul mood by the time I make it to the north barrier of my kingdom. Vivia lands next to me, her black wings spreading wide as she catches her balance. We are about fifty miles from my castle on land bordering Nephilim territory and Kraken waters. The wards only protect my people; each king has their own method of protection.

I blame my bad mood on lack of sleep and the pressures rising as more of my people succumb to the curse. Last night, another dragon fell victim, totaling nearly half our population now. However, there is another reason I'm ready to bite the head off another pretentious nobleman who keeps pressuring us to act now.

Rose.

The human roams freely in my mind, taking up space that doesn't belong to her. I thought keeping my distance would allow me to think straight and not about those red lips I want to see wrapped around my co—

"Here. The tear is forming here," Vivia says, pulling me

away from my wayward thoughts. I remind myself why we are here in the first place and that is to secure the barrier.

Night patrol had felt a weakness in the north side of the kingdom, approaching the kraken's waters. This was the second occurrence this week of a disturbance, and I have an inkling these tears will only multiply the more powerful the Nephilim become.

"There's reports of more Nephilim escaping their mountain prison. The barrier has to hold or we need to prepare to defend our territory."

Vivia isn't telling me anything I don't already know, but it frustrates me all the same. *"Let's prepare the wards. We can regroup when we get back to the castle."*

Vivia nods, prepared to assist me despite knowing it will take a lot of energy from both of us. The barrier is only as strong as the king and his inner circle. Since we are losing members to the curse almost daily now and I'm not willing to bring every council member away from the castle, the magical barrier protecting Dragon's Keep is eroding at an alarming pace.

This is why you need Rose.

The annoying thought hasn't left my mind since she arrived. She has to be here to help me strengthen the wards. What other reason would Ender leave her here as my wife?

"Now," I say, pouring strength and protection into our barrier. The magic within responds immediately and I feel the magical barrier start to knit itself back together. It's a slow process with just the two of us and I hear Vivia begin to pant from exhaustion after a few minutes.

By the time we are done, fatigue takes over our bodies and I feel as if I could sleep for an entire day. If only I had the luxury.

My wings span out, preparing for the flight home, when the dragoness beside me goes still.

My body tenses in response, prepared to find a stray Nephilim roaming nearby, even though we haven't had any close encounters. I know it's only a matter of time. *"What is it?"*

Vivia doesn't answer for a moment and I'm tempted to snap in her direction to get her attention. Luckily that is not needed, but her words make my blood run cold. *"Mina. She's talking to me through our bond. There's trouble."*

Before she even finishes her sentence, I take to the sky, fatigue all but forgotten. I desperately try reaching out for Rose, praying that our marriage ceremony is enough to create a mating bond, but no tethers connect us. All I feel is Vivia and her projecting the location to me.

Garden.

I was foolish to think I could leave Rose alone. She is literally a human in the dragon's den and dragons like nothing more than finding new, rare items. I practically served Rose up on a silver platter and presented her for slaughter.

I pump my wings harder, ignoring the strain I put on them. I close the distance between us fast, though the last mile feels the longest. Even though I can sense Rose is nearby—and alive, thank goddess—I still don't know if she's okay.

The moment my feet hit the ground, I switch forms, sending a silent thank you to my late father who taught me a simple clothing spell for switching between skins. Next to me, Vivia lands and curses.

"Cool party trick," she mutters and usually I would tease her about it, but I'm not in the mood. I have only one focus.

We round the corner and assess the scene. Mina's

dragon is out, crouched low in a defensive position. Rose's eyes are blown wide with fear and the man holding her is... Aeron?

Seeing him stops me momentarily in my tracks, wondering if we have completely misread the situation. I believe that until I see the way he holds Rose's arms, his hand half shifted so his talons keep her from pulling out of his grip.

Aeron holds very little love for me and our friendship is precarious at best, but I also felt there was a certain level of respect between us. He pushes me to face problems that threaten the kingdom and I allow him to disagree with me. At the end of the day though, we usually have the same goal in mind.

An anger like I've never experienced sinks its talons into me and refuses to let me go. My dragon sees red and threatens to break through the surface again, but I keep him at bay. Only barely.

"Remove your hands from my wife or I'll remove your hands from your body."

My voice has all three snapping their heads in my direction. Relief washes over Rose's face before she quickly schools it into a more neutral expression. I briefly notice Vivia run to her wife's side, whispering calming words to the worked up dragoness.

For a second, Aeron looks as if he won't obey my command and my body tenses in preparation. But then, ever so slowly, his hand drops away from Rose and Mina's tail wraps around Rose, pulling her close.

Aeron smiles, one that doesn't reach his eyes, as he takes a step closer to me. A growl leaves me, low and threatening, and he stops.

Smart man.

"You haven't formally introduced us to your new wife. My curiosity got the best of me, My King. You understand why people might take interest in the new queen." Aeron has been in politics his entire life, just like me. But the dragon has decades on me. He's been playing the game since my father was king.

The men were best friends; my father appointed Aeron as lord chancellor. A position that is extremely coveted and respected, second only to the king and queen. When my father and mother perished and I took up the title as king, the Nephilim were already our biggest problem. I let everyone keep their previous title, which means that Aeron still technically holds the position.

"Chancellor, you've forgotten your place. You have no right to touch the queen or question her. If she wants to speak with you, she'll seek you out." She won't though because I'll make sure she's never alone with Aeron.

"I've forgotten my place?" Aeron's brow cocks up. "Or have you, My King?"

"Tread carefully, Aeron." The air around us sizzles as our anger threatens to boil over.

"We are running on borrowed time. Your *queen*—" He sneers the word like poison on his tongue. "—has a job to do. Her time as queen will be short if you aren't focused on the same goal. As part of your advisor committee, allow me to advise. Find her strengths and exploit them."

Aeron casts one last look over his shoulder and his gaze lands on Rose. She flinches under his gaze. "Until next time, My Queen."

Aeron walks past me and I let him, even though everything in my body tells me I need to put him in his place. If I wasn't in desperate need of able-bodied dragons, I wouldn't think twice about challenging him.

The truth is I need Aeron and he knows it. I fucking hate this dynamic we always seem to fall into.

Though Aeron did remind me of something. I need to keep a better eye on Rose because I don't want to end up in a situation where she's left vulnerable and I'm not quick enough to get to her in time.

"Rose," I say, my voice still taking on a deeper tenor than normal because of the adrenaline coursing through my body. "Let's go."

"No."

Rose steps out from behind Mina. The fear from earlier is long gone, replaced with rage. And damn if my cock doesn't twitch in excitement at the sight of her flushed cheeks and heaving chest.

"No? It wasn't a question, little dragon."

"And my answer is not negotiable. No." She stalks across the garden so that she stands only a foot away from me. This close, I can smell her floral scent and the seductive taste of her ire.

"You think you can ignore me for days, then swoop in and rescue me and suddenly I will follow you like a lost puppy? Fuck that. And fuck you, too. As far as I'm concerned, Aeron isn't the problem. You are. If you actually gave a damn and introduced me as your queen, maybe they wouldn't feel the need to corner me."

"Rose—"

"I'm not done!" She stomps her foot, nearly on top of mine. "You're leaving me in the dark and I don't like it. I get it, we are nothing to each other, but considering this is now my home too, I would like to live long enough to explore it.

"So no, Malix, I won't follow you like an obedient child. I'm going to stay out here with Mina and we are going to finish watering the garden. Then I'm going to your bedroom and locking your ass outside. Slither into the bed of whoever will have you because it's not me."

Rose turns away from me and I'm tempted to pull her back to me and bend her over my knee until she learns her damn manners. That mouth on her will be my downfall. She is both insufferable and extremely fucking alluring.

Vivia smirks at me. *"I like her,"* she mouths. Mina, now back in her human skin, looks torn between wanting to do as her queen told her and not wanting to anger me. I dip my head, giving her the permission she wants.

"Let's get you something to wear and then we can finish up here. If you still have the time," Rose says to Mina before leading her through the castle doors, leaving Vivia and me alone once again.

"You have your hands full with that one. And I'm actually excited to see how long you'll be able to handle it before you snap." Vivia laughs. "I think you've met your match, My King."

Yeah, me too.

ROSE

I wake up with the start of a tension headache. I used to get them all the time back when my parents just died and I had to learn how to take care of myself and my sister. There were times I would black out and work on autopilot, going through the motions of a normal human, but not being able to remember what I did when the headache finally eased.

Yesterday's events made me long for Grym Hollow, and the predictability of the small town. I'm a guppy in shark-infested waters here; yesterday proved as much. Aeron serves as a reminder that although the dragons may look human, they most definitely aren't.

After finishing watering the garden last night, blatantly ignoring Malix who took it upon himself to hover over me the entire time, despite the fact I was—am—angry with him.

When I hugged Mina goodnight, I half expected Malix to follow me into his room. After all, it belonged to him and he has every right to be in here, but he stopped at the end of the hallway, making sure I got into the room safely. After I shut the door, I'm not sure where Malix went.

A knock on the door has me groaning. I expect my visitor to be Mina—she promised we would meet up again today—but it isn't the female dragon that walks through the door.

It's Malix.

And I'm extremely aware that I hadn't been able to find anything suitable for sleep last night, since my nightgowns haven't been restocked yet, and I wound up in bed naked.

"What the fuck are you doing here?" I scramble to pull the sheets up, not wanting to give him full access to my boobs. Jerk doesn't deserve to see them.

"I was hoping you were awake." Oblivious to my nudity, or just not caring, Malix moves to sit at the edge of the bed, body turned toward me.

I hate to admit that he looks good, damn good, in his black pants, which stretch across his thighs in a way that should be illegal. His white, buttoned shirt is only partially buttoned, allowing me glimpses of the muscular, tan skin underneath.

It would be a lot easier if my husband was ugly. Then my traitorous body wouldn't demand his touch.

"I wanted to apologize for my absence."

Of all the things I expect for him to say, that isn't one. Malix doesn't seem like a guy who apologizes to anyone, especially those with less power than him.

I ask the burning question that has been eating me up inside since the day we shared our first kiss and he walked away from me. "Why did you agree to marry me if you don't want anything to do with me? Is your plan to keep me in the dark?"

The role of queen was thrust onto me the moment

Malix married me, but it feels like a title with no responsibility or purpose. Feeling useless is the worst feeling when you spend your entire life trying to be useful to those around you.

Malix's silence is confirmation he isn't as ready to talk as he presented.

"You know what, never mind. If you're not interested in figuring out how I'm supposed to help you keep your kingdom from crumbling then neither am I."

My lack of clothes is the last thing on my mind as I fling off the covers, determined to put some distance between us. I make it approximately five steps before I'm being hauled back and pressed to a firm chest.

Malix's touch is scorching hot on my bare skin. His eyes darken and a soft growl leaves his lips. "Do you always sleep naked, wife?"

I shouldn't be wet for a man that has been avoiding me at every turn and not forthcoming when it comes to information, but goddamn, I'm only human. A fucking horny human who hasn't been with a man in over a year. Longer really, since toward the end of our relationship, Stefan and I rarely had sex.

"Only when I can't find something to sleep in, *husband*," I spit. "You also didn't get me any panties.'

For the first time since I arrived, Malix smiles. And, oh fuck, if it isn't the hottest thing I have ever seen. If I had panties, they would be soaked. Frowning Malix is sexy, but smiling Malix is devastatingly irresistible.

"Yes, I'll thank my maids for that little oversight." Then he drinks me in unabashedly.

His eyes trail down the curves of my body and it's like an invisible hand caresses each part he views. I've been with men before, but none of them have ever looked at me the way Malix is currently looking at me. Like he would worship me if I asked him to.

"If this is how you accept apologies, then I foresee many apologies in my future."

Despite myself, my cheeks burn. "I didn't say I accepted your apology." My voice comes out more breathless than I want it to, only deepening Malix's smirk.

"No, I suppose you didn't. And what can I do to make my wife accept my apology?" He's so close to me now, his lips hovering inches from mine. Having him this close is distracting, especially when he dips his head and brushes his lips against my neck. Not quite a kiss, but not accidental either.

"Perhaps there are other ways I can show you just how sorry I am."

It would be so easy to give in to him, so easy to shut my brain off and just feel. Let our bodies do the talking for once.

But I know that he's trying to distract me and it's working pretty damn good. I put my hands against his chest and I feel him growl in response. Then, with all the strength I can muster, I push him off.

Malix stumbles back, more out of surprise than my ability to over power him. I grab the sheet and wrap it around my body, hiding from his view. "If you want me to forgive you, then fucking talk to me. Don't try to distract me with sex."

To his credit, Malix doesn't look insulted...just resigned. Perhaps fucking people into oblivion has been his way to deal with people in the past, but it isn't going to work with me.

But it almost did.

"I'll make you a deal, Rose."

I roll my eyes. "Yeah well, my last deal isn't turning out so great, so forgive me if I'm hesitant."

He ignores the clear jab directed at him. "I will tell you about the reasons I've been so distracted, if you agree to tell me the reason you agreed to this deal in the first place."

Information for information. It's a powerful tool to have in one's arsenal and one that can be used to blackmail another if the information presented is good enough. Not that I believe Malix would do that, but there is a certain vulnerability in the truth and I'm not sure if I'm ready to face that.

I also don't have much of a choice, not if I want to live longer than a few weeks here. There is really only one option.

"Fine."

"Good. Get dressed and meet me in the dining hall for breakfast. We have a lot to discuss."

CHAPTER 12
MALIX

My control is slipping. I am holding on by a tether but the ends are frayed and threatening to break at any moment. That was never more evident than in what happened in my room only moments ago.

Rose is naked. *Naked.* And in my bed. The moment the sheet came down and she tried to walk away from me, I was no longer in control of my body. I had her there and I was so close to saying fuck it and taking her right then and there.

I couldn't deny this pull I have for her, one that Ender said would be there, but I hadn't believed him. I should have known better than to doubt him. Yet here I am, doubting the people who want to help me and pushing them away. This has become the rule these days, not the exception.

The doors to the dining hall open and my wife is there —fully clothed—but looking nervous. Though I miss the tempting curves laying in wait underneath the dress, I can't help but notice she unknowingly chose my favorite color.

Green. It compliments her hair and brings out the flecks of golden brown in her eyes.

She doesn't attempt to greet me as she walks in and I take a certain satisfaction in the look on her face when she realizes the only set spot at the table is the one directly next to me. It's not the best placement for conversation, but it allows me access to her.

Rose settles in next to me and we fall into a companionable silence as the kitchen staff brings out an array of breakfast items including an assortment of meats, eggs, and fruits. A sweet wine is poured for us and then we are blissfully alone.

Rose peers at me from under her dark lashes and then busies herself with her cutlery when she notices I'm staring at her.

"Are you going to speak or do you plan on staring at me the whole time?" she asks, taking her first bite of the spinach, egg, and cheese omelet the staff prepared.

"I think I'll do that later."

"Malix."

This is the first time she has said my name and even in annoyance, it's the sweetest sound I've heard in a long time. I want to pull it from her lips when I'm buried to the hilt inside of her.

"You promised me answers. I'm only here because I'm curious."

"You want to know the threat to Dragon's Keep." It wasn't a question, but she nods all the same.

"Then you need to understand the beginning. In the early days of our settlement, our biggest threats were creatures known as Nephilim. Giant creatures set on destroying everything in their wake. They strive to create a world of chaos."

"So these Nephilim, are they still around?" Rose discards her fork, angling her body to give me her full attention. Her white corset pushes her ample chest up, and I force my gaze to stay on hers.

"Yes"—I nod—"though not in the way they once were. It took decades to get to a place where the rulers of Mescos could finally entrap them. My father was leading the group—"

"Were you there?" She cuts me off and something akin to worry crosses her features.

"No, little dragon, it was before my time." My words ease the tension from her body and she gestures for me to continue. "The six rulers managed to trick and trap the Nephilim within the mountains, but not before their leader, Gadreel, cursed our kingdoms and destroyed the only portal between our world and the human world."

"Curse you? What did he curse you with? Is this why you agreed to marry me because you think I can somehow help you break this curse?"

"That's complicated."

Rose isn't satisfied with my answer and she narrows her eyes. "Well uncomplicate it and explain it to me. I'm keeping up."

This woman really will be the death of me, but I think I will welcome death with open arms. She's not afraid to challenge me, despite the fact that I'm considerably more powerful than she is.

"By destroying the door to the human world, Gadreel took away one of our biggest power sources. Supernaturals and humans have mixed for years and a human mate acts as a conduit for our power. They make us stronger, so dragon rulers have always taken human mates."

"So your mother was..."

"Human, yes," I confirm. "She was the last human. She stood besides my father during the first Great War and their combined power helped keep a strong barrier. They knew that the Nephilim would return one day, so the protective barrier around Dragon's Keep was their last attempt at saving them."

"What happened to your parents?"

I'm momentarily caught off guard, which rarely happens these days. Everyone in Dragon's Keep knows of my parents' love story and their need to be together, even in the end, that it has been so long since I've had to retell it.

"I was ten when my mother got sick. My father hired the best healers from around Mescos, even those from other kingdoms, but my mother's sickness was aggressive. No one knew how to make her better and eventually she succumbed to her illness. My father died the next day, most people say of a broken heart."

Rose's eyes shine with unshed tears. She surprises the hell out of me by reaching for my hand and squeezing it. It's a reassuring touch that is meant to bring comfort, but it's so foreign to me.

"That sounds awful. I can't imagine losing your parents so young. Mine died when I was eighteen and it had been hard enough then. Who raised you?"

"No one." The day my parents died was the day I became a man. I had to, there was no other choice. "There was a kingdom to lead and no king. I had to step up and take on the role."

"Oh, Malix..."

"Don't," I grit out through my teeth, unable to hold back the knee-jerk reaction every time someone looks at me with pity. "I got that look plenty as a boy. I don't need it from my wife."

"Well too damn bad. Why do people think pity is a bad thing? It means people care and don't think you deserve the hand life dealt you. So, I'll look at you any way I damn well please." There's a delightful flush to her cheeks when she's finished and she goes to pull her hand away, but I tighten my hold on hers.

She stiffens but ultimately relents.

"So, let me get this straight," Rose starts. "Ender brought me here as your human mate in hope of...strengthening the barrier?"

"That's what I have to assume. Though that will only work if we are actually mates." Considering how she has occupied every one of my thoughts since arriving, I don't foresee that being a problem. It's the actual mating that gives me pause. "I can also strengthen the barrier with my entire council, but most of them have fallen victim to the curse."

Even if I had the power of the entire council at my disposal, the barriers wouldn't be as strong as they could be. No, that can only be achieved with a bond as strong and unbreakable as that of my parents. I'm attracted to Rose, I'll no longer deny it, but love is not something I know. All my experiences with love have ended tragically.

"What is the curse?"

"I can show you." I hadn't planned on showing her, but just as well. Admittedly, Rose needs to know, despite my reluctance. It's the only way to figure out a solution together. I search for fear in her expression, but find none, only a hard determination. With a single nod, she says, "Show me."

CHAPTER 13

ROSE

There's a warning about following strange men into a new, dark location, but I can't think of it right now. There's no reason for me to trust my dear husband, but I do. Maybe that makes me naive, but if he wanted to hurt me, he would have done so earlier.

He needs me. He admitted as much.

We wind down a dimly lit staircase, my hand on his back. I tell myself it's because it's hard to see and I don't want to miss a step and face-plant down the rest of the never-ending stairs, but that wouldn't be entirely accurate. Touching him brings me comfort.

"We're almost there," Malix assures me.

The farther we descend, the darker it gets. It also seems like the lit torches are becoming sparser and farther apart, creating limited visibility. Malix doesn't seem affected by this and I wonder if it has to do with his dragon side. Seems like a dragon would have better visibility than a mere mortal.

"Stay close," he says as he rounds the final turn and

leads us into more darkness. Malix moves away from me and panic sinks in. Did he really bring me all the way down here to kill me? That thought is squashed in the next instant when one by one, the torches around the room illuminate.

It takes my eyes a moment to adjust and when they finally do, an involuntary gasp leaves my lips. "Holy fuck."

The room is the size of a football field. But I can't see the floors because nearly every inch of this space is covered with dragons. Small and large ones of various colors. The rise and fall of their chests tell me they aren't dead, but the waxy sheen to their scales let me know they aren't okay either.

"What happened?" From the looks of it, half of Malix's kingdom is lying underneath the castle.

He doesn't answer right away. There's a lost look in his eyes as he moves through the horde of sleeping dragons. "It's the curse." Malix stops just shy of a small dragon, the size of a calf. He's a deep red color with a black strip down his back. Compared to the other dragons, he is so tiny. Just a child.

"The curse takes on different forms in the different kingdoms. It's dark, ancient magic that makes the Nephilim the biggest threat to Mescos and impacts victims at random. Dragons are most vulnerable when they are asleep, and the Nephilim feed off our vulnerability. We sleep like the dead and we take a while to fully regain consciousness.

"The curse only affected a few dragons at first and happened infrequently," Malix continues. "It has since gained traction and we haven't gone a day without losing one of the dragons to the curse. We try to keep as many of them here for safety purposes, but some families prefer to keep their loved ones with them."

I think I'm beginning to understand. Malix has given me a lot of information today and I'm still wrapping my head around it all. The Nephilim are powerful creatures and are gaining power daily. A sense of hopelessness rings through the air when looking at all of these incapacitated powerful creatures.

But it couldn't be helpless, could it? Ender wouldn't have sent me here to die. I didn't know The Guardian well, but I knew that his job was to provide protection. There had to be a reason he chose me for Malix.

"It's only going to get worse. You see why my attention is elsewhere."

I did, and honestly I couldn't blame him. Didn't excuse his absence, but it did explain it.

"What happens if you can't win against the Nephilim?" My question hangs heavy between us. I've seen Malix angry and I've seen him amused, but I don't think I have ever seen him worry. It's there in his eyes one minute and gone the next. I doubt he meant to show me his vulnerability.

"If we cannot strengthen our border and break the curse, our lands will fall to the Nephilim. Their power will grow and the rest of Mescos will be even more vulnerable than it already is."

"Shit."

Despite the tense topic, I hear Malix bark out a laugh. "So eloquently put, wife. That about sums it up."

I move closer to the young dragon I noticed when we first arrived, crouching down next to him. "What have you tried to break them out of this sleep?"

"I've hired mages and healers from around the kingdom. The healers could only keep them comfortable and make sure their bodies were taken care of while they are under the spell. The mages haven't been able to identify the magic, let alone how to counteract it."

Malix is behind me now, the heat of his gaze scorching my skin. "These are your people now too, Rose. You are their queen."

I roll my eyes. I'm queen in name alone. I don't even know what the title means or how I'm supposed to rule alongside a man who finds it difficult to share information. There have been some improvements in our relationship—I obviously know he's attracted to me—but mutual lust only lasts for so long before it simmers out.

I reach out my hand to touch the young dragon in front of me, but before I can make contact, I hear footsteps descending the stairs. I drop my hand, turning my attention to the new figure joining us.

I tense immediately when I see him.

Malix is there, standing in front of me, acting as a shield between me and Aeron. He had left in such a rush yesterday and I hadn't expected to see him so soon.

"What is it? I don't wish to be disturbed when I'm with my wife." Malix's tone is low and threatening, bordering on cold. I would think it was sexy to see him standing between us, but my body is wound too tightly with Aeron so close.

"I know, but this is important." Aeron descends the last step and hovers near the bottom. His gaze meets mine momentarily before looking back at Malix again. "We had an entire family fall victim to the curse today. Their bodies are being transported to the temple, where Solaris has agreed to house them."

"They should come here."

"Yes, well," he starts, looking around the room. "And where do you suggest we put them, My King?"

Aeron has a point. Every square inch of this room is occupied by a sleeping dragon. Malix seems to realize this at the same time I do, because he curses softly under his breath. "Fine, we will open another room for dragons who have been affected at the temple. Make sure Solaris is prepared to house many bodies."

The men launch into details and seem to forget I'm here. Which is fine, I would rather Malix deal with Aeron than drag me into their conversation. I turn back to the young dragon and gently caress his skin.

His scales feel rough under my fingertips. How long has he been down here? Do the dragons dream or are they left in darkness and suffering?

I can't quite stand to think about them suffering, especially the little ones. To my horror, he isn't the only child among the sleeping masses. The adults in their lives are helpless to protect them.

"I will protect them. I will keep them safe," I murmur under my breath, as a sense of rightness washes over me.

I close my eyes as a montage of all the times I've felt completely protected in my life flashes through my mind. There are only a few. The times my parents would read to me before bed, tucking me in with sweet kisses. The time my sister and I went to Granny's house and baked cookies until the entire kitchen table was covered in more chocolate chip cookies than we could eat in a weekend.

And then to more recently, when Malix swooped in between Aeron and me at the rose garden. I had been so mad at him for ignoring me, but I also knew at that moment he wouldn't hurt me. I was safe with him, at least physically, and that's more than anyone has made me feel in a long time. It was both a scary and exhilarating feeling, but something I wanted to pursue.

Smiling, I slowly open my eyes...and stared directly into the red, cat like eyes of a dragon.

CHAPTER 14

MALIX

Rose's scream accomplishes two things: fear and action. The only way I know how to describe the coldness that enters my body is that of overwhelming dread rooted in fear. Not for myself but for Rose. The moment reminds me of just how human my wife is, despite her larger than life personality.

"My gods..." Aeron says, eyes wide with disbelief.

I mentally prepare myself for the worst as I turn around, taking in the scene. Suddenly I realize why Aeron's face is the way that it is.

A hatchling is awake.

The red hatchling is disoriented and unsteady on his feet. Small cries of confusion and helplessness erupt from him, but none of it is coherent. Compared to full-grown dragons, the hatchlings are small, but compared to a human? They could cause serious damage, especially if they aren't fully in control of their bodies.

"Rose." The deep tenor of my voice catches her attention immediately. My heart lurches at the fear in her eyes, but I clamp it down, hardening my features even more. "Don't move and stay exactly as you are."

Rose looks ready to dash, but I fear any sudden movements will cause the hatchling to attack. "Malix, I—" The hatchling responds to Rose's voice, crouching into a defense position. "Shit..." she squeaks, which would be adorable in any other context, but this one.

"Aeron," I bark out for my advisor to join me. To his credit, he's at my side immediately, staring at Rose and the hatchling with more interest than appropriate. "Make sure Rose is unharmed and keep her away."

I don't wait for his response as I move in between Rose and the hatchling. This close, I can make out his features better and he's younger than I originally estimated. Young hatchlings are always unpredictable, especially when spooked.

"No one's going to hurt you, hatchling. Tell me your name," I order.

Instead of answering, the hatchling lunges for me. I hear Rose gasp behind me and I can only hope Aeron is doing as I instruct and keeping her out of harm's way. The young dragon swipes at my legs with his talon, shredding the bottom half of my pants.

He tries to come at me again, but this time I'm ready. The moment the hatchling lunges for my legs again, I make a grab for his head, holding him tightly in my grasp. "Name," I growl, letting my dragon peek through the surface.

It was enough.

The young dragon stops moving, whimpering softly. Recognition colors his features and his body slumps into my grasp. "Cyrus, My King."

"Do you know where you are, Cyrus?"

His head swivels from side to side, taking in all the bodies of the sleeping dragons. "N...no," he chokes out, barely containing the sobs.

"I can hear him," comes from Rose behind me, surprise in her voice. I can't acknowledge her yet.

"You're in my castle. Or rather, underneath. You've been asleep for some time now." I don't know when Cyrus was brought to the castle. It could be anywhere from a month ago or a day ago. "How are you feeling?"

"Scared. Where's my mommy and daddy? My sister?" This time Cyrus doesn't try to hide his sobbing. His whole body shakes and his tail curls around his body, making himself smaller.

I'm shit at trying to comfort people. Give me a battle to fight with brute strength, but present me with tears? I'm as well equipped to handle that as a penguin is to flying.

My movements are awkward as I pat the top of his head. "It will be okay," I say as if I'm reading from a script. Even Cyrus eyes me warily.

"That was pathetic." I turn to see my wife glaring at me, pushing away from Aeron. He goes to grab her, but I hold up a hand. If anyone is going to restrain my wife, it's me.

"Care to do better?" This woman infuriates me and challenges me at every turn. And yet I find myself enjoying our small battles.

Rose is back to crouching down in front of Cyrus, clearly forgetting that she had been terrified of him mere seconds ago. "Will he understand me when I speak to him?"

Cyrus and I both answer 'yes' at the same time. "The cup you drank from on our wedding day allowed you to communicate with our people."

"Good," she says out loud. Then her gaze softens at Cyrus, a warm smile spreading across her face. Something simmers deep in my belly. Jealousy? No, but it feels awfully close.

"Cyrus, that's a strong name."

The hatchling nods. "It's my grandfather's name. He was a warrior."

"I can tell. You must take after him." She tentatively reaches out to caress his face. Cyrus lets her, leaning into her touch. "We are going to find your parents. And your sister. I just need you to be brave for a little longer. Can you do that for me?"

Cyrus sniffles, but nods. "Yes." Then after a moment of hesitation adds, "Who are you?"

"My name is Rose. I'm..." I hear her hesitation and I don't like it.

"Queen. She's my queen," I supply for her, making a mental note to remind her later of her status at my court.

"Oh. Oh! I'm sorry. I didn't know, My Queen." Cyrus scrambles to bow, but Rose stops him.

"Don't worry about it. I'm still getting used to it myself," she assures. "You must be hungry. How about we get you some food and then we can work on finding your family, okay?"

Rose stands, dusting off her dress before addressing me. "We need to get him food."

I don't hesitate. "Aeron. See to it that the hatchling is fed. Then start looking into his family."

"No."

"Absolutely not."

Rose and Aeron speak at the same time. Annoyance dampens my mood. I'm really getting to hate that fucking word.

"Rose just broke the sleeping curse on one of our drag-ons. Something we have been trying to do for weeks. Send someone else for the boy. We must call the council together and have the girl tell us how she did it."

"The girl," Rose hisses, "is not your interrogation subject. You want to know how I did it? Well, so do I. The one thing I know for certain is that I'm getting this child food. I can't trust you with his well-being."

"You have an obligation to your people. We must learn how you broke the sleeping curse and harness that ability to restore the rest of the sleeping dragons."

"Don't speak to me about obligations! I know why I'm here."

"Do you?" Aeron growls. "Seems like you should be reminded."

"Enough." Aeron has been playing a dangerous game ever since my wife arrived in Mescos. He's purposely pushing the line because he knows I need him. Aside from me, he holds a considerable amount of power and knowledge about our realm. Acting too rash could set me up for an internal battle I'm not equipped to fight. Not yet.

"The queen," I start, reminding Aeron of his place. He does little but narrow his eyes at the term. "Will see that the boy is taken care of. Then we will gather everyone into the meeting room."

"But I don't have anything to say!" Rose argues. "I don't know how I did what I did and I'm not even sure it was me."

"It was," Aeron insists, but we both ignore him.

"Be that as it may, a dragon was revived tonight. The council needs to know this and you need to be there to share your experience. I wouldn't ask this of you if I didn't think it was important."

Rose bites her lip. I wonder for a second if she will fight me on this as she has fought me on everything else. I'm not above forcing her into the meeting, but I also don't want the council's first impression of my wife to be her attending against her will.

Slowly, the steam inside of her deflates, and Rose sighs. "Fine. But I'm not going to be any help."

"On the contrary, My Queen, you will be more help than you can imagine." Aeron breezes past us, heading toward the stairs. "I'll tell the council we will meet at dusk."

I don't stop him as he leaves. The council will be informed of what took place here and will undoubtedly have questions. Luckily, Rose has a few hours to get her bearings and to tend to Cyrus like she seems so keen to do.

"Will you call Mina? I'm going to need her help," she says, just as Cyrus sheds his dragon skin in favor of his human skin since he's probably too weak to maintain his dragon. He's far too pale and skinny. A good meal and warm clothes would do him well.

Mina is the obvious choice to help her. She's a mother and nurturing, far better suited than I will be in this situation. Still, I can't help but feel disappointed that her first instinct isn't me.

And why would it? We've been at each other's throats every step of the way. A perfect dance of mutual disdain and something that runs deeper than lust. A pull that I can't quite shake and am not prepared to act on yet.

"It will be done." She nods and gives her attention back to Cyrus. "There are a few blankets by the stairwell. He can wrap one around himself until he gets clothes," I say as Rose and Cyrus walk away from me.

My wife seems to be fond of that these days and I can only blame myself for that.

CHAPTER 15

ROSE

Cyrus is still shaking by the time we make it up the stairs, and into the main part of the castle. I fumble my way through a few hallways until I find the dining hall, cleaned up from breakfast.

Mina rushes over to us. I'm impressed with her ability to get here so quickly. I guess Malix made sure she would be here when I need her. That almost makes me warm to him. Almost.

"I grabbed some clothes from my son's room, though I'm not sure what will fit," Mina says, looking over Cyrus in a way only a mother could. The overwhelmed boy next to me relaxes slightly, as do I. Mina just has the ability to make everyone feel safe and secure around her. "He'll need to eat afterward; poor boy is skin and bones."

Mina ushers Cyrus off somewhere private, promising to be right back. I nod, keeping myself together a moment longer. Once they leave and I'm blissfully alone, I sink down into the closest chair.

My body is *tired.*

Everything happened so quickly, and I wasn't lying

when I said I had no clue how I broke whatever sleeping curse Cyrus was under. Maybe it wasn't me? Perhaps the curse is losing its strength or was never as strong as Malix and his council originally thought.

Aeron seems to think it was something I did. Maybe he's right, but that still doesn't magically make me understand what happened back there. And if my body wasn't so fatigued, maybe I could put a little more thought into it.

The door to the dining hall opens again, and I turn to smile at Mina and Cyrus, but it isn't them who walk through the door. It's my husband.

Malix takes one sweeping glance around and crosses the room in long strides. I pretend like I don't see his pants strain against his muscular thighs with each step.

Seems criminal that he's only seen me naked and I haven't had the chance to appreciate his naked form.

"See something you like, wife?" Malix says and I realize how hard I've been staring at him. Hard enough to get fucking caught. I feel the blush burn my cheeks and neck as I avert my gaze from his powerful thighs to his smirking face.

"Nothing of importance," I say and I swear I see him flinch. I elect to ignore it. "What do you want?" I don't attempt to hide how tired I am with niceties. I want nothing more than to slip back into bed and sleep for the next twelve hours.

"How are you feeling?" He's next to me in an instant, looking me over with what I might say is actual concern if it belonged to anyone other than Malix.

"Tired. Very tired." It is a testament to just how tired I am when I can't even come up with a snarky remark for him.

"Let me make you some tea with honey."

"I'm fine, I don't—"

"I insist," he says, reaching out his hand for me. I hesitate for the briefest moment, before taking it.

"I can't be gone for long. Mina and Cyrus will be back soon and I'm not going to leave her alone with him. He's my responsibility."

"He's ours," he corrects, "and Mina is more than capable of taking care of Cyrus. I already informed her I would be stealing you away."

"Always pushing off your unwanted tasks to other people, I see," I murmur under my breath, but my husband's a damn dragon so of course he hears it.

Malix stops walking and turns to face me. The look on his face is equal parts pissed and resigned to his fate. "You'll let me care for you before you give me a verbal lashing. Hate me all you want, I deserve your ire. But I'm going to make you some damn tea, so stop being stubborn for one damn second and let me cater to my wife."

It's not often I'm rendered speechless, but this is one of those times. I have no witty retort nor the energy to deny him, at least for the time being. My silence is acquiescence enough and he takes my hand again, pulling me to the kitchen. I have no choice but to obey.

"Sit." He gestures to the high bar stool by the island as soon as we enter the kitchen. A few of his staff members are working, but Malix barks something to them that I don't quite understand, and the staff begins to file out one by one until we're alone.

Malix works in silence as he heats water in a kettle. His movements are soothing, and I find myself getting lost in his motions. The kettle sounds and he pours the hot water into a teacup with tea leaves. After adding a healthy dose of honey, he places the steaming cup in front of me before taking a seat next to me.

"If I didn't watch you make it, I would think you poisoned it," I say and pick up the cup and saucer, giving it a quick taste. The warmth spreads from my head down to my toes and the honey adds the perfect amount of sweetness.

"I believe the words you are looking for are 'thank you.'"

A smile tugs at my lips, which I quickly hide behind my cup. "Thank you, Malix."

He pauses at my gratitude. A smirk crosses his face before he says, "My pleasure. Drink every last drop. It'll help." Even being helpful, my husband can't let go of his commanding attitude.

I find that I like it a lot.

For once, I do as I'm told and finish my tea, placing down the empty cup and saucer on the island. "How did you know I needed that?"

Malix shrugs. "My mom used to drink this when she had a hard day and was feeling extra tired by the end of it. It always seemed to make her better. Thought it might do the same for you."

"Wow, that was...sweet?" I hate how I made my compliment into a question, but this Malix is so far off from the Malix in my head.

But is he really?

This is the Malix who left me after we were married, but the same Malix who looked ready to claw out Aeron's eyes the time he stopped me in the garden. The Malix who kept busy and avoided me, but also did cute shit like this, making me tea because I was tired. He also hasn't once pushed me to tell him about what happened back with all the sleeping dragons. No, he came to make sure I was okay.

My head—and heart—is a complicated place to be right now.

Do I want to kiss him? Scream at him? Fuck him? Leave him?

Yes. To all. Yes.

I'm a damn fool.

"I don't understand you." I sigh, my body feeling tired for new reasons. "I don't know if you want me here or if you would have preferred I'd never come." On a surface level, I understand it. He's a king in need of saving his kingdom and his people. I'm the woman that can help him achieve that. Still, I don't enjoy feeling like a chore he never wished to have.

I don't need love. We won't ever achieve that, and I've made peace with it. But I do want to be more than tolerated.

Struggle plays out on Malix's face like a movie. For someone so cold and distant, he is certainly easy to read when he doesn't have his guard up.

"You confuse me too, Rose." My name sounds foreign on his lips. Wife or little dragon are the only things he's called me. "Like why you choose to be here in the first place. Don't think I have forgotten our deal from earlier about sharing.

"But in all seriousness," he continues, "I don't know how to act when you are around. You do things to me, Rose. Things you shouldn't be capable of doing, but my beast wants you. Wants you more than anything he's ever wanted, and I can hardly be around you without tempting myself."

Oh.

How the fuck do I respond to that?

It's like my mind has short-circuited and no amount of

rewiring will fix it. Words leave my lips, but I'm running on autopilot. "Your beast wants me but what about you? Not King Malix, but *you*."

Do I want to know the answer? Do I care?

If you asked me a few days ago, my answer would have been no. Now...well it feels like I can't breathe until he tells me.

Malix moves closer, his knees bump into mine and neither of us pulls away. "No one's ever asked what I've wanted."

"Maybe more people should."

"Maybe," he agrees, reaching out to gently press his hand against my cheek. It's innocent enough, but we both suck in a deep breath. "I...want to kiss you."

My heart does a weird lurch and I wonder if I'm about to have a heart attack. No words form, but I feel my head nod, consenting to his will.

I shouldn't. I shouldn't want to kiss him. It will only make everything between us even more complicated. I've been down this road with another person before and it did not end well for me. This has the potential to end worse. Catastrophically worse.

I can't seem to stop us, though. Together, we are a runaway train, going straight toward the cliff at the end of the tracks.

All those thoughts leave my mind as soon as his lips are on mine. They are soft and he tastes vaguely of honey. Or maybe that's me.

I kiss him back, my body reacting on instinct. I bring my hands up to rest on his chest, feeling the strong muscles that lie underneath his tunic.

The innocence of the kiss doesn't last long. Malix grabs the back of my neck and pulls me closer until our bodies crash together and I'm straddling him. What started out as a spark has quickly turned into an inferno as his tongue parts my lips and tastes me. I groan softly, wanting, no, needing more.

I want to take and take, peel back every damn layer he's hiding from me.

So I take.

Like a dog in heat, I begin to rub myself against his leg, needing to feel friction between my thighs.

"Fuck, wife. You're a wanton thing, aren't you?" he groans, nudging his leg harder against me and I moan out. I desperately seek the pressure my clit so eagerly wants.

"Maybe you shouldn't have ignored me and I wouldn't be this way."

"No, I quite like you like this," he purrs, running his hands up my sides, stopping just underneath my breasts.

More. More. More.

"Please," I beg, but I'm not entirely sure what I beg for.

"What is it you need, My Queen?"

You. To stop. To continue. To...

My racing thoughts soon cut off as he rubs his knee harder against me. "Fuck..."

"Well, I should say," a new voice speaks up and I scream, jumping away from Malix as if he burned me.

We both turn to see who the voice belongs to, and my face burns when I see Mina—just Mina, thankfully—smirking at me like she knew this would happen all along.

"I thought you'd like to know that Cyrus is fed and we are trying to locate his family. Also, the council has requested to meet as early as possible and are awaiting your company. Both of your companies. But clearly, another meeting started here." She laughs.

I am never going to hear the end of it.

"Right, we were just...ah..."

"Oh, I know exactly what you were *just doing*."

I don't meet the eyes of my friend, knowing I would find amusement at my expense. I'm feeling too vulnerable as it is. "Right, well, we should go then."

"Rose." Malix reaches for me, but I quickly step out of his grasp. I don't trust myself around him right now. Clearly I can't help but rub my pussy all over him after a simple act of kindness.

"We should get this over with," I say and do my best not to sprint past him.

It's not until I'm out of the kitchen and past the dining hall that I realize I have no clue where the meeting room is.

CHAPTER 16

MALIX

Progress.

At least that is what I would have called what happened between me and Rose back in the kitchen before we were interrupted. I saw the moment realization hit Rose—eyes blown wide like a gazelle who wandered too close to the lion's den.

"Thank you," I reply to Mina, perhaps a bit too curtly. Mina is used to my antics, and does little to hide her smile as I go after my wife. She is particularly fond of running away from me. A game of cat and mouse I'm growing tired of playing.

Except this mouse is clueless about where to run.

I find my wife pacing just outside the dining hall, scowling when she sees me approach. So, we are back to that.

It would be more convincing if moments ago my wife wasn't rubbing her pussy all over my thigh. Even now, I can smell her desire. She wants me, but she doesn't *want* to want me.

Too bad, little dragon, you are mine.

Despite her anger toward me, I need her to be prepared for what is coming. "Are you certain you're ready to speak to the council? We can wait until morning." Which would be my preference, but the meeting isn't about me.

There's hesitation in her expression, but in the end, she shakes her head no. "I want to get this over with. But, I really don't have the answers they are looking for. I don't know how I did what I did. It just sorta happened."

"Then I suppose it will be a short meeting."

"But—"

"Need I remind you that you are their queen?" I interrupt her. "You hold the power. This meeting isn't dictated by the council's wants, but by your rule. *Our* rule."

Rose bites her bottom lip, and my mind conjures up pictures of her biting her lip in the throes of passion while I settle between her thighs and devour her. Will she taste like her namesake? Or be sweet like honey? I have half a mind to hike up her dress now, drop to my knees, and find out.

Rose's scoff brings my attention back to the present where I'm, unfortunately, not inside of her. "I'm not their queen."

"Are you not my wife?"

"I am, but—"

"Then you are their queen. In every way a person can be a queen, you are. And I fully plan on standing by My Queen's side."

Rose's breath hitches, a flush coloring her cheeks a dainty pink. She's looking at me as if she has never seen me before. Like I'm not the man she once thought I was.

That makes two of us.

"Okay." No snark. No refusal. Just quiet acceptance. I think I might have broken my wife. "Let's go."

A HUSH FALLS over the room once we enter. I may as well be invisible with how much attention I garner. Curious eyes roam over Rose. For most, this is the first time they are seeing their new queen. That's not what interests them the most though. It's her humanity.

And how a mere human could awaken a sleeping dragon.

Any lesser woman would fold under the gazes of the council, or find ways to make themself appear small in the hope that they go unnoticed. But my Rose isn't wavering as she walks by my remaining council members.

Something tells me that Rose is no stranger to judgmental stares. What the fuck kind of life did she lead not to blink in the face of deadly dragons? They all wore their human skin—for Rose's benefit, I'm sure—but it does little to hide the predator lying underneath. I vow to learn more about her past later, even if I have to steal it from her lips.

My council barely allows my wife to sit before their questions begin.

"So, it's true then?" Otis asks, ever so impatient. "Your wife was able to wake up a sleeping dragon? Aeron claims to have witnessed the feat."

"It's not a claim. It's fact," the dragon in question growls.

Otis puffs out his chest, trying to appear bigger than he is. Strength is coveted among our kind. Appearing weak can cost a dragon their life. "Be that as it may, we would prefer to hear from the source."

All attention is back on Rose once again. A new voice speaks up, Aracelia, the only other woman on my council.

She's a force to be reckoned with, born into a family of warriors and nobles. She, besides Rose, is the only person younger than me at the table. "Everyone here has family or friends affected by the sleeping curse. What these men are trying—but failing—to say is that we would appreciate any insight you can give us, My Queen."

Rose sweeps her eyes through the room, taking in the remaining dragons on my council, before landing on me. My dragon preens at the attention. She's looking at me for...what? Comfort? Permission? Our bond does not give me the answers I seek. Rose has so many walls up, I fear I'll never be able to break them all down.

Taking a gamble, I reach for her. My hand covers hers, providing the only comfort I can give her right now. I half expect her to pull away, but she doesn't.

And fuck if my dick doesn't harden at her touch.

"Malix believed showing me the sleeping dragons would help me understand the curse plaguing the kingdom. Neither of us thought I was capable of doing what I did. I can't rationalize it in my mind. One minute I was staring at Cyrus and the next, we were looking into each other's eyes."

"Maybe it would be helpful if you take us through the process? Starting from when you arrived under the castle," Vivia suggests.

Rose nods. "I was looking around at all the sleeping dragons, and I felt an intense sadness. That only increased when I saw Cyrus and realized he was just a child. I don't know what possessed me to reach for him; I just did."

"Was there anything in particular you were thinking about other than the sense of melancholy?" Aracelia asks.

Rose doesn't answer immediately. She ponders the question and after a moment she says, "I guess 1 was thinking about protecting him and wanting to provide a safe place for him and the other dragons who can't protect themselves." There is a slight pause before she adds, "And I thought of the last person who made me feel safe."

"And who was that?" Aeron inquires.

"I hardly think that's relevant." Vivia glares at Aeron.

"Of course it's relevant. Everything she did leading up to that moment is relevant." Aeron's heated gaze sweeps the room until they land back on my wife. "My question still stands, My Queen. Who did you last feel safe with?"

"You don't have to answer that if you don't want to," I assure her, despite the death glare Aeron sends my way. If looks could kill, I would be little more than ash right now.

The older dragon is on thin fucking ice. If he doesn't adjust his damn attitude soon, I will be forced to put him back in his place. He could stand to be humbled and I would take great pride in being the one to do it.

Fortunately for him, my wife is more understanding than me. "It's okay, I don't mind." Her words say one thing, but her hardened expression says, *I'm not afraid of him.*

"Since you're so curious, councilman," Rose starts and her next words send my beast into primal mode, "I was thinking about my husband."

CHAPTER 17

ROSE

Fatigue is quickly setting in. My eyelids feel heavy, threatening to stay closed with each blink. The questions come more frequently, but my answers rarely change. However, one in particular stands out among the rest.

Can I do it again?

Even after explaining to the council I hadn't meant to do it the first time, Aeron and Otis insist I try again. I'm not opposed to trying—I want to help—but the little strength I have left is slowly slipping from my grasp. I feel like I could sleep for a full twenty-four hours.

Throughout the bickering, Malix stays silent and this unnerves me more than anything. An angry or cocky Malix I can handle because I can dish it up as well as I can take it, but the silent man sitting next to me is not one I'm equipped to handle.

The intensity in which he's staring at me makes me both afraid and a little aroused. Images from the kitchen replay in my mind like my own private porn movie. The way he kissed me like a starving man and I'm the last morsel of food to be found. I rub against him, desperate to feel friction between my legs. I should feel embarrassed about that, but I don't. I won't feel ashamed to explore my sexual desires.

Except it stopped as suddenly as it had started and neither of us got what we wanted. I left in a hurry, embarrassed about getting caught, not the deed itself.

Even sexy thoughts of my husband can't suppress the yawn that escapes from my lips. Malix snaps out of whatever hold he is under and stands abruptly. "Enough for tonight. Rose needs to sleep."

"My King—" Aeron begins to argue, but Malix snaps.

He whirls around so fast, I barely see him move. One moment he's beside me and the next he's across the table, grabbing Aeron by the neck. "One more fucking word out of you and it'll be your last."

The dragons around the table stand up, but only Otis goes to Aeron's aid. Vivia and Aracelia seem to be enjoying Malix's outburst. Aeron is clearly not a favorite among the two women on Malix's council.

"Sir, I believe what Aeron is trying to say is that it's extremely important that we have Rose recreate what she did. To even stand a sliver of a chance against the Nephilim, we need our people back." Otis's confidence wanes as he takes in the two dragons.

Indecision is written all across his pale face. To help the king or to help the most powerful council member. I do not envy his decision.

To his credit, Aeron doesn't struggle in Malix's grasp. His face is red from either lack of oxygen or anger...or a combination of the two. The loathing in his beady black eyes makes the hair on the back of my neck stand on end.

Suddenly, I'm afraid for my husband's safety.

Another tense moment passes between the two powerful dragons before Malix loosens his grip on the older dragon's neck, letting his feet touch the floor again. Aeron pulls in a deep breath, slowly backing away from Malix.

"This isn't over," Aeron murmurs, almost imperceptibly. Before anyone can do or say anything, he leaves the room without so much as a backward glance.

Otis, realizing that he is in the direct line of my husband's wrath now, takes a step back. It's subtle, but may as well have been an entire leap since I'm told dragons do their best not to show their fear.

"Make yourself useful, Otis, and see to it that Aeron doesn't find his way into trouble or to my wife. If he does, it will be your heads displayed on spikes," Malix threatens, draining the color from the poor man's face.

"Of course, Your Highness." Otis makes a quick dash to the door, but before he leaves, he turns around and bows in my direction. "It was a pleasure to meet you officially, My Queen." With that, he leaves to trail Aeron.

"Well, this has all been entertaining," Aracelia muses, pushing her chair in. "Perhaps it is best to reconvene tomorrow—if the queen wishes," she adds quickly after Malix growls at her. "As always, it has been a pleasure. My Queen"—Aracelia moves so she's standing in front of me. The stern-looking, but gorgeous woman offers me her hand —"I look forward to working alongside you. Please don't judge us too harshly based on Aeron's actions. We aren't all completely insufferable."

I smile, despite the tension and fatigue coursing through my body. "Thank you, Aracelia. I'm looking forward to getting to know you. But please, just call me Rose. No titles."

"Very well, Rose then. Sleep well." She winks at me, leaving only three of us.

Although I haven't ever spoken to Vivia, I feel as if I know her through Mina. She talks about her wife often and she is well respected by my husband. I already feel a budding friendship forming.

"I should find my mate," Vivia says. "I hear we are keeping Cyrus until we can locate his family."

My face heats. "Yeah, sorry about that. He can stay with me if that's too much trouble."

"No trouble at all." Her gaze flickers over to Malix, who still stands tense and looks as if he wants to break a window or two. "You already have your hands full. Good luck, Rose."

Vivia is the last to leave and I'm alone with a man with murder in his eyes. If I could scrounge up enough energy, I might be fearful. But with each second that goes by, standing upright is more of a chore.

My body sways and I reach for the chair to steady myself. Did this sudden exhaustion come from reviving Cyrus? Before I can contemplate the thought, Malix curses and comes to my aid. His strong arms engulf me in an instant. "You're tired."

I bite back my laughter. "Really, what gave it away?"

He growls at my answer. My husband, the growly dragon. "We shouldn't have conducted the meeting. I should have trusted my gut and made you go to bed."

"Made me? And how would that have worked out for you, hmm?" I glare at him. "You can't make me do a damn thing, Malix. I agreed to this meeting and I don't regret that. You need to trust that I can make my own decisions."

"And you need to listen to your body and not push yourself to the brink of exhaustion. I'm taking you to bed, little dragon." He doesn't wait for my answer as he picks me up, carrying me bridal-style.

I shouldn't want this.

I can't want this.

But I don't want to fight it either.

The truth is, I *am* fucking tired. Drained physically and emotionally. Walking all the way back to Malix's chamber—our chamber—was not something I was looking forward to. This damn castle is so huge and maybe if I had wings, getting from point A to point B wouldn't take so damn long.

Needless to say, I relish the fact that Malix wants to carry me. There would be no protests on my end. I rest my head against his chest, eyes drooping. "This is nice. You should carry me more often."

He chuckles and I feel it deep within his chest. "Maybe I will."

"See to it that you do." Talking to him like this comes so naturally. For once I feel completely at ease and don't feel the pressures of daily life trying to crush me.

It is...refreshing.

And terrifying, because yesterday I wanted to punch him in his too-handsome face.

By the time we make it back to our room, I'm half asleep. I hear Malix mumble something about changing. Sleeping in this dress with the corset isn't ideal, but my limbs feel like mush. My body has molded to the bed and I don't want to move.

I say as much, but it comes out as more of a groan. Hands turn me over until I'm lying on my belly and slowly I feel the laces on my dress loosening.

Malix is...undressing me?

My brain reminds me that he's already seen me naked, but this is more intimate. I should smack his hand away and demand he leave so I can change....but I don't. Malix's calloused hands roam over my body, being mindful of the vulnerable position he has me in.

My body shivers as soon as he moves me and discards my dress. I tell myself it's from the cold and has nothing to do with the man that took off said dress. I wait for his hand to slide between my legs or caress my breast, but Malix is being a gentleman as he pulls a loose sleeping gown over my head.

I'm only a little disappointed.

My body flops down on the bed and I pull the covers tightly around me. I fall asleep almost instantly, but not before I feel the bed dip beside me and strong arms wrap me in a tight embrace.

CHAPTER 18
MALIX

Sunlight flickers in through the gaps in the curtain, shining light across my bed. My eyes flutter, slow to wake up entirely. A warm body presses up against me, limbs entangled with my own.

Last night I put my wife to bed.

And joined her.

I could lie and say I planned on leaving as soon as I tucked her in, but the truth is that I planned on staying with her the moment she told the council she thought about me when she wanted to feel safe. It lit a primal part of me and the need to stay close to her.

She is mine and it's about time we stop denying this pull between us. I tried and made myself keep my distance, but it was a battle I lost all too quickly. The pull has only grown stronger the more we try to push the other away and I'm done denying this part of me.

My wife is my mate.

I'm her mate.

It's that fucking simple.

I lean down, nuzzling against her neck. Hints of floral

and clean linen invade my senses. She smells so fucking good. My tongue flicks out, wondering if she would taste just as good. Her skin is cool to the touch, tasting vaguely of salt and lavender from the oils placed in her baths.

Delicious.

Rose squirms, moaning softly, but not waking up entirely.

Doesn't matter. Her body still arches toward me, even in sleep. Pride like I've never experienced surges through me and I bring my hand up to rest on her hip, pulling until our bodies are pressed tightly together.

"Malix," she speaks my name, raspy with sleep, but there's nothing tired in the way her ass presses hard against my cock, waking it up within the confines of my pants.

"Good morning, little dragon. I trust you slept well?" I trail light kisses up her neck, stopping at her jaw, just shy of her lips.

"You slept with me." I wait to hear anger in her voice, but it never comes. Only mild curiosity.

"I did. It is my bed after all."

"It is, but you haven't been sleeping in here. Where have you been sleeping? In another dragon's room?" She tries to appear nonchalant, but I hear through her facade.

She's jealous.

I should reassure her, but that wouldn't be nearly as fun. "And if I was?" It's a dick thing to say, but I never claimed not to be one.

Rose huffs and tries to scoot away from me, but my arms tighten around her, keeping her in place. She continues to try to wiggle away from me, but all it's doing is pressing her ass tightly against my hardening cock. I moan softly in her ear.

"Bastard," she hisses, and immediately halts her movements. "Why don't you go to one of your concubines to get the attention you clearly crave."

I laugh, which only proves to piss her off more. She manages to get her leg free and is about to swing it back to hit me in the shin, but I manage to wrangle her until her lithe body lies underneath mine, arms pinned above her head.

"Malix!"

"I've slept in my study."

"What?" Rose stops struggling and looks up at me. "You...really?"

"Really. It's terribly uncomfortable."

"Oh," she whispers and just like that, she's far away from me again, protected behind the walls she's created. "I see."

It's almost as if she wanted me to be in the bed of another dragon. To make it easier for her to hate me, but I won't allow that to happen. My wife will soon learn I'm a persistent man when it comes to something I want.

And I want her.

Slowly, I loosen my hold on her, pulling back. I lie back down, pulling her next to me. For once, she doesn't fight as I lay her across my chest.

"It's your turn." I'm cashing in on the long-overdue history of her life. I want to know everything that brought her to the moment I met her in my hallways.

Was it only days ago?

Feels like a lifetime.

"I don't know what you mean." My wife is many things, but a liar she is not. I feel the way her body tenses on top of me.

I rub her back, trying to bring a semblance of comfort.

Seeing my wife retreat back into her shell makes me feel particularly violent. Still, I want to know.

When she realizes I'm not going to give up, Rose sighs, turning her head so she's looking up at me. "It's not a fun story."

"I don't need a fun story. I just need your story."

Rose hesitates for a fraction of a second before asking, "If I share, you'll share your story too?"

"That's the deal." I nod.

"I'm not sure where to start," she admits. I don't respond, giving her time to collect her thoughts. Of course I want to know all of her history, but I'll take what she can give me.

"I come from a town called Grym Hollow. It's a small, secluded town. Basically you are born there and die there."

"Like this kingdom?"

"I suppose, in a way." She shrugs. "But also different. We don't have a king or queen. It's just a normal town, except we have The Guardian. Many avoid him though. He lives on the outskirts and never wanders into town. He protects Grym Hollow."

Interesting. I don't know why Ender has set up his home in this human town, but he has a reason for everything he does. The Guardian always has knowledge that others don't, so I can only assume this place is important in some way.

It brought me Rose, after all.

"I had a pretty good childhood, not anything I can complain about," Rose continues. "But when I turned eighteen, my parents died in a car accident." She pauses before asking, "Do you know what a car is?"

"My mother was human. Yes, wife, I know what a car is

—or rather was. I expect they've changed a lot since her day," I muse.

"Right, anyways, I was left to take care of my sister and I don't think I would have made it through that time if it wasn't for Stefan."

This time I'm the one that tenses, my hand stilling on her back. Rose notices my change in demeanor and laughs. "Simmer down, dragon. Let me finish my story."

The smile quickly vanishes from her lips as she says, "Stefan was there for me when the whole town decided an eighteen-year-old who had just gone through the most traumatic moment of her life was too much to handle.

"Neither one of us meant for it to happen, but we fell in love. I was still fucked up and not really taking care of myself, but I was so sure that those things wouldn't matter as long as I had the man I loved by my side. I just had to stay positive.

"That worked...for a while. Until it didn't. The sadness always came back and I just couldn't put on an act some days. I retreated and would get resentful when people told me to get over something that happened so long ago. As if losing your parents and the grief that comes with it should have an expiration date.

"My sister was the opposite. She sought out people to escape her misery, always becoming the life of the party. I suppose people cope differently," she adds.

Tears start rolling down Rose's cheeks. Anger and despair like I've never known flare to life within me. "Anyone who has not lost their parents in a horrific way can't even begin to understand the deep sadness and emptiness we feel every fucking day. Shame on those people."

Despite her tears, Rose offers me a smile. She places a

hand on my chest and says, "It is an awful feeling, isn't it? I always feel like I have my grief in check and at random times it unleashes, surprising me.

"Anyway, apparently I didn't have as good of a hold on my grief as I thought I did. I pulled away from Stefan. I couldn't keep pretending to be happy and all he wanted to do was move on from that incident. He said I can't keep living in the past and I should think about the future. It was only fair for our relationship."

I've had relationships before Rose; I wasn't celibate, but I've never been in love. Infatuation and lust? More times than I could count. But it was never serious and always fizzled out in a few months. That was the life I knew, the life I was content with.

But it isn't the life I want anymore.

I want Rose in every way a man could have a woman like her.

"So you grew apart. Is that why you agreed to come here? To get away from Stefan?" I ask the question, but I'm not certain I want to hear the answer.

"Sort of," she admits. "Stefan actually betrayed me. Him and my sister. I found out he was cheating on me with my sister. Both of them connected over their mutual disdain for me, apparently. The grief and sadness I held were too much for them. My sister's the reason I'm here, though. She got pregnant and it wasn't an easy pregnancy. There was a chance she would die in childbirth.

"So, I made a deal with Ender to save my sister. I'm sure she, Stefan, and my niece are one big happy family." Bitterness laces her tone, but I can't blame her.

If her sister and Stefan were here now, I'd burn them to a crisp. They don't deserve Rose's sacrifice, especially since the last thing she did in her mortal world was save her sister.

But if she hadn't done that she would have never ended up here, wrapped up in my arms.

"You will never feel that pain or loss here, Rose. Never. It is the one promise I vow to keep for you." No matter what it costs me, I'm not going back on my word.

There is fear in Rose's eyes. My little dragon is overwhelmed, and I'm willing to let those words rest between us. She will believe them soon enough. "Thank you for telling me." It means more to me than she knows.

"Yeah, well, someone should know." She shrugs and makes me wonder what rampant rumors spread back in her town about their devastating breakup.

I hold Rose a little tighter, scared she would slip through my grasp at any moment. "We're staying in bed all day." I don't care about my duties or figuring out how Rose can break the curse on another dragon again, I just want her.

A surprised giggle leaves her lips. "No, we aren't. We have things to do."

"Fuck those things." I'm fully aware I sound like a child, but I also don't care.

My tone amuses her because she giggles. It's the cutest fucking thing I've heard all day. "We can't. You heard your council. They want to see if I can awaken another dragon."

"Absolutely not," I growl. "You can rest. You don't need to jump back into things now. We have a little time to spare."

"I'm not certain we do. Besides, I'm also curious. Aren't you? I mean, I could really help if I learn how I'm able to awaken them. It would help you against the Nephilim, wouldn't it?"

"Yes," I say begrudgingly. "But if this takes too much out of you, then jumping back into it so quickly might not be the best plan of action."

"Maybe. But I still want to try. And I would prefer it if you were there when I do it." Then my wife gets a wicked glimmer in her eyes, it's there so suddenly, I'm not sure how it happens.

She moves and my eyes trail her every movement. She shifts her body until she's stradling me. My cock presses against her spread thighs, begging to be seated deep inside her.

"Let's make a deal," the wanton woman atop me says.

"I'm listening."

"Come with me to where the dragons sleep and let me try to awaken one. Once I have my answer, we can come back to our room and find"—she rolls her hips over mine and we groan in unison—"ways to congratulate me on my efforts."

"Mmm, I suppose you've convinced me. How can I say no to an offer like that?"

"You can't." She grins and gets off of me before I can protest. "I'm going to bathe. Wait for me here."

And I do.

CHAPTER 19

ROSE

My body still tingles from Malix's touch. Warmth and desire flood me, and I can't deny it any longer. I want my husband.

Even more shocking news: he wants me.

I do my best to keep my lust under control as we reach the cellar underneath the castle. Malix's body is tense as he follows closely behind, reminding me he isn't a fan of this plan. I understand why he wants me to wait another day, but I have to know if I'm able to wake up another dragon like I did for Cyrus.

At some point, Malix sent word to the rest of the council members because they now slowly make their way into the cellar. I look back once, meeting the eye of Aeron. His smug face makes my stomach churn. Did he feel like he won? His outbursts during last night's council meeting solidified my unease around him.

I want to yell that I'm not here because he demanded it. I'm here because I want answers and I want to help.

But it would be a moot point. Men like Aeron only care

if they get their way and not the circumstances surrounding it.

Malix's hand grazes my back and I look into those deep, green eyes of his. "Are you certain, little dragon?"

I steel my resolve and nod. "Yes, I can do this."

"Of that, I have no doubt." The soft smile he gives me nearly makes me call this whole thing off and drag him up to bed and have my wicked way with him.

Calm down, Rose, I know you're cock deprived, but geez.

It was so much easier when I thought my husband was a dick and not *about* his dick.

When I reach the bottom of the stairs, I'm once again hit with a sense of melancholy at the state of these beautiful beasts. *My* beasts. In the short amount of time I have been here, I've started seeing Malix's people as my own. I'm not sure when that shift happened or how.

"My Queen, do you want to try awakening another hatchling?" Vivia asks, coming to stand next to me. I wonder if she has any loved ones slumbering down here and how hard it would be to know you can't do anything for them.

Of course I want to wake a hatchling; I want to wake all the hatchlings, but I want to test out my ability on a full-grown dragon. Maybe I should work up to it, but I've never been the patient sort and I'm not going to start now.

My eyes roam the room. In my shock from seeing the sleeping dragons for the first time, I missed the dragons who lay asleep in their human form. My gaze stops on an older, brown woman wearing a thin, white dress. Her curls frame her face, graying at the roots and fading to black toward the ends.

"Who is she?" I point. Vivia and Malix turn to see who I'm referencing.

"That's Elain. She's an elder, the matriarch of her family," Vivia answers.

"Is her family cursed?"

Vivia shakes her head. "No, she's the only one."

Before Vivia finishes her sentence, I head toward the elder, kneeling at her side. I'm drawn to her, probably because she reminds me of my own grandmother and the endless summer days we would spend at her pool, pretending we were mermaids.

I reach out and gingerly touch my hand to her cheek. She's as cold as ice and if I didn't see the slight rise and fall of her chest, I would think the worst.

What did I think about the last time when I woke Cyrus up? I felt a fierce need to protect him and make sure he was looked after. I made a silent vow to keep him safe.

Safety. Protection. Pure intent. These are the things I need to think about. My eyes close as I try to block out the stares of the council behind me and the expectations falling upon my shoulders.

A warm body presses against mine, but instead of tensing up, I fall into his embrace. Malix's strong arms wrap around me in what I can only describe as possessiveness. His hot breath singes my neck and I shiver.

Focus.

A small part of me though, a part that I just can't ignore, wonders what would happen if I fail. What if I can't wake the dragons and what I did to Cyrus was just a one time thing?

Ender brought me here because he believes I'm the answer the dragons have been searching for. That I'm fit to be the human mate of the dragon king, a title that should scare me shitless, but instead intrigues me in ways I'm not prepared for. But what if I'm not enough?

My heart pounds faster in my chest and my hands begin to shake. From behind me, I hear Aeron growl in annoyance at my lack of progress. This is too much and I'm not prepared for the task.

I go to pull my hands away, but before I can, Malix stops me. His large hands cover mine, keeping them firmly in place. "No, wife. You'll finish what you started."

"I can't...I don't—"

"You can." The faith he has in me almost makes me believe I can. "You did it once and you can do it again. Show them the type of queen you are."

The type of queen I am?

I want to be the same thing I always want to be. Useful. Like what I do matters. From a young age, I dedicated my life to helping others. If there was ever a time I needed those traits, it's now.

Okay, I can do this. I *can* do *this*.

I must have said those words aloud because Malix squeezes my hand and says, "Yes, you can."

The words center me and I close my eyes once again. I remind myself why I'm drawn to this dragon and memories of my grandmother resurface, playing out like an old picture show in my mind.

The warm nights we had jars to catch fireflies. How we would name them and then release them back to their families. The chocolate chip cookies with peanut butter chips she made after I had a bad day. The way her bed squeaked each time we got in to cuddle and read a story before bed.

These were my favorite moments with my grandmother and I miss her dearly. Probably just as much as this grandmother's grandchildren miss her.

A smile forms on my lips and I open my eyes. Almost as

immediately as it came, my smile vanishes when I realize the dragon beneath me didn't stir. "It didn't work," I whisper incredulously.

Disappointment rolls off the council in waves. Even Vivia looks crestfallen, but offers me a tight lip smile when she notices I'm looking. I don't want to look at Malix out of fear I'll see disappointment in his eyes. Coward.

I failed.

"Impossible. Try again, My Queen. I saw you do it once before, you can do it again." Those words might have been encouraging from anyone else, but they came from Aeron. There is a thinly veiled threat behind everything he does. Promises of consequences yet to come.

"It's too soon," Malix says. He moves and I feel the absence of his body heat immediately. I can only assume it's to face Aeron. "She needs more rest. Another day and we'll try again."

"My King, we have no time." Aeron is beginning to sound like a broken record, but one that is quickly gaining traction. For the first time, I see doubt in Vivia's expression. It's brief, here one moment, and gone the next, but it was there all the same.

"Our wards are steadily crumbling, and more Nephilim have been spotted roaming the mountain land. It's only a matter of time until they're at our front door. We have no time!"

Everyone begins to shout at once and I feel the room close in around me. This is my fault. I'm fucking worthless. I had one job and I can't even do that right.

"The queen needs to try again!"

"We are in the end times, My King."

"We should discuss this elsewhere."

All the voices swirl in my head until I can't decipher

who spoke. It's too much. Too much pressure that I obviously can't live up to. Too many voices. Too many doubts. Too many—

Elain's body jerks once and big, brown eyes snap open, blown wide with terror. The elder thrashes, her hand colliding with my cheek. My head snaps to the side and the faint metallic taste of blood fills my mouth. The hit wasn't hard, but I ended up biting my cheek in the process.

Vivia and Aracelia are at my side in an instant, restraining the fighting elder. "She's midshift! Malix!" Aracelia barks as Elain attempts to kick her off. That's when I notice Elain's hands have transformed into sharp talons. One slash of those and a person will be in ribbons.

Before I can fully let that idea sink in, Malix moves, pushing me behind him. He takes over Vivia's place, holding Elain by her arms. For such a small woman, she is sure putting up a powerful fight.

"Elain, stop shifting." My husband's voice is a command that makes even me want to obey. There's a power in it, one that demands to be heard and obeyed. To her credit, Elain tries fighting it, but Malix repeats his command and the elder dragon slowly goes limp in his arms.

Her talons fade back to wrinkly brown hands, but the fear in her eyes never leaves. "Where am I? What happened?" Her voice is hoarse from lack of use. She needs water. It was exactly how Cyrus acted when he broke through the curse. Confused and disoriented.

"You're safe, Elain. Let us take care of you," Malix says. "You've been under a sleeping spell. Aracelia and Vivia will fill you in." The female dragons give curt nods, before helping Elain up. They speak in hushed whispers as Elain weeps softly into Vivia's shoulder.

I can't even begin to know how she's feeling right now.

"We're done for today." Malix's declaration surprises me, but I also don't particularly feel like doing this again. My cheek throbs and fatigue is already setting in, though not as bad as last night. I'm now certain waking the dragons depletes me of my energy.

"Just one more—"

"Lord Aeron, I'll kindly ask you to shut the fuck up before I rip your head from your body."

Wisely, Aeron purses his lips together, though his eyes hold his own murderous intent. I fear that Malix is turning Aeron against him, and as much as I don't care for the older dragon, I also know he's a valuable asset to Malix's council.

He also isn't wrong.

We don't have time.

Not that I'm going to say that to Malix, though. No, I like my head firmly attached to my body.

With a stiff bow, Aeron departs, taking Otis along with him. I have a feeling the other man is little more than the dragon's lapdog. Harmless until provoked.

"Aracelia, Vivia, do you have this handled?" Malix's tone still hasn't gone back to normal, but it also doesn't hold the same venom it held with Aeron.

"Yes, My King. We will get Elain fed and back to her family." Vivia is already leading the elder dragon to the stairs.

"Good. My wife and I are not to be disturbed. You and Aracelia are in charge until tomorrow morning."

Both women nod, taking Elain up to get her fed and clothed, as they try to explain what happened to her.

Then Malix is in front of me, kneeling down. He tilts my head to the side, gaining access to my cheek. It still stings, but it's something I can easily ignore. "You're hurt," he points out.

"I'm okay, really—what are you doing?" I squeak as he lifts me up into his arms, just as he did last night.

"Taking you to bed."

I scoff. "Stubborn male. I'm okay. It was just a hit to the cheek. I swear, I'll live."

The look he flashes me is equal parts terrifying and incredibly alluring. My traitorous body snuggles closer to him.

"We are going back to our room. Don't fucking argue, Rose." I bite back my retort, but glare to convey my annoyance. "And I'm going to soothe your cheek and then I'm going to fuck your stubborn ass into our bed to show you my gratitude."

Gratitude.

I think I'm going to like gratitude.

CHAPTER 20
MALIX

Some would say I'm overreacting. After all, there's only a faint red flush to my wife's cheek. Elain's hit was pure surface level and didn't break her skin, but that doesn't matter to me or my beast. My mate is hurt and all I can think about is taking away her pain.

I sit Rose down on our bed and reach in my bedside table for the healing lotion. "This is really unnecessary," she says again as I unscrew the lid. "I don't even feel it anymore."

That is irrelevant when I can clearly see her reddened cheek. The lotion feels cool on my fingers, and I gingerly touch her cheek. Rose doesn't flinch, so I know her cheek isn't causing her pain, but I need to be certain. Since I'm the reason she got hurt in the first place.

Rose is only in this situation because my kingdom is crumbling. She has done more in a few days than I have achieved in a year, since the Nephilim attacks began. Seeing my wife crouch down next to Elain and her attempts to break the curse has me on edge.

Admittedly, I was nervous when nothing happened at

first. I shamefully believed that she couldn't do it again. Horrible thoughts of my dying kingdom played through my head, and it made me sick to think about losing my people and Rose.

But I shouldn't have doubted her. She's proved herself capable and in front of my entire council, nonetheless.

Ender was right.

Rose is mine. My mate. My queen.

"How does your cheek feel?" I ask, wiping my hands on my pants.

"It still feels fine. Just like it did before you rubbed the lotion on." It's not a thank you, but coming from her it may as well be.

I've always liked my women with a fiery edge to them anyway.

"What about your strength? Are you tired? Need food?" When did she last eat anyway? I'm not doing a good job of meeting my human mate's needs. It's been so long since I've had a human around, I tend to forget their needs differ from dragons. My mother required three small meals a day and lots of water, otherwise she grew lethargic and moody.

"Malix." Rose laughs and cups my face between her hands. They're so fucking soft. It makes me wonder if every part of her will be this soft. "I'm okay. A little tired, but fine. I promise. Besides, there's something else I need." Her features change from playful to something that has my cock aching with the need to be inside of her.

"You know, in my world, in order for a marriage to be complete, we have to consummate it," Rose says, walking her fingers up my chest. She's drinking me in and I'm keen on letting her.

The scent of her arousal fills the room and I clamp

down my beast who's ready to shred her dainty little dress and sheath himself deep inside her pussy.

Soon. But not until she was begging for it.

"Is that so?" My voice is little more than a purr. In truth, bondings aren't fully complete until the mates join through passion. Once that happens, it will be impossible for me to deny Rose. I'm going to want her in my bed, screaming my name every morning and night.

Dragons go through a period of nesting. It usually lasts about a month, depending on the dragons, but in that time, the mates spend their entire time creating their love nest and fucking in it until they pass out in each other's arms. They only leave their nests to eat and drink, but then it's right back to their nests. Bothering a nesting couple could end in the intruder's death. It's best to leave them alone if you don't want to be ripped limb from limb.

Nesting with Rose has crossed my mind multiple times, keeping me up at night with the need to fucking claim her. Every day of our month-long nesting, I'd worship Rose until she forgets all the men that came before me, and I forget any woman other than my wife. If we were lucky, she might fall pregnant with our child by the end of it. I need heirs.

But time is not in my corner. The Nephilim are waking up and the tension with my council threatens to burst each day. Those who I trust are slowly dwindling, so I can't afford the luxury of nesting. Not now. Because if we don't live through this...

No, I can't think this way. We will defend our territory, there's no other fucking option.

This is my home.

My people.

And Rose is my mate.

"Malix?" Rose's soft voice brings me back. Her head is

slightly tilted and the compassion in her eyes nearly sends me to my knees. "I lost you there for a moment. Where were you?"

A loaded question and not one I can easily answer. The price a king pays is his own well-being and I've paid it again and again. Though having a queen to ground me is something I'm not yet accustomed to.

"Our people," I finally settle on. It isn't a lie, now is just not the time to discuss it in depth.

Rose nods like she understands and I've no doubt she does. "You have given enough for your people for one day. We both have. I think it's time for us to enjoy our marriage bed."

I've never heard sweeter words.

"I'm not a gentle lover, Rose. You should know this before we continue." I don't want to hurt her, but I'm part beast. That beast likes to come out during heated moments, and it has been desperate to get its hands on Rose since she got here. My beast always knew Rose was the one for us.

"You and gentle don't belong in the same sentence, husband."

Husband. That's what does it for me. A simple word, but one that carries so much importance, far more than the title of king ever will.

I kiss her. Not a sweet, exploring kiss. No, this kiss is meant to claim. To succumb to my will. I drink Rose like my favorite wine, nipping at her bottom lip. Her tiny gasp goes straight to my cock.

I can't nest with her, but I can give her one night of orgasms.

It will have to be enough for now.

My hand travels up her thigh, inching her dress higher

up her leg. She's so fucking soft and responsive to my touch. Her scent fills the air, and I crave to taste her.

When we break apart, Rose's golden cheeks are flushed red. She pants, her chest heaving, giving me a good glimpse of her cleavage. My mouth waters at the thought of her nipples, teasing them until they become hard points.

"Lie down," I command, expecting a sassy response. Instead, my wife complies, lying down on her back. I move between her legs, hiking her skirts up higher until the cotton of her panties shows. Damn the maids for remembering to supply my wife with them.

"You're drenched for me." Unbridled satisfaction warms my body.

"Don't get too cocky. It's just because I haven't been with someone in a long time." My wife attempts to play her sass card, but the breathiness in her voice tells me her wetness is all for me.

She wants me.

Just as much as I want her.

And I plan on taking my damn time.

I both curse and praise the existence of panties. The white cotton hugs her mound and seeps with her desire. But it's still a barrier between her and me. I need it gone.

My hands slide up her ivory skin, squeezing her thighs between my hands. Rose lets out a dissatisfied whine and I chuckle. "So, impatient, wife."

"If you don't touch me, I'll do it myself," she huffs and reaches her hand down between her legs.

I almost let her.

But her cunt is mine.

"Mine," I growl, pushing her hand away. I grab the band of her panties and slowly slide them down her thighs. Rose kicks them the rest of the way off for me and she is bared from the waist down.

The scent of her arousal only amplifies, sending my beast into a frenzy. *Need her now,* he hisses at me and I'm helpless to do anything other than obey. I lower myself to my knees—Rose is the only woman I'd get on my knees for. My queen deserves to be worshiped.

I spread her wide; her pussy glistens in anticipation for me. "Malix…" Rose begs, arching toward me. "Please—ah!"

The first lick through her folds draws a deep moan from both of us. Her juices explode on my tongue, a sharp sweetness that is distinctly her. I make a V with my fingers, spreading her lips wide.

My tongue dances over her clit, eliciting a cry of pleasure from her lips. "Fuck!" she groans, rubbing her pussy in my face, riding my tongue with wild abandon. Images of her sitting on my face, riding my tongue until she comes over and over again fill my mind.

My dick throbs at the thought.

I tease her clit before taking the sensitive bundle of nerves into my mouth. I suck. *Hard.* Rose's back arches off the bed and she begs for more. "Malix, please. Don't stop. Fuck, husband, don't stop."

"Never," I growl. I'll eat her pussy until she goes limp, squeezing out every orgasm she is capable of.

My girl is wanton, grinding down on my face with moans of ecstasy. She's not quiet. Good. I don't fucking want her quiet. I want everyone to know that my queen is being pleased and enjoys every second of it.

Rose's thighs shake, squeezing around me. My two fingers holding her open are coated with her slick and I move them inside of her. She tightens around them, cursing softly.

My fingers and tongue fuck her, pushing her closer and closer to the edge. My own desire amplifies and the need to be buried deep inside of her is so strong.

"Malix, I'm going to come...fuck—" The words barely leave her gasping lips before she tightens around my fingers. She screams through her orgasm, coming on my face. Her scent will not be easy to wash away, and it thrills me.

I lick her through her orgasm, lapping at her release until she goes limp underneath me. A self-congratulatory smirk plays on my lips as I pull back slowly.

"I hope you aren't getting tired, little dragon. We are just getting started."

CHAPTER 21

ROSE

The last man I had in my bed was a local man from Grym Hollow, shortly after I broke up with Stefan. He was definitely a rebound brought upon by sadness and a little too much alcohol. I don't even remember his real name, just that he went by Jet. In hindsight, that should have been my first clue.

The sex wasn't bad, but Jet grossly overestimated his sexual abilities. I all but had to draw a road map to my clit for him and I could tell that frustrated him. After that little misunderstanding, the sex was fine. We both came—me much later than what Jet probably had hoped for—and went our mutual ways.

I didn't feel any better after fucking him, but I also didn't feel any worse. So I took that as a win.

Sex with Stefan had been good, but only because we had years of love and time to learn one another's body. I didn't think I would ever find someone like that again. A person that made me orgasm and cared for me.

Malix is...everything I didn't think I needed.

I came into this deal not knowing I would be a bride

and ready to throttle The Guardian for that oversight, even though it was technically my fault for not reading the contract thoroughly.

But now...

I think I'm falling for my husband.

"I hope you aren't getting tired, little dragon. We are just getting started." Malix's voice is husky, full of lust and self-satisfaction for making me come so hard. Usually, I would knock him down a peg, but I don't have it in me. Not after that orgasm. It was as if he had already learned my body and knew exactly what I liked.

"Not even close. You haven't come yet."

He's not even naked yet. Neither am I, but I have less clothes on than he does and that just seems unfair.

Malix stands up, licking my arousal from his lips. A shiver goes down my spine at the sheer intensity in which he is staring at me. From this height, his groin is exactly level with my face. A rather impressive bulge outlines his leather pants and my mouth waters with the need to have him down my throat.

I've never been super into giving head, but I've done it because I knew my partner enjoyed it. Sometimes I found pleasure in it as well, but I never craved a cock down my throat as much as I crave Malix's.

I peel his tight leather pants off while Malix takes off his shirt. My breath catches in my lungs upon seeing him naked for the first time.

His shirt teased at the muscles that lay underneath and the tightness of his pants always gave me some indication of what he is working with—which is a lot—but it never did it justice. I know that now.

Malix's body is hard as stone, sculpted from marble as if by Michelangelo himself. Each valley and divot of his body is a delicious temptation made of sin. My eyes trail down his torso to the V of his hips. Farther still to see the dragon of a cock standing at attention.

"Holy fuck, that's a weapon," I murmur, not meaning to speak the words out loud.

"See something you like, wife?" The arrogance in his tone, for once, is a turn-on.

"Fuck yes." Very much.

On instinct, my hand reaches out, wrapping around his shaft. My fingers don't touch and I'm slightly terrified that his cock will rip me in two.

Well, what doesn't kill you makes you stronger.

I'm about to have the strongest vagina in Dragon's Keep.

"Your mouth, wife. Give it to me." Malix's command is liquid heat straight to my core.

I've never considered myself a submissive lover, but I'm happy to play the part now.

My mouth opens, tongue out and ready to taste. Malix curses and guides his erection into my eager mouth. I lap at his tip tasting his salty precum.

Only half of him has entered my mouth, but already he's deep down my throat. I hollow my cheeks and relax my throat the best I can. Breathing in and out through my nose.

"Fucking perfection," Malix growls and I preen at his praise. "I'm going to fuck this pretty mouth, wife, and I want you to take it."

My answer is a moan. Malix reaches down, one hand pulling my hair out of my face and the other holding the back of my head. My body braces itself, prepared for the rough face-fuck he's about to deal me.

Malix starts thrusting his hips, keeping my head in place. I take his cock down, down, down, farther than I have ever had a man. I moan and gag around him, keen on letting him move me to his will. Spit runs down my chin and tears spring to my eyes.

This is so fucking hot.

He's relentless with his thrusts, moving in and out of my mouth like his life depends on it. He loosens his hold on my head, and I bob my head in time with his movements. His low moans fill the room, along with the obscene sounds of my gagging.

"Are you going to swallow my cum like a good girl, Rose?"

My thighs drip with my arousal. I can only nod.

Yes. Give it to me.

Malix grunts, jerking his hips once more before he sputters into my mouth. His warm, salty cum coats my tongue and I do my best to swallow his entire load, though some of it dribbles down my chin.

He pulls his cock out, leaving me gasping for breath as if I had just run a mile. I'm amazed to see that he's still so hard. Do dragons need no time between their orgasms? Because if that is the case, I'm about to have one sore body. And I'm pretty certain I'm okay with that.

I barely have time to steady myself before Malix pushes me back on the bed and hovers over me. His body towers over mine, pining me in place. "I need to be inside of you."

Even though I saw the evidence with my own eyes, I can't believe Malix is ready to go again. No downtime. Is this man even real?

Reading the surprise in my eyes, Malix laughs. "Dragons are sexual beings. We have a high sex drive."

"I'm starting to learn that," I pant, voice hoarse from his brutal mouth-fuck. His tip is teasing my entrance, ready to sheath its way inside me.

"Are condoms a thing in this world?" I ask, the thought coming to my brain, and I ask before I can stop myself. Judging by the puzzled look on his face, I have my answer.

"Doesn't matter. I have an implant," I say. Still, he looks at me like I had just sprung an extra head. "So I don't get pregnant," I explain.

Understanding colors his face finally. "Dragons have an herbal mixture to prevent pregnancy if we decide we don't want children."

And I definitely don't want to talk about *that* right now. Later, but not now.

I hook my legs around his waist, pulling him closer and meeting his lips with a searing kiss. It does its job and distracts him from the whole baby talk. Our combined orgasms mingle on my tongue as we kiss. His tip notches at my entrance, slipping in.

I brace myself, knowing he's going to be a tight fit. All at once, he pushes in and I scream out, both from surprise and something that straddles pain and pleasure.

Our hips are flush, pressed so tightly together. I look down to where our bodies join and I blush. My pussy lips are spread obscenely wide, allowing him access to the most intimate part of me.

"You take me so well, wife," he purrs in my ear, kissing his way down my throat, nipping as he goes. His mouth reaches my breasts, and he takes a nipple into his mouth. I moan, no longer focusing on the pain of him inside me.

He flicks his tongue over my nipple, and it stiffens to a painful point. In every way possible, my body is adjusting to him. "Malix, take me." If I didn't feel him move inside of me, I felt like I would explode from overstimulation.

"Whatever my queen asks." He pulls away from my taut nipple with a soft pop and drives his hips into me. It is fast and hard, exactly what I need. I don't need nor want to feel the gentle strokes and caresses of a lover. I need Malix in a way a lioness needs her lion.

Or like a dragoness needs her dragon.

Already I can feel my climax quickly approaching and judging by the way Malix is looking at me, with open admiration and possessiveness, I know he's not far away either.

The room fills with the vulgar sounds of us fucking, his balls hitting my ass with each thrust, the bed bumping up against the wall, and our mutual sounds of pleasure.

Together, our bodies spasm and I clench around him. Malix roars in pleasure and we come as one, toppling over the edge together.

Neither one of us speaks at first. I'm too busy trying to catch my breath and I take pride in the fact that I made Malix just as breathless.

For the first time, I don't need words to express how I'm feeling. I simply let my lips on his convey every emotion I'm feeling.

I can't feel my body and I'm thinking I should be concerned. It was foolish of me to think one time with Malix would be enough.

Spoiler alert, it wasn't. And now my body is ultimately paying the price.

Definitely worth it.

Malix comes back from the washroom, holding two towels. He starts to clean my body and I'm slightly mortified when he cleans his cum from between my legs. I just let this man do terribly delicious things to my body and I'm feeling self-conscious because he's cleaning me? Doesn't make sense to me, either.

Eventually I surrender to his cleaning because although I don't want to go to bed sticky, I also don't think my legs would be able to carry me to the washroom for a bath.

With the second towel, Malix dries me off and tosses both towels to the ground when he finishes. He produces something out of a capped vial and pours the thick lotion substance onto his hand, and starts to rub it between my legs.

"What's that?" Curiosity gets the better of me.

"This," he says, rubbing higher up between my thighs, "is for the soreness."

"Oh," I manage and decide I most definitely am falling for my husband.

I struggle to keep my eyes open, not yet ready to fall asleep, but my body has different plans for me. "Malix?" I murmur.

"Hmm?" He pulls a blanket over my naked body, and I hum as the warmth engulfs me.

"Are you sleeping with me tonight?"

"Tonight, and every other night, little dragon."

I smile at the nickname, his chosen term of affection. That too is growing on me. That or I'm too sexed out of my mind to think properly.

My dragon husband gets into bed next to me and another thought comes forward in my mind.

"Malix?"

"Yes, wife."

"Why haven't you shown me your dragon yet?" I don't know why it popped into my head, but for a dragon husband, he's seriously lacking on the dragon part. I want to meet his beast and that introduction is long overdue.

"My apologies. I didn't know you were interested in seeing my dragon."

I scoff weakly, my eyes fluttering closed. Sleep is an incessant son of a bitch, and I curl up on his chest. "I think it's obvious that I would want to see him. I bet he's cute."

A low rumble leaves his chest, and he chuckles. "I'm not sure cute is the word I would use."

"No, it's definitely the word I'm going to use. My cute dragon husband," I say between yawns.

Malix rubs my back and I feel myself start to drift off.

"I'll introduce you to him tomorrow."

"Good," I murmur and finally let sleep claim me.

CHAPTER 22

MALIX

The mood in my meeting chambers is somber as we listen to the reports from last night. It's not good. Not fucking good at all.

Early this morning word was sent to my chambers, drawing me away from my sleeping wife. Rose looked so peaceful and thoroughly fucked. I didn't have the heart to leave her. I also didn't want her to think I ran out on her so I left her a letter on her bedside table, telling her I would meet her tonight.

Last night something changed fundamentally between us. Before, I couldn't say with full certainty, but this morning I can confidently say Rose is mine. In every sense of the word. Our bond has grown stronger, though it's not at its full potential yet. Even now, I want her. To fuck her. To taste her. To nest her properly.

But that isn't in the stars for us. At least not yet.

"The entire west border is flooded with Nephilim, far more than we have ever experienced before. We tested the strength of our wards in the west, and they are waning quickly. I fear the worst, My King," the young soldier, barely past the age of a hatchling, says. Since when did we start robbing the nests of babes to produce a full team of guards?

We have no time.

Aeron's words reverberate in my mind. I know he's right. I hate that he's right, and I can't deny that anymore when the evidence is staring me in the face.

We need more of our dragons awake. Which means I would require more from Rose and be unable to provide her with much in return. My Rose is so damn caring that she would wake the entire kingdom if I let her, but I know how much energy an awakening costs her. I'm not willing to risk her.

But she's only one person.

The heinous thought enters my head. Rose *is* only one person and Ender did bring her here to help my people. I should be taking full advantage of her talents, but if I push her too far, the only person capable of breaking the curse will be out of commission. She needs to be protected too.

However, I refuse to see Rose as a pawn in my war. She's my queen and I vowed to protect her. I won't go against that promise. Not when everything between us has changed so drastically.

"Did you catch sight of Gadreel?" The only hope we have for time is if the Nephilim king is still imprisoned in the mountains. His people won't act until their king is free.

The guard shakes his head. "No, My King. None of the guards spoke of seeing Gadreel. We can only assume he is still in the mountains."

I don't like assumptions. I need facts. Assumptions allow room for mistakes and mistakes lead to death.

"We need to send a warning to the other territories," I say to the table. The guard, sensing he's dismissed, bows, and leaves the room. Aeron, Otis, Vivia, and Aracelia all turn to me. For once, everyone agrees.

"I can arrange a messenger," Aeron supplies, but I shake my head.

"No, I must go. This is business between rulers, just like how it was in the past. Besides, there's too much to say that we can't convey in a simple message. I also want to investigate the infestation of Nephilim." I need to see with my own eyes if Gadreel has awoken.

"I'll go with you," Vivia is quick to offer, and I nod. I couldn't do this alone and she's the only one I trust by my side.

I also want Aracelia to remain at the castle. I don't trust leaving Aeron and Otis alone to their own devices and Aracelia is a good council member. She doesn't always agree with me, but I trust that she has the best interest of our kingdom at heart.

Perhaps Aeron did too, but his ideals are also filled with greed and exploitation. He will climb over anyone if it means he achieves his desired outcome.

I don't know what my father saw in him.

"We will leave at first light." I stand, ending the meeting. My gaze locks with Aracelia. "You're in charge while I'm gone. Keep the castle closed. No one comes in or out until I get back."

"Yes, My King," she answers automatically.

I don't miss the death glare Aeron shoots my way. As one of the senior members of my council, palace responsibilities fall to him while I'm gone. It's an insult I didn't choose him, and he knows it.

I can't worry about that now because I have a date with my wife I can't miss.

ROSE AWAKENED another dragon today and I'm glad to see she doesn't look as fatigued as she did when awakening Cyrus and Elain. I wish I had been with her during it, out of my own selfish curiosity. My beast has other reasons he wanted to be there, and they all have to do with protecting our mate.

She's with me now though. She's safe.

"So, how long do you think you'll be gone?" I hear the hesitation in her voice. I updated her on everything that happened at the council meeting today and I can see my wife struggling with the reality of me leaving.

I don't want to leave her, especially after last night. I just want to fuck her into our bed every night and morning, but our enemies grow stronger. If I want more time with Rose, I first need to assure we have a future that spans past the month.

"A week at most. Vivia and I need to see the growing numbers of Nephilim for ourselves. We also need to speak with the other leaders of Mescos. They need to prepare for the worst."

"Does that leave me in charge?" The horror on her face makes me smile. One day she won't fear her title. She'll thrive on it.

"Decisions will be passed to you for final approval. I left Aracelia in charge of the daily tasks while I'm away. She's familiar enough with the procedures and a good leader. You can focus on—"

"Awakening the dragons," she finishes.

I was going to say her garden because I'm not thrilled with the idea of Rose awakening the dragons without me here. It's not a control thing either. I don't give a damn what she does, I just want her safe. I can see herself pushing herself to the brink of exhaustion for the dragons, all the while ignoring her own well-being.

"I'll be careful." She smiles, reading me like an open book. "I want to help."

"You already are." I stop walking once we reach her garden. The revival process is slow, but she's out here most days with Mina, attempting to resurrect life into the neglected garden. There are glimmers of life peeking through the dead foliage, so whatever she's doing is working. I haven't seen this area blossom to its full potential since my mother. I find I miss how it once was; a small piece of her.

"Enough doom and gloom. We came out here for one reason. Now let's go, let me see him." Her contagious smile affects me, and I return it.

She's making me soft.

No, she's making me stronger.

She's making the whole damn kingdom stronger.

Show her. My dragon is impatient, wanting Rose to view all of us. She needs to accept every piece of me and that includes my beast.

I start to strip, feeling Rose's eyes on me. I hear an appreciative hum and turn to see my wife blatantly checking out my ass. "See something you like, wife?"

Rose doesn't even pretend to look chastised. She meets my heated glare with her own, smirking. "I do. Do you always get naked before you shift?"

"The majority of the time, no. I know a trick to make my clothes shift with me. But I like how you look at me when I'm naked."

"Hmm. You are allowed to always shift in front of me."

"I'm glad I have your permission." If I don't start to concentrate, I'm going to take my wife right here on the grassy floor. The excitement in her eyes is the only thing keeping me grounded. She may want me right now, but she wants to see my dragon more.

When I finish stripping, I hand my clothes over to Rose who drops her eyes to my not-so-subtle erection. A throaty laugh leaves my lips, getting her attention.

"Well, it's just there. Of course I'm going to look at it," she mumbles with the slightest hint of a blush to her cheeks.

"You are going to do more than look at it when I take you back to our bed."

"Promises, promises," she sings.

This is a promise I intend to keep.

I put some distance between us, giving me enough space to shift. I reach for my beast awaiting deep down inside of me. Shifting is as easy and as natural as breathing. I don't have to think about it, my beast comes when I call him. There's a slightly uncomfortable feeling as the switch happens, but I hardly notice it anymore. My body is accustomed to the change.

The shifting process takes seconds if that. I stand tall, all ten tons of pure fiery beast. My scales are black, with black spikes framing my face and trailing down my neck. They flatten when they reach the rest of my body. My onyx-colored wings stretch, spanning the size of over half the courtyard.

My yellow cat-like eyes adjust to my surroundings before landing on Rose. Our bond is alive with wonderment and curiosity. There's an underlying fear, which will go away in time. Rose will know that I would never hurt her.

I'll hurt others for her. Rip to shreds any dragon or Nephilim that defies my queen.

"Wow," she whispers, taking a tentative step forward. Her emotions fight each other, grappling with the idea of touching me or staying back.

"You can touch. I won't harm you," I speak through our bond, startling her.

Rose composes herself quickly and closes the distance between us. I bow my head to get to her level. *"You're safe,"* I assure, and push that emotion into her, filling our bond with security.

I watch her steel her resolve and soon her hand is on my snout, feeling the textured scales underneath. She sees dragons walking around every day, but she's still in awe when looking at my dragon.

Pride and intense alpha satisfaction fuel me. I flick out my tongue, licking her arm and she pulls away with a giggle.

"Satisfied little dragon?" I ask, curling my tail around her small frame.

"So very satisfied. You look..." The word seems to elude her, amplifying my already cocky demeanor.

"I fucking love how you look at my dragon," I murmur and nuzzle her neck. Her soft skin is a stark contrast to my rough, leathery scales.

"I want to see you fly, but before that, I need you. Now. Shift back."

Not normally one to take orders, I obey hers without any questions.

CHAPTER 23
ROSE

Malix left early this morning, but not before leaving me with a tender ache between my thighs. It was slow, sensual sex, far different than the fucking we did a few nights ago. There was something different in the way our bodies collided and how we watched each other fall over the edge together.

Pure bliss. That's the only way I can describe it.

Although the hour is early, I find myself not able to go back to sleep. It is crazy to say, but I missed Malix the moment he left. Emptiness settled over me, along with the fear of running a kingdom I know little about. Malix has faith in my abilities, and I desperately want to live up to those expectations.

Breakfast is a simple meal of oatmeal and berries with apple cider. I don't have much of an appetite for it, but I manage to eat about half of it before giving up. I need the fuel for the things I have planned for today.

Mina meets me at the entrance to the castle cellar. The smile she gives me is melancholic and tired. It hits me for the first time that not only did Malix leave, but her wife followed him as well. I should have realized this earlier, but I was too wrapped up in my own husband leaving.

"How are you doing?" I pull Mina into a hug. The woman sinks into me and I feel the weight of her sadness.

"I know it's silly to be this upset"—she sniffles into my shoulder—"but I hate it so much when she's gone. I never sleep well and I'm in a constant state of worry. I try to put on a brave face for our son because I don't want him to be scared, but it's so exhausting."

On a minuscule scale, I understand how she feels. My relationship with Malix is still so young and new. The attraction happened on day one, but it wasn't until recently that we allowed ourselves to give in to those desires. Now I feel connected to him in a way I haven't ever been connected to anyone else. Even Stefan, and we dated for years.

What was it he called it?

Mates.

The word doesn't seem so heavy as it once did.

"Well, you don't need to be strong around me. Cry if you want. I've done a lot of that in the past few years, and I can confidently say it makes you feel marginally better."

Mina laughs, pulling away from my embrace. Her eyes are shiny with unshed tears and cheeks tinted pink. "How are you holding up?"

I inhale a deep breath. "Honestly? I didn't expect to miss him as much as I do. It's such an odd feeling to care for someone this deeply after only knowing them for a short period of time.

"Yeah, that would be the intensity of the mate bond. It's the best thing, but times like this make me hate it just a little bit."

"I'm beginning to see that."

A somber silence falls between us, and I loop my arm through hers. The saying misery loves company has never been truer than in this moment.

"So, what is the plan for today?" Mina says after a while, probably tired of listening to our feet tread down the stairs.

I fill her in on what I plan to accomplish today. I made a promise to Malix that I wouldn't overextend myself when it came to waking the dragons. It's a promise I intend to keep, but that doesn't mean I plan on sitting down and twiddling my thumbs until he returns.

The goal today is to awaken two dragons, an adult and a hatchling, something I have not yet attempted. I've kept the awakening process to one dragon per day, but at that rate, it will take forever to wake the rest of the kingdom. We don't have time for that, as Aeron likes to remind us daily.

Two isn't much of a difference either, but it's a start in the right direction. This process will take time and I can't go too hard too fast. No matter how much I wish to wake every single one of the sleeping dragons.

We reach the bottom of the stairs and the sheer number of dragons still in need of help overwhelms me. Mina reaches for my hand and gives it an encouraging squeeze. "How about we start with those two over there? Mother and daughter."

I look at where she's pointing and see a medium-sized brown dragon curled in on a small girl in a blue, long-sleeve dress.

"Do you know them?" My heart breaks for the mother and daughter, but the only silver lining is that they are together in their slumber. How much harder would it be for the little girl to be without a mother? Or the mother's pain of not knowing if her daughter would ever wake up again.

"Not well, but yes, I know them. They are sweet people and don't have any other family as far as I know. Just each other."

Mina stays a little behind me, making sure I have enough room. "How long have they been cursed?"

"I'm not certain, but I want to think it's been close to a month."

A month. A month of your life stolen from you. No wonder these dragons wake up disoriented. Nephilim are doing more than simply cursing them with sleep, they are taking away their time and memories that could have been made during the days, weeks, or months they've been asleep.

I place my hands on the mother's rough scales and the child's hand. The love between a mother and a child is supposed to be the purest kind of love there is. I don't have children and frankly, I don't know if I'll ever want to have kids, it's a discussion Malix and I need to have, but I know how much my mother doted on me and my sister.

She was the person I ran to if I had a bad day. The person I would tell all my secrets to. She knew how to make me laugh and knew exactly what I needed even if I didn't always want to hear it.

I got eighteen years with my mother, and I wouldn't trade a single day of them away. Of course, I wish I had more, but I didn't. That's life. It's fucked up and messy. Unpredictable and draining. But it can also hold the most exciting and thrilling time as well. It can lead you down paths you never saw yourself on and make you realize how much you deserve the good when it comes your way.

I want this mother and daughter to have more time together. Despite the dangers outside our borders, despite the lack of promises for tomorrow, I know if they had to choose, they would choose to spend their time together and be conscious.

"Rose, step back." Mina's voice cuts through the fog in my brain. Soft hands tug me backward and I stumble. And not a moment too late. The dragon thrashes once and shifts before us. Her frail body drapes over her daughter's and she sobs. Long wails of agony and fear.

The faintest of movement underneath her has the mother pulling back. "Zuri?"

"Momma?" The girl—Zuri—cries. "Momma, what happened?"

Mother and daughter turn toward Mina and I, pupils blown wide with terror. "What happened? Where are we?"

Mina is at their side in an instant, taking off her own cloak and draping it around the mother. She pulls it taut around her neck, more so to keep the chill out and less for her own modesty.

Mina speaks softly to the pair in the gentle way I've come to associate with her. I'm glad that she's here because I don't think I could conduct myself in the same manner she does. There is a certain motherly quality she possesses that I'm not sure I have, despite the years I spent raising my sister.

"Let's get them to the kitchens for food and water," Mina says, helping the mother up. I reached for Zuri, but the dragoness lurches and pulls her daughter close to her chest. A deep inhuman growl leaves her lips.

I put my hands up in a way that I hope conveys that I mean no harm, but her hold on Zuri doesn't loosen. I try not to take it personally because this woman doesn't know me or know that I'm their queen, but it still stings. It's a stark reminder that just because I'm queen doesn't automatically make me one of them.

"On second thought." Mina smiles apologetically. "Let me take them upstairs and fill them in on the happenings while you rest."

Unlike the others, I don't feel the same fatigue or grogginess I did before. If anything, I feel slightly winded. So maybe that's progress?

Even though I want to help, I see logic in what Mina is saying. She's a familiar face and someone the dragons can trust. I nod my acquiescence.

"I'll check in on you later. We can have dinner together," she suggests.

"I would like that."

I offer the two awakened dragons one last smile before Mina leads the mother and daughter upstairs, leaving me to decide my next moves.

I DON'T GO BACK to my chambers to rest. My mind is alive and buzzing with thoughts of Malix and the work I can do here while he's gone. Although the fatigue hasn't hit, I don't go back to the cellar to awaken more dragons. It would be a foolish task to do on my own.

Instead, I go to my garden.

My watering can is where I last left it, perched by the well. I fill it and start on the north side where budding roses have begun to bloom. It's a small victory, but a victory all the same. I like seeing my efforts come to fruition.

Tending to the garden here is easier. It's maybe the soil or air or...something. Things grow faster here. More vibrant and beautiful. There's so much beauty in this kingdom and I haven't even seen half of it.

As I water my rose bushes, my mind wanders to Grym

Hollow. How the town appears so picturesque, but where secrets run deep. To be honest, it was stifling there. Some people are meant for small towns, but I'm not one of them. There was never any change and no one ever let you forget your past, no matter how far you ran from it.

My sister thrived in the small town. She had friends, far more than I ever had, even when my parents were alive and when I didn't push people away. She was—still is—popular, despite half the town knowing my boyfriend cheated on me with my sister. The townspeople enjoyed rationalizing the second-most traumatic incident of my life by blaming their infidelity on my declining mental health.

It must be so much easier now that I'm not there to remind her every day of what she took from me. Not that I ever said anything to her about it, no, just my presence was enough to remind her of their betrayal. Perhaps this deal brought peace to more than just me. She gets to have her perfect family and I get to...

Fall in love all over again.

It's new and fragile and completely scary, but it's there, budding like the roses are. And if I'm not completely wrong with reading people, I think Malix feels the same way.

"My Queen."

The voice jolts me back to now and I spin. My heart immediately drops at the two approaching figures.

Aeron and Otis.

Don't show fear. They are part of my husband's council and while my husband isn't here they would defer to me. Though Malix did mention Aracelia could handle most of the day-to-day happenings.

"Lord Aeron. Lord Otis. What can I do for you?" *And how can I get you the fuck away from me?*

Aeron smiles, though it reminds me of a lion who just

found a herd of zebras. "We were in the dining hall when we heard Mina speaking to a mother and daughter. Ones you just awakened."

I nod, though there isn't a question in his statement.

"You are getting stronger, My Queen. You hardly look put out at all."

I'm not sure whether his words are praise or an insult to my appearance, all the same, I smile. "Thank you. I'm glad I was able to bring a daughter and mother back to one another."

"Yes, it is quite a sweet reunion," Aeron says, though he seems disinterested. "How are you feeling?"

If this is a trap, I'm not sure how to navigate it. Something feels off about the two men. Aeron being Aeron isn't a surprise, but the way Otis squirms under my gaze and how he can't quite meet my eyes has me on edge.

"I feel fine," I say slowly. "So, I decided to tend to my garden."

"Yes, we see that."

"We want to know why you are tending to your garden and not awakening more dragons," Otis blurts, words tumbling out of his mouth before he could stop them. Aeron huffs, clearly annoyed with his partner.

So much for subtlety.

I bristle at his tone and clear accusation. "It's not safe for me to push myself. Malix or Mina should be there in case anything goes south. I also promised my *husband*," I emphasize to remind them of our places, "that I would not overexert myself in his absence."

"If it is a chaperone you need, then Otis and I would gladly offer our help," Aeron says.

I do my best not to roll my eyes, but I don't think I'm

successful. It's the same song and dance over and over again and frankly, I'm getting tired of it.

"That won't be necessary. Mina is a great companion, and we will awaken more tomorrow. If you'll excuse me, I need to get back to watering." With all the effort I can muster, I turn my back on the councilman and his lackey.

I expect the conversation to be over. I *want* the conversation to be over, but the two dragons can't take my no for an answer.

"I will ask you one more time, Rose, will you come with me to awaken more dragons?" Aeron's voice is so close, I feel his hot breath on the back of my neck.

I whirl, my curls bouncing and hitting Aeron in the chest. "It's Queen Rose to you, and I have already given you my answer. Learn to accept no and go back to whatever hellish hole you crawled out of."

Aeron's much taller frame shakes with mirth. I take a step back, only to run into a hard chest behind me.

Otis.

I didn't even see him move.

"Unfortunately, *My Queen,*" he snarls, "that answer doesn't work for us."

Arms wrap around me, pinning me in place. I try to scream, but a cloth covers my mouth.

"This could have ended differently," Aeron tsks.

That's the last thing I hear before everything goes black.

CHAPTER 24

MALIX

The Nephilim infestation is worse than the reports say. West of Dragon's Keep is territory not claimed by any of the five other kingdoms and has been the imprisonment for Nephilim for the last century.

We fly high above the wandering Nephilim; careful not to alert the creatures of our presence. I've never seen so many in one place and never this close. They are tall creatures, about the size of two or three average men. Their brute strength and ability to dip into magic make them a deadly foe.

According to every text I've found on these creatures, Nephilim are a conquering species and have been since the discovery of Mescos. Under their rule, every other supernatural creature would be a slave to the Nephilim; beat, murdered, and assaulted for their sheer amusement. If the Nephilim were to ever succeed and bring down the six kingdoms, Mescos would no longer be a country where supernatural creatures lived in relative peace.

It would be a place of torture and death.

I can't let that happen.

Vivia flies beneath me, taking in the same sight as me. Even from here, I can sense her fear. Not for herself but for her family and the life they created together. It's exactly how I feel when I think about losing Rose.

"There are dozens of them, if not one hundred. How many did the guards report on?" Vivia asks through our bond all dragons share when in our natural form.

"The most? A dozen."

"This is more than a dozen."

"No shit," I huff. Not mad at Vivia for pointing out the obvious, but upset the reported numbers have grown exponentially. Time to act is approaching rapidly and I wouldn't be caught unawares.

"Let's land. Kraken's Lagoon is close by. We should be out of Nephilim detection range there." I just hope the kraken king won't mind the intrusion. He's a good man, but a powerful leader. His people, like my own, come first. As long as he doesn't feel his people are threatened, we shouldn't have a problem.

I lead Vivia to the southernmost tip of Kraken's Lagoon, landing with a loud thud reverberating the soggy ground around me. As soon as I get my bearings together, I switch forms.

Behind me, I hear Vivia do the same. "Stupid magic," she murmurs, rummaging through the pack she carried for clothes. I smirk at her comment and silently thank my father for bartering with a Pixie for this particular magic that allows my clothes to transform with me.

So much more convenient.

Vivia is dressed in under a minute, slinging the pack over her shoulder. "Did you see Gadreel?"

One of our biggest reasons for flying all the way out here is not only to see how many Nephilim have escaped their imprisonment, but to see if their king has as well. Gadreel is easy to spot among the horde of giant creatures. He stands a few feet taller than the rest of his people and the entirety of the left side of his face is burnt to a crisp, thanks to my father.

"No. For now, he seems to still be in his prison, but it won't be for much longer." This problem will expand outside Dragon's Keep if it has not already. Nephilim are tricksters as well as conquers. They invade in surprise attacks and thrive on chaos.

"We need to warn the other rulers of Mescos. Everyone must stay vigilant and prepare for war."

"I agree with that, My King, but," Vivia starts, "how do you expect us to get the word out to the other five kingdoms? Time isn't on our side, and we don't have messengers to spare."

I thought of this. I thought of every angle possible because if I don't, it means someone I know or love can get hurt. There's only so much guilt a king can carry, keeping him up at night, agonizing over it all.

Landing here was not a random thought. The other leaders of Mescos will need to be informed and gathered for a meeting. The best way to get that information out is through waterways.

The krakens have access to any body of water whether it be fresh or saltwater. I'm not certain how they do it, and none of the krakens I've ever met are willing to part with that information, but it serves us right now.

"We won't need to," I say, "he should be here any moment."

"Who?"

Before the word is even out of her mouth, the calm water starts to ripple. Vivia steps away from the edge and we watch as a figure appears from the watery depths below. Inky, purplish-black tentacles ascend from below. I have seen those tentacles crush a man's skull and drag others down to their water grave. They are an extension of his body and a powerful tool he wields with precision.

The kraken king greets us in his hybrid form. Part monster, part human. From the waist up, glistening muscles flex as he moves closer to the bank. His skin is the shade of tree bark after a night full of rain. His black locs hang low down his chest.

"King Malix," his voice booms in the otherwise quiet evening air. Although I can't see any others, I know he hasn't come alone. "I received your message this morning. What urgent matters elicit a visit from the dragon king?"

"King Allarick, it's been far too long." Honestly, I don't remember the last time I've seen the kraken king face-to-face. We aren't close allies, but we are cordial. "I've come for two reasons."

"Oh?" His green eyes glimmer in the low light. "And what are those?"

"I have a favor to ask—"

"Ah, there it is." He stops me before I can get the rest of my reasoning out. "You only visit when you need my people to benefit yours. Otherwise, us krakens are supposed to fend for ourselves, is that it?"

"No." There isn't time for this conversation now, but I entertain it all the same. "Ask for what you want and if it's in my power, it will be yours. If you agree to help me."

Allarick pauses, considering my offer. Truthfully, I don't know what the krakens would want from us. They are one of the most self-sufficient kingdoms in Mescos. It makes me wonder just how self-sufficient they truly are.

"What is it that you'll need from us?" Allarick finally asks.

"I need a message to go out to all kingdoms. I have information about the Nephilim. It's imperative that we prepare for the worst."

Allarick doesn't speak for a long time. I've learned over the years it's one of his favorite tactics. Prolong the silence in hopes that others will continue to speak to cover up the awkwardness.

Too bad I take solace in silence.

"Very well. I will send my men to deliver the message and bring them here. But in return I need something."

"And that is?"

Allarick produces a closed clam from god knows where and hands it to me. It's wet and slimy, but I school my face to remain neutral.

"There's a list inside of supplies I'm in need of as soon as possible. Vow you'll get them to me in a timely manner and I'll send my men now."

Before I agree to anything, I pry open the clam and take out the soaked seaweed paper. I look over the supplies and frown. "Dresses, toiletries, and nonperishable foods?" I inquire.

Allarick doesn't elaborate. "Do we have a deal?"

"We do. You'll get what you requested as soon as the meeting is over and I'm back home to gather these items for you."

Allarick gives a curt nod. "There are cabins a mile from here. You are free to use them for the night. The others, if they agree, to which I make no promises, will be here over the next few days."

That means I'll be away from Rose longer than I intended, but it is the best bet we have.

I nod solemnly. "Then it's settled."

Allarick nods. "So, it is. We will meet again soon, Dragon King."

CHAPTER 25

ROSE

The stone flooring is cold on my cheek, but my groggy mind doesn't understand why I'm here. My muscles ache from the odd position I awake from, and I groan as I push myself off the ground. The room is poorly lit and it takes my eyes a moment to adjust.

It only takes me a moment to recognize the room. I've grown familiar with it over the past few days I've spent here.

I'm in the cellar...but how?

Then it hits me all at once.

Otis. Aeron. The garden. The verbal fight that followed and then a hand—no, a cloth?—covered my mouth. The last thing I saw was Aeron's smug face before darkness took me.

Fear settles over my body, and I contemplate my next move. I still feel slightly sluggish from whatever they used to knock me unconscious, but I test my body's ability and stand up.

"Ahh, you're awake. Finally." Aeron steps out of the

shadows like a vampire who just lured their next victim into his home.

Or a dragon into its nest.

Otis, ever the loyal lapdog, appears next to him. Unlike Aeron who stands with the confidence of a man who is used to getting what he wants, Otis appears meek and unsure next to him. That could be a good thing, right? It means he could be persuaded to my side.

That dream quickly deflates when Otis catches me staring at him and shifts his expression to a glare.

"What did you do to me?" I ask, backing up to put more distance between us. Didn't all those detective shows I used to watch say something about keeping your captive talking while you assess your situation and find ways to escape?

I doubt those victims ever faced dragons before.

"Interesting stuff, isn't it? A simple mixture a demon once taught me. Inhaling the substance causes temporary loss of consciousness."

Explains how I got into this situation but doesn't explain why. "Why are you doing this to me?"

"Don't take it personally, Rose. I would have done this to anyone if I knew they could awaken the dragons. Unfortunately, you are the only one with that ability, so you are useful to me," Aeron says, looking entirely too smug with himself.

I still don't get it though. I understand wanting to wake up dragons, we can both agree that we share that goal. But he's been insistent on it since the moment we learned of my abilities. What is his angle here?

"We could be working together, Aeron. We *should* be working together. I want to awaken the dragons as much as you do, but Malix believes—"

I don't see it coming until it was too late. Aeron's hand

collides with my cheek, whipping my face to the side. I stumble, nearly falling from the force of the slap, but I catch myself. The pain doesn't hit immediately. It's the shock that outweighs the throbbing in my cheek.

He hit me. A man has never hit me before.

"Malix is wrong," he snarls, his body towering over me. Despite my best efforts, I flinch away. "He's ignored the danger time and time again. He hesitates when he should strike and because of that, our people suffer. But *I* won't let that happen. I will be the king Dragon's Keep deserves and their hero when they realize it was I, not Malix, that ordered them awakened."

"This is all because you want to be king?" My words come out slurred as a coppery taste fills my mouth. Fuck, that really hurt. And the bastard made me bleed. "Do you even care about your people? The ones you claim to want to save." I know the answer before he even speaks.

Men like Aeron never care about others, not when power is involved. He just wants to take the kingdom and the throne.

"I wouldn't expect you to understand, human—"

"I'm your queen!"

Aeron roars with laughter as if I had just told him a joke and not that I was his superior.

"Queen?" he scoffs. "No, you are a pawn and Malix should have been utilizing your potential from the very beginning instead of using you as his own private whore."

The words feel like another slap in the face. I'm not Malix's whore or pawn. Right? I hate the doubt that creeps in, even though I know Malix cares for me and refers to me as his queen when around others.

"Enough of this. The hour grows late, and we have a

limited time before your pathetic husband comes home," Aeron says, pulling away from me.

"But sir," Otis's weasel-like voice says, "the king will kill us when he comes back and discovers what we've done. Perhaps we are being too harsh—"

Aeron whirls on him and I almost feel bad for the fury etched on the intimidating dragon's face. Almost.

Otis's eyes widen and he takes a few steps back. I half expect him to drop to his knees and beg Aeron for forgiveness. "Malix won't be a problem. But if you continue to prove yourself to be so idiotic, you'll meet his same fate."

"Yes, sir. I won't let you down," Otis squeaks.

"See that you won't."

My mind is still on the 'same fate' part. What the fuck did he mean by that? Did he plan on hurting Malix? "You can't touch him." The words are out of my mouth before I can stop them.

Now it's my turn to accept Aeron's wrath. "Is that so? And what are you going to do about it, human?"

The bravado I felt only moments ago fades and fear takes its place. Aeron must see it in my face because he smiles. There is nothing friendly in the way he is looking at me right now. I'm a sheep and he knows it.

"That's what I thought. Now, Rose, you have a job to do. Every single one of these dragons needs to be awakened. Otis will see to it that you do your job like a good little human." Aeron reaches out to caress the cheek he slapped, but I jerk away.

"I won't do it. I don't fucking take orders from you." I want the dragons awake and reunited with their families, but I'm not giving in to Aeron's demands. We have to do this the right way and what Aeron proposes will drain all of my energy and more. I need to be alert, now more than ever with the sinister duo before me.

"That's too bad. Otis, bring in our visitor," Aeron commands.

Visitor?

I watch as Otis disappears up the stairs. He's gone for only a minute, but it feels like a lifetime, and he's not alone. As soon as I see her, the breath is stolen from my lips.

Mina is bound and gagged, with bruises and scratches down her arms and cheeks. Whatever they did to her, she fought and fought hard. Pride for my friend swells in my chest but it leaves too quickly because Mina is in danger.

Even now as Otis pulls her down the stairs by the chains around her wrists, she fights, but I note her sluggish movements and the way she is limping on her left side. "What the fuck did you do to her?"

"Another fun substance from a friend in another territory. It prevents shifting. Usually used on wolves, but Mina seemed like the best person to try it on. She did put up a fight, so I suppose she can be proud of that."

"Let her go, she has nothing to do with this!" I think of Vivia and their son. *Oh god, their son.* Is he okay? Did they hurt him? Kill him? No...I can't get distracted. I push those harrowing thoughts to the side and focus on my friend in front of me.

"She does, actually. She's the unfortunate woman who befriended the false queen. She's here to ensure your compliance."

Before I can ask what he means by that, Aeron signals Otis and the weasel-man hesitates for the briefest second before his fingers and nails stretch into talons. Realization of what he is about to do hits me and I scream, "NO!" But it's useless.

Otis slashes his talons across Mina's face and screams fill the air. I don't know if they are mine or hers, or a combination of both of us, but angry tears start rolling down my cheeks. Blood pours from the wound and Mina's soft cries break my heart.

This is my fault.

I'm so sorry.

"Please. Don't hurt her," I beg, the fight leaving my body. This feels a lot like giving up. Maybe Aeron is right, I am the false queen. Queens protect their people, but my friend is hurt because of me, and my husband's life is in danger. Giving in is the only option I have that keeps those I love out of danger for a little bit longer.

"What is that, My Queen? Are you ready to obey?" Aeron mocks me with my meaningless title and all I can do is nod. I'm afraid if I speak, only sobs will come out.

"I'm glad you see it my way. Perhaps you aren't as stupid as I thought. Otis," he barks at the other dragon. "Leave Mina down here. Oh, and ladies? Before you try fighting your way out of here, the chains around Mina are laced with the same substance we used to stop her shifting initially. Meaning, she is little more than human right now."

Otis tosses Mina down the last few steps. She loses her balance and slides down the steps before she awkwardly catches herself.

Aeron no longer pays us any mind. He's barking orders at Otis to remain with us while he keeps people away from the cellar. He's gone shortly after, not sparing Mina or me one last glance.

For a moment, it looks like Otis wants to say something now that Aeron is gone, but I don't want to hear his worthless explanations. "Malix will kill you."

Otis bristles at the vitriol in my tone. He puts on a mask of indifference and says, "You have five minutes to get yourself together and then it's time to begin your task. You know what happens if you don't obey."

I ignore Otis and reach for Mina. I read so much in the look she gives me. Fear, anger, hurt.

"I'm so sorry," I whisper, unable to stop the tears as I pull the gag free from her mouth. I use the bottom of my dress to clean the blood off her face. She winces at my touch.

"Not your fault," she murmurs and tries to smile, but it's a bloody mess. "We'll get out of this."

I nod and let her have her fantasy. I know there isn't a way out of this, even if I manage to wake every dragon in here. Aeron isn't going to simply free us for a job well done. I keep these thoughts to myself, and I silently pray to any god or goddess that will listen to keep Mina and Malix safe.

I can't lose the people I love.

CHAPTER 26

MALIX

Five days.

That's how long it took for Allarick's men to gather the four other kings of Mescos. Each day ticks by agonizingly slowly and is another day lost. Another day the Nephilim grow stronger and risking our livelihoods.

Another day away from Rose.

I tried to sense her through our bond, but we haven't had enough time to nurture and grow it. I can't communicate with her from this far of a distance. I can vaguely sense her, so I know she is alive—what little comfort that brings —but I don't know if she is okay. If she misses me.

Admittedly, that last one is my own selfish desire.

Checking in with Vivia does little to ease my nerves. Her connection to Mina is spotty at best, but she reasons that is because we are far from home. She's probably correct, but I still feel a sense of unease.

I force those thoughts to the back of my mind as I prepare for this morning's meeting. Not too long ago, one of Allarick's errand boys sent word to Vivia and me. The last ruler, the demon king, arrived ten minutes ago. Initially I was irritated by the demon's lack of punctuality, but then I heard he had considered not coming at all and my anger morphed into something else entirely.

Was it wise to pull each king away from their territory amid the brewing war? Perhaps not, but there is no other option. Not when death is knocking at our door.

I dress in my normal black breeches with a leather vest over my brown tunic. It's simple, but effective to get my point across. I'm taking no shit today.

I meet Vivia outside my cabin. She's dressed similarly in black breeches and a black tunic, her preferred color.

"You ready, My King?" she asks, looking me over once.

There's no use in lying to Vivia. She sees right through my bullshit, so I just shrug. "Let's get this over with."

We walk in companionable silence to the spot we met Allarick at a few days ago. Only this time we aren't alone. Four powerful men stand in a semicircle, their bodies tense as they size one another up. From the corner of my eye, I see Vivia roll her eyes.

"Too much damn testosterone," she murmurs, and I'm inclined to agree.

For as long as I can recall, each territory has held peace with one another. A few spats occasionally creep up, but none that would jeopardize the relative peace of Mescos. Still, we are wary of one another and for good reasons. Our loyalty first and foremost is to our people, and we will cut down anyone who threatens us. No one is off-limits.

Rip, the wolf alpha, notices me first. His honey-colored eyes bore into mine. I allow myself a moment to take him in. He's let his hair grow out since the last time I saw him, pulled back into a tight knot on the back of his head. He stands shirtless, his bronze muscles comparable to dragons, which makes sense. Both our species are built to withstand our beasts inside us.

Shifters are leery of other shifters, but we have created a mutual respect. Like me, Rip lost his parents at a young age and was forced to take over his pack. He fought for his place and has earned every bit of his feral reputation. Not that I would ever admit it to him, but the wolves are lucky to have him as their alpha.

"Malix," he greets, inclining his head in a gesture of respect.

I returned the gesture. "Rip."

The other three rulers size me up, but don't speak. Which is fine with me, I'm not up for small talk. The semicircle is tense enough without forced conversation. We wait in awkward silence until Allarick appears from the depths, his body dripping with water and his locs thrown over his shoulder.

"We better get this started," he says, and everyone nods in agreement.

"Let's make this fast. I'm meeting with Ender," Oziel, the demon king, says.

Naturally, his words pique my interest. "You're making a deal with Ender?"

Demons are known for their deals and contracts. They are businessmen at heart, and make sure their deals always favor themselves. Some call them corrupt, but it's in a demon's nature to cause a bit of mischief and chaos.

Oziel's mouth widens into a toothy smile, one that would make a lesser man's hair on the back of their neck stand up. Oziel is unpredictable on a good day and outright hellish on a bad. "Why, yes. Similar to the one you made, I've heard." Oziel looks around the room at the other rulers.

"And one that every man here has made. For the good of their people, of course."

It never crossed my mind that Ender would offer the same deal to the rest of the rulers of Mescos that he did for me, but I can't say I'm surprised. The Guardian works in mysterious ways and I yearn to know what his role in all of this is. What does he get from helping us?

It's a question I can't possibly answer right now. Not when other pressing matters demand my attention.

"What is it you called us here to discuss, Dragon?" the fae king, Niko, asks. Niko possesses a terrifying beauty. It is what makes all fae so dangerous. People tend to underestimate the deadly creatures, but I have heard stories of Niko ripping people who wronged him limb from limb. Out of all the rulers here, Niko is the one I know the least about. He keeps his secrets close, wearing them like armor.

Everyone's attention is on me now. Five of the most powerful creatures in our world await my next words. Instead of intimidation, I feel power, and I soak it up.

"The Nephilim have started to escape their imprisonment."

My words are followed by hushed curses, from all except Allarick. His people are close to the Nephilim's imprisonment site, so my news doesn't shock him.

"And what of Gadreel?" Taivan, the pixie king asks. His translucent wings flutter behind him, looking angry in their own right.

"The last we checked, Gadreel was still imprisoned."

"And how long ago was that?" Rip asks.

"Almost six days," I say easily. It's not good news and I don't like sharing it, but these men have a right to know what's going on. My people might take the brunt of their attack, but none of their territories are safe either.

"I'm down dragons—"

"What do you mean you're down dragons?" Allarick cuts me off and narrows his eyes at me.

I haven't told them about the curse. None of the other kingdoms speak about how the Nephilim's magic is affecting their kingdom. Perhaps out of shame or something else entirely, but I wasn't ready to disclose that problem yet. And now it seems inevitable, so I explain the curse wreaking havoc in my kingdom. About the sleeping dragons, but I leave out Rose's involvement with it. I'm not ready to share her with the others yet.

"So you're telling us that our first line of attack has dwindled in numbers?" There's anger in Rip's voice, but I don't know if the wolf's anger is with me or with the situation.

I tense, but nod briskly. "Unfortunately, so. Even if we were at my full numbers, we wouldn't have the capacity to take the entirety of the Nephilim down. Each one of you should be prepared for destruction and war."

"We suffer because of your inability to keep your people safe," Niko says flatly. I don't realize how tense my body goes until Vivia reaches for my arm, giving me a warning squeeze. I slowly deflate, letting the anger ease out of me.

Before I can answer, Rip speaks up. "His people aren't the only ones cursed. It has reached my lands too." Rip doesn't elaborate what he means by that, and no one asks him. Clearly he's not ready to give that information up. "So, it's only a matter of time before your lands are cursed, if they aren't already."

"Fucking hell," Allarick curses.

"So, what does this mean?" Oziel addresses the group. I rarely see the demon without his usual smirk, but right now he's frowning. If I didn't know any better, I would think the demon king is rattled by the news.

"That means prepare your warriors over the upcoming days and weeks. The Nephilim are nearing my border as we speak and if I can't strengthen my wards soon, more Nephilim will cross and make their way over to your lands."

There is no good outcome. Even if we win the battle and the Nephilim are pushed out of my kingdom, the others will still have to face the enemy and defend their homes. The Nephilim will continue to look for weaknesses in our land, meaning every kingdom is vulnerable to their attacks and must hold their own.

"You've given us a lot to think about, Dragon," Niko says.

"And none of it good," Tavian mutters.

"No, none of it good," I agree, "but all important. You see why I needed to meet and why this information had come directly from the source? We do not want to prematurely alarm our people. We need them to believe in our victory." There couldn't be any other way.

"We need to keep our lines of communication open." I look at Allarick. He's the only one with easy access to everyone's kingdoms.

The kraken king notices me staring and sighs. "I suppose I will be your messenger boy. But those things I asked for? Double it," he says. I nod, knowing I can provide the clothes and supplies he needs.

"Are we done here?" Rip asks. "I need to return to my pack and prepare."

"We are, for now. Be vigilant and wait for further communication," I say and feel the weight of not only my kingdom, but the entirety of Mescos, on my shoulders.

I can't fail.

Rip is the first to leave. He shifts right before us, turning into his large, gray dire wolf, and sprints away. Taivan is the next to go, his wings carrying him out of sight in minutes. The rest simply take off on foot, having other means to get home.

Allarick lingers once everyone else is gone. Only once we are alone does he speak. "I will send someone soon. Make sure you have the items I requested."

"For your new wife?" He doesn't confirm or deny it, but I know that to be the reason. I wonder what Ender promised Allarick.

"We will speak again soon. Please don't get us all killed."

Absolutely no pressure.

"I'll do my best," I say as Allarick nods once and then disappears into the water.

Vivia is at my side, pulling my attention to her. "We've done what we came to do. Now let's go home."

Nothing sounds better. I nod and without another word, I let the switch transform my body and I take to the skies.

I'm coming back, Rose.

CHAPTER 27

ROSE

I lost count after twenty awakened dragons.

That was two days ago.

At least I think that was two days ago. Time is meaningless in this damp cellar. The only marking I have for the passage of time is when Otis delivers meals twice a day. One I presume is breakfast because it's usually some oatmeal and fruit and a dinner meal consisting of dry chicken and bread.

My body feels heavy and sluggish. I desperately want to sleep, to close my eyes and transport myself away from here, but every time I close my eyes, I'm startled awake by Otis. Dark circles under his eyes tell me he is just as tired as me, but I hold no sympathy for my captor.

As much as I worry about my body failing me, I worry for Mina more. She hasn't recovered from the deep slashes of Otis's talons. The blood has crusted over, but her eye is swollen shut and she still favors her right side. Otis and Aeron insist on keeping her in chains to weaken her, which I know is halting the healing process.

Despite the obvious pain she's in, Mina has smiled and

supported me through each awakening. Even when I was in tears due to the lack of sleep and the strain this is putting on my body, Mina held me and made sure I was comforted. I don't deserve her. Not after all the pain I caused.

My eyelids flutter closed as another dragon thrashes to life. Before the awakened dragon gains their bearings, Otis swoops in and ushers them away. I'm not sure where they are taking these newly awakened dragons nor do I know who is helping them through this transitional period, but I hope they are receiving the care they need.

With the hatchling gone, I move closer to the wall and slide down. I let my head fall back and try to pretend that my body isn't revolting against me.

Mina is by my side in seconds, pressing the back of her hand against my forehead. "You're warm."

I murmur something indecipherable and hear Mina curse. "Water. You need water," she says, reaching for the canister of room-temperature water Otis so graciously supplied us with.

Mina brings the canister to my lips and I drink. Even that minuscule task takes a Herculean effort. "Why are you doing this?" I ask when she pulls away. My voice is hoarse and weak.

"What do you mean?" Mina genuinely looks confused.

"Helping me. Why?" Still, she doesn't seem to understand why I would ask this question, so I elaborate. "I got you hurt and captured. This is all my fault."

"Oh, Rose." She sighs softly, moving to sit next to me. I don't miss her wince as she adjusts herself as comfortably as one can when still in chains. "This isn't your fault. This is the fault of a simple-minded man in search of power. He will get what's coming for him."

"You truly believe that? But what if he hurts Vivia? Or

Malix?" My heart sinks to the pit of my stomach. If anything happened to Malix because he was trying to save me…how could I ever forgive myself? Or if my friend's mate died because of me—

"Stop it. I can see you spiraling," Mina says, resting her hand on mine. I wonder what I look like to her right now. Pale as a ghost and scared out of my mind, probably. "Our mates' lives are threatened almost daily. I think Aeron is in for the fight of his life when they return, no matter what he claims to have up his sleeve. Vivia and Malix will persevere. We can't afford to think any other way."

She's right. Thinking of Malix as hurt or dead will cause me to spiral into a darkness I'm not sure I'm strong enough to pull myself out of.

We fall into silence, our heads moving to rest against one another. It's the only comfort we can offer each other, but it's enough.

I'm not sure how long we sit there—long enough for Otis to leave with the hatchling and come back with a new fire in his eyes. He takes one look at the both of us and snarls, "This isn't break time, *My Queen.*" He throws out my title like a dull sword, useless in practice, but pretty in name. "Get back to work. Aeron is growing impatient."

Because he was so patient before, I think, but don't voice.

"She needs rest. You can see how much this is affecting her. Give her time!" Mina comes to my defense, but Otis is quick to argue.

"We have no time!" His loud voice bellows around the room. "Every single dragon in here must be awakened. It's the only way Aeron will be satisfied and—"

"What has he promised you? Otis, you don't have to do this." I hope to garner sympathy. I can't wrap my mind around what hold Aeron has over Otis besides being more powerful.

"I'll be by his side, as his second, and we will finally restore our kingdom to how it once was. The dragon king needs to be ruthless, and Malix makes us all weaker."

I feel Mina tense up beside me at the same time I see Otis's hand form talons. He's on a precipice, one push will send him hurtling down and take us with him. I can't have that. I *won't* have that.

Before the argument can escalate, I push myself up, off the wall. My head spins and my vision gets hazy around the edges, but I ignore it. "I'll do it."

"But Rose—"

I cut Mina off with a soft smile, trying to convey how much I appreciate her help. Unfortunately, we aren't in a position to barter.

My eyes sweep the room. Only about 15 to 20 dragons remain, most of which are hatchlings. I should be done by now, but more dragons appear each time I wake up. Mina said something about a temple housing the sleeping dragons as well.

It's not going to be easy, but at least now there is a clear finish line. "Give me another few hours and he'll have all his dragons."

Otis narrows his eyes. I steel myself, ready for the fight brewing inside of him. However, Otis sighs deeply, the tension in his body deflating some, but not going away entirely. "Three hours. That's all you have."

"That's not enough time—"

"I'll do it." I speak over Mina. She protests behind me, but I quickly move on. "But promise me, after three hours, you'll return Mina to her son and let her see a healer."

"Fine, whatever." I'm under no delusion that Otis holds

any power here. Ultimately it will be up to Aeron what happens to my friend, but I want to at least try to keep her from whatever dark fate awaits me.

"Three hours," Otis repeats one more time. "Start now."

I'm in no position to argue, even though I'm barely holding myself up. Mina is at my side, bracing me against her. Without her, I fear I'll fall straight on my ass.

I survey the room once more and mentally prepare myself for the task ahead. And then, I start.

By the time the last dragon awakens, I don't have the strength to stand up. My body falls to the ground in a crumpled heap the moment Otis leaves with the last hatchling. Everything hurts and a tension headache is starting to form.

Mina flits around me, trying to ask if I'm okay and what I need.

She's sweet. A good friend. Probably the best friend I've ever had.

My eyes start to droop. I just need to sleep. For a second...or a year. Doesn't matter. I'm so tired. So, so tired.

"Rose, we have to go." Mina is in my head. Or ear. Or something. I feel her hand on my shoulder, gently shaking me.

Doesn't she understand that I just need five minutes?

I think I say that out loud because she says, "We don't have five minutes. Rose, listen to me. Otis, idiot that he is, left the door to the cellar open. I didn't hear it close when he rushed out of here. This is our chance to leave. We'll find Aracelia. She'll help us."

Aracelia. Right, Malix's council member. One that he trusted since he left the kingdom to her. Not me.

I don't blame him for that. Look at how well I'm doing.

"But we have to go now before he discovers his mistake. Please, Rose. Get up." This time Mina pulls me hard and I'm up on my feet. Not steady, but I'm standing and using Mina as support. She's not much better off than I am but seems to possess a little more energy.

We struggle up the stairs. Mina's left side is hurting her. I can tell by the grunts she makes each time she takes a step. I'm half walking, half being dragged by Mina. We move slowly and stop on occasions when Mina says she hears something. Her strong hearing is the only thing that is saving us now.

When we finally reach the top of the stairs, both of us are panting, gasping for air to fill our lungs. "Mina, I want to rest." Even as I say it, I know it's not a possibility and I can't hinder Mina's escape.

"Just a little bit longer. I promise," she pants, looking left and right before deciding to head left, toward Malix's meeting room.

We don't pass a single dragon, which is odd. After awakening the entirety of the cellar, I expected to see some of them walking around. I'm instantly on alert, momentarily forgetting my fatigue.

"Where is everyone?"

Mina shakes her head. "I don't know. Safe, I hope. We will figure it out later. I think I hear Aracelia up ahead."

"Thank god—"

"Hey! You two! Get back here!"

Our heads whip around at the sound of Otis's command. The man is midshift, but instead of freezing like me, Mina pushes me forward. "Run!" she screams.

"But—"

"Rose, go!" Her command rings throughout the hall and tears sting my eyes. I take a few steps back, just as Otis advances on Mina. Him, fully in his dragon form, and her, unable to shift due to whatever the hell Aeron put on her shackles.

"Now, Rose!" she screams again and I bolt as Otis leaps onto Mina. A scream rips out of my lungs and my feet move on their own accord. "Don't look back, keep running!" I hear Mina scream before I hear nothing at all but a terrible ripping sound.

Oh gods.

Tears pour down my face and I nearly trip as I hurry down the hall. When I finally reach the door, my body collides with it, unable to stop my momentum. I fumble with the doorknob, while my body shakes with sobs.

I think I just killed my best friend.

The door opens a moment later and I stumble in, slamming it shut behind me as if a single door will protect me from a godsdamn dragon.

"Shit. Queen Rose?" A familiar voice says.

I'm not alone, but I hadn't noticed anyone when I barged in unceremoniously.

I raise my gaze to see who else is in the room with me. Aracelia's face is a mask of concern and confliction. She doesn't quite know if she should go to me or see what I am running from.

My blood runs cold when I see who is standing next to her, his eyes narrow into tiny slits. I have never been more afraid of Aeron than I am at this moment.

"What has happened to you?" Aracelia asks, moving to my side.

I know she's a friend. Or I think she is one anyway, but I

don't want to be touched. I jerk from her grasp and point at the man who has been running me ragged all week and may have just killed my friend. "Ask him!" The venom in my voice astounds even me.

Aracelia backs up. "You," she murmurs softly, as if working out something in her mind. She turns to Aeron, her posture rigid. "You said the queen was sick but being looked after and cared for."

For a man having been caught in a lie, Aeron doesn't look the least bit ashamed. Instead, he appears agitated that this conversation is taking place.

"Aracelia." Feigned patience laces Aeron's voice. "You must understand that dire situations call for extreme action. Not many people are willing to do what needs to be done, so that burden must fall upon me."

"What did you do, Aeron?" Aracelia crouches low, blocking me from the sinister dragon.

"What needed to be done. And now, our dragons are back and ready to defend our territory."

"She could have died!"

"One death compared to hundreds seemed like the best scenario!" Aeron shouts. "And I would make that choice over and over again."

"You defied your king."

"No, my king defied me. He defied all of us. Now I'm here to fix the mess he has caused to fester for so long." His cryptic statement lingers in the air before his attention is on me. "Now, give me the human so I can complete what needs to be done."

Aracelia barks out a humorless laugh. "You'll have to kill me before I let you harm our queen. She has a purpose here and it's not death."

I don't deserve this loyalty from her, but I appreciate it

all the same. Aracelia's body begins to morph and her clothes rip to shreds, falling to the ground around where she once was.

Now, a large midnight-blue dragon stands in her place, her spiked tail pushing me farther away.

Aeron only sighs like he knew this would happen but is disappointed all the same. "I'm sorry it came to this. You're a fierce dragon, but you put your faith in a king who doesn't deserve it."

I don't hear if Aracelia responds. I watch the older dragon shift into something that can only be described in nightmares. A gray dragon, roughly twice the size of Aracelia, growls from the other end of the meeting room. His leathery skin is full of spikes that could pierce through my human flesh easily.

But that's not what scares me.

What scares me is Aeron's open mouth, a glowing red light building deep in his throat. I realize too late what he's doing. Because a few moments later, flames engulf the room.

CHAPTER 28
MALIX

For the better half of the day, Vivia and I travel home. Neither one of us spoke much on the flight home, both too consumed with thoughts of our mates. I don't want to admit it, but I grow wary the closer we get because I still can't feel Rose.

We land on my kingdom's soil just as the sun sets for the day. Instead of shifting like I thought Vivia would do with me, her body goes rigid next to mine. She doesn't leave me in suspense for long though. *"Something is wrong. Mina, she's..."*

A loud, feminine scream pierces the night, rattling the windows. *"Mina!"* Vivia growls and flies forward. I don't think, I just follow and try desperately to get a message to Rose.

I'm here. I'm coming.

But Rose doesn't understand our mating bond and doesn't respond. In fact, her mind is almost entirely blocked off from me, but I can feel some of her strong emotions trickle through, despite the barrier.

Fear. Anger. Betrayal.

My dragon rears with the powerful need to find my mate and protect her. If she is in trouble, it's only because I made the decision to leave her alone.

Fucking idiot, my dragon roars in my head and I'm inclined to agree with him.

Vivia soars through the doors of the castle, seeking out her mate. The halls, normally busy with my staff, are quiet and barren. I hear my own beating heart and the low growls from Vivia.

Then a scream. Familiar, but not Rose.

Vivia's roar is anguished and feral. There's no stopping her as she flies down the corridor, abruptly turning left at the fork. I don't know what it's like to love someone so deeply and completely for two decades like Vivia and Mina do, so I can't begin to imagine the anguish and fear going through my friend at the sounds of her loved one in turmoil.

But I think I'm beginning to understand.

Where the fuck is Rose?

I don't get the luxury of reaching out for her though, because as soon as we round the next corner, two figures occupy the hallway. It takes my brain a moment to register what I'm seeing. Perhaps I have been too complacent in my privilege that I had never considered any of my people betraying me. Even now, with the evidence right in front of my face, my mind is refusing to believe it.

Otis, in his dragon form, crouches over a bloodied and battered woman. The room smells of decay and copper. The woman is in chains, blood pouring from a gash on her face, painting most of her body red. Despite the obvious serious wounds, she's a feisty thing and refuses to give up without a fight.

I don't immediately recognize Mina until Vivia tackles

Otis to the ground. Otis isn't a large dragon, but he's no hatchling either. He hits the stone wall hard, causing small fissures to form in the stone.

Vivia doesn't allow him to regain his balance. She swipes her talons across his chest, her fire coming to the surface shortly after. Normal fire doesn't affect us much, but dragon fire can melt straight through our skin.

Otis roars out, but it's not a roar of triumph. It's fear, filled with pain. I could stop this. Spare Otis from the death that Vivia will more than likely rain down on him, but I'm not feeling particularly sympathetic. In fact, I'm in a very volatile mood right now.

I shift back to my human skin, running to Mina's side. When I get to her, I crouch and silently curse. The left side of her face is completely shredded, blood pouring freely. She has another slash across her breast, down to her hip, but it doesn't look as deep. Probably hurts like hell, but it's thankfully shallow.

Why didn't she shift? I've seen Mina fight. She's ruthless, even with her lack of formal training. There are chains around her arms and neck, but those shouldn't keep her confined. I go to reach for them, but Mina jerks away from me.

"Don't touch them!" she shrieks and for a second I think I hurt her, until she shakes her head and says, "They're poisoned. Or cursed. They won't allow me to switch."

My hands drop to my side, and she must see the question written all over my face. "Aeron. He did this. All of this and—oh gods, where's Rose? I'm so sorry, My King. I tried to protect her. I really..." Mina trails off into sobs. I want to reassure her that she didn't do anything wrong, but my mind has only one thing it wants to focus on.

"Where did she go, Mina?"

"D-down the h-hall..." she manages to get out. "I'm okay...just g-go."

Mina is far from okay, but I don't have the luxury to argue with her. Vivia will see to it that her wife's okay after she finishes disemboweling Otis. Let his blood feed the stone and serve as a reminder that turning against your people has consequences.

Mina all but pushes me away. She clearly needs the attention of a healer and leaving her feels wrong, but inside, my dragon rages. My control slips and I shift back, letting my dragon take the lead.

Fucking finally, he growls at me.

Rose's presence is a beacon now, leading me to her. I feel her and every emotion running through her. She's so scared and her soul calls out to me, even if she doesn't realize what's happening.

I fly down the hall, but not before I hear the sickening crunch of bones behind me. I spare a glance down to see Otis's neck bent at an odd angle. If he isn't dead, he will be shortly and I have no capacity to mourn him.

Rose is just beyond the door at the end of the hall that leads to the meeting room. Screams erupt, sending a chill down my spine. I don't bother using my tail to open the double doors. I soar right through the petrified wood, splintering it into hundreds of tiny pieces.

Fire engulfs the room and I hear Rose scream. My head jerks to the side, seeing my wide-eyed wife trembling and completely vulnerable. She doesn't possess the leather scales of a dragon. Her skin will burn immediately.

And I'm too far away from her.

Time slows and the sound around us silences.

Aeron's fire comes in hot, burning the wooden table and

chairs. Flames lick at the floor and ceiling, coming closer and closer to Rose. Even from this far away, I see the sweat dripping down her forehead.

Before the fire can stake a claim to Rose, Aracelia wraps her body and tail around Rose, taking the brunt of the fire. A small grunt is the only indication Aracelia gives to show her discomfort.

Rose's head pops up behind Aracelia, her eyes fixated on me. Joy, that seems so out of place in this room, spreads across her face. "Malix!" she gasps, before Aracelia pulls her back down and away from Aeron.

My presence is known if it hadn't been before. Aeron is slow to turn around and for a lesser dragon, I would assume it's because they're fearful. But not Aeron. Never Aeron. He only fears a future where what he wants doesn't come to fruition.

"*My King,*" he spits, moving his hulking body closer to mine. "*Welcome home. You've missed so much while you were gone.*"

"*You had no right.*" My voice is barely my own. Low and gravely, a predator just begging to come out.

"*I have every right to protect my people! Someone has to. Dragon's Keep doesn't need a weak king. I did what you couldn't. All dragons are awake and getting the care they need. I used the human like you should have. Now we might actually stand a chance against the Nephilim.*"

All dragons? "*What the fuck did you do, Aeron?*" I hiss, crouching low.

"*I kept your precious human in the cellar until she awakened my people.*"

"*Your people?*"

"*Yes.*" The word is like a purr on Aeron's lips. "*I challenge you for the title, young Malix. To the death.*"

There hasn't been a challenge for the title of king in over two centuries. Kings are revered and respected among our people and in return, we provide for our kingdom. This much power is easily corruptible and if Aeron had his hands on the title, Dragon's Keep would be only one step above a prison.

I may be more cautious in my approach to the kingdom, but not once did I ever think about anything other than giving my people the best opportunity for survival. I made deals that sacrificed my well-being to keep my kingdom's best interests at heart in order for the kingdom to thrive.

I will not have a power-hungry tyrant take it from me or my wife now.

"To the death," I agree.

And Aeron strikes.

Aeron is just shy of being an elder dragon, but his age isn't a detriment. If anything, his experience aids him. He has studied and known me since I was a hatchling. For that reason alone, I know this fight isn't going to be easy.

Aeron's teeth make contact with my flank. Pain laces up my body and I hear Rose scream my name. Her tortured cries are almost enough to make me regret my choice to agree to this death match, but there is no other way to settle this.

Aeron must be stopped. I should have seen it a long time ago. A mistake I don't plan on making again.

Aeron's dragon is large, standing a few feet taller than me. I'm far bulkier though and much angrier than this bastard is. He messed with my mate and because of that, I can't allow him to live.

I roar, shaking him off me. He's a persistent fucker though and tries to swipe at me. His talons scratch across my scales, not even breaking the skin. I snap my jaws at him, backing him up before I lunge.

My teeth sink into his legs and blood fills my mouth. I shake my jaw, tearing chunks from his leg until it's completely mauled. *"You'll pay for that,"* he hisses.

Soon we are a blur of teeth, fire, and talons. I feel each time he gets a hit on me; at this close range, there is no missing. Each hit is meant to hurt or kill. Nothing is holding Aeron back. A crazed look gleams in his eyes and I no longer recognize the dragon who has been my advisor since I became king all those years ago.

My father had warned me Aeron was hot-tempered, I just never believed him until it was too late.

Aeron's jaw comes close to my throat. Too close for comfort. But he's getting sloppy. He no longer has the endurance of a young dragon and with the amount of blood he's losing...well, it's only a matter of time before he makes a mistake.

I could be merciful and let the older dragon live. Imprison and rehabilitate him. Let him prove his worth in society.

But he hurt my mate.

The dragon has to die.

"This could have been different, Aeron. We could have been a ferocious team." I'm surprised to feel a pang of sadness at my words. It's true. Aeron is a powerful dragon, but he lets his greed and selfishness color his decisions. I agreed with him on many goals, just not the approach.

Things could have been so different.

"The kingdom will fall in your hands. You useless, piece of—"

I'll never know what he would have called me, though I can guess. I take advantage of his distraction and lunge straight for the jugular. Dragons are built for endurance and killing one is extremely hard, but no one can live with their throat ripped out.

Blood gushes from the open wound and Aeron's eyes widen. He honestly hadn't expected to lose. To die when he had gotten this far.

"May the goddess take pity on your soul, traveler," I murmur. Aeron opens his mouth, but nothing comes out except a trickle of blood. I watch as the light leaves my advisor's eyes and he sags against me.

I dump his body unceremoniously onto the floor. His last shift takes place and soon the great dragon is reduced to nothing more than an older man. Naked with his throat ripped out. His unseeing eyes remain open.

It's done.

"Wife. Come to me." I speak silently through the bond only Rose and I share, testing out its limits now.

Soft footfalls work their way around Aracelia until I see the entirety of my wife. She's ghostly pale and looks like a strong gust of wind could blow her over. There are dark circles under her puffy, red eyes.

My eyes trail down her body. Not in a sexual way, but I take in every injury on her. The one that disturbs me the most is the almost healed busted lip and the slight purplish color to one of her cheeks.

If Aeron wasn't already dead, I'd kill him again for touching her.

"Come," I repeat.

I barely have the chance to shift back before Rose runs toward me, throwing her arms around my neck, and sobs into my bloody shirt.

CHAPTER 29

ROSE

I feel like I could close my eyes and never wake up, but the nightmares of the last week plague my every thought. My body sags against Malix in relief and I dissolve into a puddle of tears and hysterics. "Mina! She's—"

"Hurt, but fine. Vivia is taking care of her." Malix has no reason to lie to me, but I don't quite believe him. I witnessed firsthand the abuse Mina was put through at my expense. I heard the sickening slash into meaty skin and her cries of pain as I ran away like a coward.

"I need to see her. I need to make sure she's okay." I'm fixating on this one thing. It's so much easier to take in one major problem at a time than take the entirety of my situation in. Even now my body trembles and threatens to war against itself if I allow myself to be pulled into the dark place that's begging to drag me down.

"Please, we have to go. We have to help her. We have to—"

"Rose." Malix reaches out to steady me before I can delve further into the hysterics bubbling inside of me. My emotions are a jar with a lid threatening to burst, ready to spill out at a moment's notice.

"Everything is going to be okay," Malix soothes, rubbing my arms to calm me. I want to argue that no, everything is not okay. In fact, everything is the opposite of okay.

"Malix, how can you say that when you are covered in blood?"

"It's not all mine."

"Like that makes a difference?!" My voice reaches shrieking levels. I can only imagine what I look like right now. Luckily only Malix and Aracelia are witnesses to my hysterics.

"I'm going to take care of you, wife. Trust me," Malix says and slowly pulls me into his arms, carrying me bridal style. I don't even protest. The moment he picks me up, my body decides it has finally had enough and refuses to move anymore.

Malix walks by Aracelia and mentions something about the bodies and cleaning up. I don't dare look back at the bloody mess on the floor. The image of Aeron will haunt my nightmares for a long time. I don't feel sorry for his death; it was his own fault. But it doesn't mean I relish it either.

Then Malix is taking me up to our chambers. I expect to be taken straight to bed, but he brings me to the bathing chambers where he prepares a tub of steamy water for a bath. Malix puts me down on the wooden stool next to the tub and slowly removes the soiled clothing from my body. He asks me a question, but I don't register it and just stare at him blankly.

Something akin to pity and sorrow glimmers in his eyes and he leans forward to press a faint kiss to my forehead.

He whispers, "I'm so sorry, Rose," before picking me up again to place me in the warm water.

I hiss at the abrupt change in temperature and Malix braces himself to get me out if I ask him to, but soon I grow used to the warm water on my skin and melt back into the tub. My eyelids—which suddenly feel too heavy—close.

I hear rummaging next to me and the weight of clothes falling to the ground. The water rises and I feel a presence at my back. Then Malix's strong arms wrap around me and he's kissing my grimy hair, whispering how proud he is of me. More apologies leave his lips, but I don't understand why he's sorry. I don't blame him for anything that has happened over the last few days, but clearly he does.

There is grime and blood over both of our bodies, but I can't produce the energy to even care. Malix takes it upon himself to clean my body. He softly caresses my skin, not in a sexual way, but in a way that fills me with such safety and love. If I weren't so tired, the love I have for my husband after such a short time might frighten me.

When he's done cleaning my body, he works a lather through my hair. It's knotty and oily, but he doesn't seem to mind. After a few minutes, he washes out the shampoo and scrubs the blood off his own body. Our once-clear bath in tinged brownish pink.

Disgusting, but I'm too exhausted to care.

Sleep calls my name and I'm so tired of fighting it. I vaguely feel Malix pick me up and carry me out to our bedroom. I'm not sure I even get dressed because the last thing I remember is his own weary face looking down at me with enough adoration to choke me.

Then sleep finally claims me.

I EXPECT to see light filtering in through the curtains when I wake up, but all I see is moonlight. I don't know how long I rested, but I feel like I'm ready to take a nap already. It takes another moment before the horrors of the last few days trickle back into my mind.

Mina hurt.

Aeron dead.

Malix hurt.

Otis...dead? I'm not sure about that one, but if Vivia is anything like Malix, I'm certain she took care of her wife's torturer.

Speaking of Malix...I reach out to the opposite side of my bed, but all I feel are rumpled wool blankets.

Panic starts setting in and for a moment, I wonder if I dreamed up Malix coming to my rescue and I'm about to wake up in the cellar, forced to obey the whims of Aeron.

Before that thought can consume me, the door to my room opens and Malix walks in carrying a tray of food. I sigh, my body visibly relaxing at the sight of my husband.

Malix offers me one of his rare smiles. "I was hoping you'd still be asleep when I came back. How long have you been awake?"

"Just woke up." My voice is hoarse. I crave the water he's carrying. "I thought I was dreaming."

Malix sets down the tray of food on the bed next to me, careful as he sits. "You've been asleep for almost an entire day."

My jaw drops like one of those old-school cartoons my dad used to watch as a kid. "A whole day?"

Clearly amused by my reaction, Malix smirks. I can't

help but notice that it doesn't quite reach his eyes though. "You needed it. Your body has been put through a lot these last few days..." He trails off and I think he's done talking, but then he finally says, "Rose. I'm so sorry—"

But before he can get any more of that sentence out, I put up my hand to stop him. "No, stop apologizing. This wasn't your fault. You didn't know this would happen. This was Aeron's. He made the decision to hurt me. Made the decision to defy you." I needed to take my own advice because there is a part of me that will always blame myself for Mina's injuries. I'm sure Malix must feel the same about me.

Malix doesn't look fully convinced, but he nods anyway and reaches for my hand. I know it's to reassure himself that I'm okay and not mad at him so I squeeze it gently. "How long have you been awake, husband?"

"I hardly slept," he admits, making me frown. We would need to remedy that later.

"How is Mina, by the way? Have you heard?"

"She visited the healers and is now resting at home. They were able to remove her chains. She has a pretty deep gash in her face that will leave a mark, but otherwise she's okay. She asked about you."

I smile. "I'll make sure to visit her soon, maybe bring her some soup from the kitchens."

"Later," he agrees, "but right now you are going to eat. You're not leaving our bed for at least another twenty-four hours." He nudges the full tray of food at me and the mound of food he brought is enough to feed a full-grown dragon.

"I hope you'll be helping me eat this." He makes a noncommittal nod and reaches for one of the bowls of fruit. Still, his gaze lingers on me, as if waiting for me to eat.

So, that's exactly what I do. The buttery biscuits melt on my tongue, and I flood them with the sausage gravy. More eggs and potatoes than I could possibly eat in one sitting are piled up in the corner of the tray. I'm particularly ravenous today—tonight?—and manage to eat a good portion of each. I wash it all down with the waters and juices Malix brought me.

By the time I'm done eating, most of the food on the tray is gone. So much for not being able to eat it all. "You are the best husband ever." I sigh contently, rubbing my bloated stomach.

"And what was I before?" I hear the smile in his voice and it makes my stomach fill up with butterflies.

"A halfway-decent roommate."

That earns me a bark of laughter. "Says the woman who has stolen my bed and room."

I hold up a finger and waggle it at him like a mother to a naughty boy. "Oh no, mister. You gave me this room and then left me in it. Alone. I will hear no complaining from you."

We smile at one another, both remembering the early days of our relationship. It feels like a lifetime ago. So much has changed in the last couple of weeks. Is it possible for a person to change in that amount of time? For feelings to change and evolve?

Malix's smile soon fades, and the mood darkens. "While I was gone—"

"I already told you not to apologize. It's fine."

"I'm not going to apologize."

"Oh." I blush. "Then what?"

"You woke every sleeping dragon, Rose. They are all awake now because of you and your ability. Otis and Aeron smuggled them over to the temple, and now they're waiting to reunite with their families. There's nothing I can do to thank you enough for what you did. This kingdom owes you a big debt, one I don't think we will ever be able repay in full."

Suddenly the tray between us is a barrier, keeping me from my husband. I push it aside, careful not to spill the remainder of my breakfast onto our sheets. When it is safely out of kicking distance, I move to straddle Malix.

The thin white dress he put me in last night bunches up around my hips, pulling tight around my thighs. It's almost indecent, and I watch as Malix's eyes drift down to my thighs. Slowly, far too slowly, he brings his gaze back up, pinning me with his molten stare.

I'm all too aware that I'm not wearing panties and my core is pressed against his legs. If I move just a little to the side, I could create friction against my clit.

Focus, Rose. Think with your brain, not your pussy.

If my vagina could pout, she'd be throwing a tantrum right now as I disregard her needs and cup Malix's face. "Am I not your queen?"

Aeron had said I was queen in nothing more than name alone. That I held no power and was simply a pawn for the dragons to achieve victory in their upcoming battle with the Nephilim. Despite my best efforts, I couldn't chase away the doubt that had started creeping in.

That doubt, however, goes away when Malix squeezes my hips. His face is hard lines and narrowed eyes. "Of course. You are my wife, Rose. The queen of Dragon's Keep."

I didn't know how much I needed to hear those words until he said them. A small smile spreads across my lips. "Then, is it not my duty to serve my people?"

"In a sense yes, but—"

"Then you and this kingdom owe me nothing," I interrupt. "Would it have been more ideal to wait and space the awakenings out a little more, so I didn't dispel all my energy? Yeah. The situation sucked, but I don't regret helping the dragons. That's why I'm here, isn't it?"

The question hangs heavy between us. There're many unasked questions, all I'm too chickenshit to ask. No matter what he says, this is my life now and will forever be so. There's no going back to Grym Hollow and honestly, I wouldn't want to. Perhaps it's crazy, but I truly believe I belong here, dragon or not.

After a tense moment of silence between us, Malix shakes his head. "No. That's not the only reason you are here, Rose. Not to just be my wife or help break the sleeping curse. Not even to help against the Nephilim. You are your own person, and you can choose your own purpose.

"But"—he pauses briefly—"we may have never antici-pated becoming husband and wife, let alone mates. You may have never considered yourself a queen before the role was thrust upon you. But this time with you has shown me how lonely I've truly been. You are mine as I am yours. I want you by my side."

I want you by my side.

If his words aren't convincing enough, his actions from yesterday were. How he fought for me. Took care of me when I could no longer take care of myself. Told me how proud he was of me.

Malix didn't have to do any of those things. Hell, he could have easily acted like Aeron and imprisoned me for his own personal gain, but that's not the type of man—or dragon—Malix is.

Emotions surge through me. Words don't accurately convey my feelings, so I do the only thing I can and hope it says what I cannot.

I kiss him.

His lips respond to mine, and we fall down until my back hits the soft bed beneath me. Malix is gentle as he climbs on top of me and the weight of him feels like a security blanket. Nothing can harm me when he's there.

And nothing can harm him. I may simply be human, but that doesn't limit me. I'm capable of more than I even dreamed of.

The kisses start out light, almost shy in nature. This is still new territory for the both of us. Feelings we are still trying to unscramble, but the one thing I know for certain is that this is right.

It doesn't take long before Malix is asking permission to deepen the kiss and I respond immediately by parting my lips, inviting him in. He claims my mouth and steals my breath at the same time.

It's not enough though. I need more. I need *him*.

"Malix." His name comes out in a moan. He tries to pull back, probably thinking he's hurt me, but I dig my nails into his back, keeping him in place.

"Yes, wife?" His gruff voice tells me he's just as affected by me as I am of him.

"Make love to me."

CHAPTER 30

MALIX

I should say no. Rose put her body through hell over the last few days for our people. She should be resting, and I should be encouraging that...not be on top of her with a throbbing erection and a need for her that can only be satisfied once I'm buried deep inside her.

My little dragon is needy though. She grinds her hips into mine, eliciting long moans from the both of us. I know a losing battle when I see one and there's no use denying my wife. And frankly, I never had any intention of denying her.

Ever since the first night with her, the way our bodies fit perfectly together and how we moved in tandem, I knew that this human was mine. Mine to fuck. Mine to protect. Mine to love. I haven't been doing a good job at any of those things recently.

We are newlyweds, but don't get the luxury of nesting. I knew marrying Rose would not allow me to have the typical nesting experience other dragons are permitted. Not because she's human, but because our marriage is one of political nature and of convenience.

I vowed to respect her. No more, no less.

My heart had other plans though.

"Malix," my mate moans breathily. There's need and lust wrapped up in my name that goes straight to my cock. "Please, I need you."

Not want.

Need.

I lean down, our noses touching lightly. Her eyes are blown wide and the tangy smell of her lust fills the air.

"You are my queen. You never beg. Only demand."

Her eyes widen for a fraction of a moment before a wicked gleam takes over. My seductress smiles, running her hand up my shirt. Her slender fingers tracing the curves and dips of my torso.

"In that case," she purrs, "I want you to fuck me, My King." To prove her point, she cups me between my legs, rubbing my hard cock through the thin breeches I wear. "Your queen requires your cock."

A low growl leaves my lips. Any inhibitions I have leave me entirely and I claim her mouth in a searing kiss. It's a frenzy, two flames meeting in the dark, needing each other's heat. Her needy moans only spur me on.

But there's too much fabric between us. Too many barriers. I need her skin against mine, heating me from the outside in.

Her damn nightgown gets in my way and I've never considered myself an impatient man, but this moment proves me a liar. I shift my hand into my sharp talon, cutting the dress down the center. I hear a soft, surprise gasp as cool air hits her skin, pebbling her rosy nipples.

My lips are around them in an instant, sucking the bud into my mouth. Rose calls out my name, her body arching closer. She fumbles with my clothes until a frustrated cry leaves her mouth.

"Something you want, wife?" I pull away from her peaked nipple, moving my attention to her other. My tongue runs along the sensitive tip as more frustration stems from my horny mate.

"Clothes. Off. Now, Malix."

I'm not one to be commanded, but my wife voicing her needs and making sure she gets her pleasure? Sexiest fucking thing ever. I bend to her will and no one else's.

I break apart from her long enough to pry the tunic from my body. My pants are the second thing to go and my dick all but weeps in relief when I free it from its confines. Finally, I'm completely nude, allowing Rose to drink in her fill.

Which she does unabashedly, hand trailing down my body, tracing the V of my hips. Her touch lingers there before dropping lower, her hand wrapping around my throbbing cock.

"Mine." She emphasizes her claim by stroking me up and down, her thumb sliding over my tip. It's too fucking much and not enough. It's pleasure and pain and I'm fucking addicted to it.

"Yours, wife," I agree and move my hands down her body to the apex of her thighs. I slide a finger down, feeling just how wet she is for me. It's fucking beautiful. "So ready to take my cock, little dragon." The pad of my thumb finds her clit, gently rubbing.

Rose's eyes roll back. "Fuck..." she draws out the word, legs parting more. This beautiful creature is on display for me, offering herself up. I'm selfish enough to take it.

I bring Rose to the edge, her thighs quivering, before I pull back. "Malix, I want—ah!"

I push inside of her, her pussy so wet I move easily through her tight channel. She clenches around me. "So perfect. So fucking perfect, wife."

Rose, who should still be recovering from her days in the cellar, flips us and quickly crawls back on top of me. I'm too stunned to do anything other than allow it to happen.

"Were you serious when you told me to demand what I want as your queen?"

"Extremely so."

A wicked smile lights up her face and she reaches down between us. She runs the tip of my cock through her wet folds before guiding me inside of her. We moan in unison.

"Good," she pants, "because I want to orgasm."

And then she starts to ride me. There are no words to describe how ethereal and sexy Rose looks as she bounces up and down on my cock, taking the pleasure she so desperately needs. Our bodies make lewd sounds as they crash against one another, and I watch her pussy lips separate each time she takes my cock all the way.

I'm not going to last.

Not long. I'm a man deprived. I need Rose more than I need oxygen. But this moment is Rose's and I refuse to finish before she does. She just needs a little help to reach her peak.

My thumb finds her sensitive bundle of nerves again and rubs in slow, teasing circles. I want to bottle up her moans and whimpers of pleasure for selfish reasons.

"Malix...I'm close—oh god!" Her words end in a scream as she comes hard, her sweet cream coating my cock. My release swiftly follows, and I fill her completely with my seed.

Maybe I'll make her walk around all day with my seed

dripping down between her thighs. The thought is tempting.

Rose falls in a panting heap on my chest, her hair framing out around her as she nuzzles into my neck.

"This is a break. I'm not done."

I bark out a laugh. "Is that so?"

"Yes, that's so. You left me for days—don't fucking apologize again—so we have things to make up for."

And make up, we do.

OUR DAY and well into the evening hours are a blur of limbs, orgasms, and sweat. Our bodies were insatiable. It wasn't just the sex we craved, but the assurance that the other was okay and still with us.

At least that was what I needed.

A heavy tiredness settles over my body, burrowing deep within my bones. I brush it off as the stress of the last few days and the amazing night I just shared with my wife catching up with me.

I barely manage to clean myself off. That minuscule task feels momentous. The bed is completely soiled, and I don't have the energy to call in a maid to clean up. It can wait until morning. Tonight, Rose and I will sleep in my nest.

I don't bother putting on clothes, I've already exerted myself enough for one night. Instead I fall into the cushions and blankets of my nest, waiting for Rose to return from the bathroom. It feels like I'm fighting to keep my eyelids from drooping, and I sigh in relief when I finally hear the door open back up.

Rose's floral scent hits me first before she tucks her soft

body against mine. My eyes close on their own accord, but not before I wrap my arms around her.

"You are falling asleep on me, husband." She laughs softly. I can't even deny it. My body feels heavy and it's becoming painful to keep myself conscious. I just want to sleep. Sleep until my body doesn't feel so heavy.

"I blame you." I try to tease, but it falls flat to my ears. Luckily, Rose doesn't seem to notice.

"Can't say I'm sorry." I imagine her cute smirk, the one she does when she's satisfied with herself. "I need sleep too. In the morning, we can go back to our normal duties. Together."

It was probably not wise to waste more of our precious time, but I don't regret it. Not even for a moment. "Together."

As soon as the words leave my lips, darkness claims me, lulling me into a peaceful sleep. One I could stay in forever.

ROSE

There's a delicious ache between my thighs when I wake up the following morning. I'm surprised to find myself gearing up for more, as if last night's sex fest wasn't enough. Since when did I become so wanton? This is normal between married couples though, isn't it? The intense need for one another.

My thoughts of a morning quickie are shattered when I turn in Malix's arms to find him still sound asleep. My disappointment is short-lived when I notice how serene he looks in sleep. The worry lines on his brow are gone and Malix looks so much younger. It's hard to remember that for a dragon king, he is young.

Seeing him this tired makes me wonder how much he was able to sleep while away checking our borders. Whatever the reasons, he needs sleep and I'm more than happy to give him that.

Untangling myself slowly so as not to wake him, I break free from his grasp and crawl to the edge of his nest. Malix doesn't so much as stir.

I leave him to rest so I can dress for the day. I emerge a

moment later in a cream lace-up dress that does wonders for my cleavage. The normal maid—I really should learn her name, but she isn't the most talkative person—strips the linens off the bed. Suspicious stains are visible over some of the sheets, but we are both pretending as if they don't exist.

"Kitchen has your breakfast prepared, My Queen." Before I can respond, she's out of the room with my soiled bedding.

My stomach growls at the thought of food. I take one last look at Malix to make sure he's still asleep before I head for the kitchen. Greasy bacon and buttery biscuits await me when I get to the kitchen. My mouth starts to water as I prepare a tray to bring back up to the room.

As I'm shoveling an embarrassing amount of potatoes on my plate, I hear someone walk in behind me. I look over my shoulder, half expecting to see Malix, but it isn't my husband who stands haggard with dark circles under their eyes.

It's Vivia.

"Vivia!" I say a little too loudly, causing her to flinch. "Sorry," I try again, only much softer. "You look..."

"Like shit." A self-deprecating laugh leaves the dragoness's lips. Her body is rigid when she walks, wound up tight like a coil.

She looks down at the food with dull eyes. It's like her body knows she needs to eat, but her heart just isn't in it. She must feel me staring because after a few moments, she starts to half-heartedly pile a random assortment of food onto her plate.

If I were a betting woman, I'd wager none of that is going to be eaten.

"How is she?"

Vivia doesn't look up. She keeps piling random fruit on her plate. Her movements are robotic; she's here, but in body alone. "Stable. She's in a lot of pain, even if she won't admit it. But her face…"

The screams. Tearing of flesh. That's all I remember before running away from Mina. No matter how long I live, I don't think I will ever forgive myself for leaving her. Even knowing Mina is the one that told me to go.

"She's calling it her battle scar. Thinks she looks pretty badass." Vivia's smile doesn't reach her eyes, but her fondness and love for her wife shine through.

"Sounds like Mina." Always the optimistic.

"She's stubborn."

"I'm beginning to think that's just a dragon's natural state."

This time Vivia's smile is real. "Yeah, I suppose it is. How's Malix?"

"Asleep," I say and finish loading my tray with food. "He needs it."

"He does."

We lapse into a comfortable silence, and I finish pouring two glasses of freshly squeezed juice. Pineapple from the smell of it. I should leave, but I hesitate by the door. "Can I visit her soon?" I blurt, very un-queen-like.

I see the brief hesitation and lie to myself that her reaction doesn't hurt. Does she blame me for Mina's injuries? Does Mina?

"Tomorrow," she says at last. "I just want her to have one more day of rest. Right now our son hasn't left her side. I think he needs to reassure himself that his mother is okay."

"Right, of course. Please, let me know if there is

anything Malix or I can do. Do you mind letting her know that I'm thinking about her?"

Vivia nods once. "Of course. She will be happy to hear that."

"Thank you." I linger for another moment before finally leaving. I hate when people around me are hurting and I can't do shit about it. The only solace I take is knowing that Mina is going to be okay and that I didn't cause the death of my dear friend.

By the time I make it back to our chambers, fresh linens cover my bed, and the room no longer smells like sex and sweat. I carefully place the food tray on the bed, buttering the biscuits and getting the food ready for consumption when I hear my name.

"Hello, Rose."

Like a startled cat, I jump, nearly spilling my breakfast all over my clean bed.

"Ender?"

I can't hide the surprise or confusion I feel when I see The Guardian is standing in my room. I haven't seen him since the day he dropped me off and left me to my fate. The fact that he's here now sends alarm bells ringing in my head. "What are you doing here?" Then a sickening thought takes form and blooms, spreading the beginning signs of panic within me. "Are you here to drag me back to Grym Hollow? Is my sister okay? What–"

Ender puts his hand up, effectively silencing my panic spiral. "I'm not here to take you home. This is your home now and where you will remain for the rest of your days. Your sister is fine, discovering the joys and hardships of motherhood. Hasn't asked around about you though."

I'm not sure if I'm relieved or disappointed about the news of my sister. I suppose I'm thankful my deal wasn't in vain, but the bitterness for how things ended between us is still there. If dragons had therapists, I would need to find one soon.

"You have a problem. I'm here to give you advice," he adds cryptically.

A problem? I laugh at the absurdity of the statement. "Couldn't have come a few days ago, could you? That's when my problem started, but I can assure you, we are all fine."

The pitying look he gives unsettles me to my core. I don't want to face Ender alone. If we have a problem, then Malix needs to be aware of it as well. But when I look over at the nest, Malix is still there; he hasn't moved a muscle. How is he still asleep after all this?

The answer is there, deep inside me, but not one that I'm willing to give voice to.

"Let me just wake up my husband." My body is working on autopilot. I feel like I'm a spectator, watching the scene take place before me without actually being part of it.

"Rose—" Ender tries to speak, and my too-big, too-fake smile cuts him off.

"Just one second," I say, my voice higher pitched, "He never usually sleeps this late."

I feel like I'm the oblivious character in a horror film who says they should go check out the basement. Everyone knows that's a bad idea, but the character insists on doing it anyway.

I know what I'll find when I get to Malix, but I choose to live in ignorant bliss a little longer.

When I reach my sleeping husband, I crouch down and gently shake him. "Malix?" No response. I wait a second.

Then another.

And another.

"Malix?" I shake him harder this time, raising my voice. The bubble of ignorance is deflating fast.

"Rose. He's not going to wake up." Ender is behind me now. He rests his rock-like hand on my back. It's too heavy. Too suffocating.

I won't let the panic consume me.

"Yes, he will. I just need time." Apparently, stubbornness isn't exclusive to dragons.

"He's cursed, Rose."

Why does he insist on giving voice to things I already know? Because he can't read the fucking room. "And I've healed every other sleeping dragon. Just give me a damn minute!" I growl with all the intimidation of a small dog against a wolf.

I can't let myself spiral, especially when I know I can fix this situation. I just need to ground myself and make a list of things I know.

I know that Malix is under a sleeping curse, courtesy of the Nephilim.

And I know I can bring him back.

So I try. Just like I did with all the others, I place my hands on him and channel my thoughts to those of comfort and security. Doing this now is as familiar as breathing.

After a full three minutes I pull back and wait.

My mind conjures up a ticking clock, each second that goes by gets increasingly louder until I can no longer drown out the noise.

"Sometimes it takes a minute," I say, not sure who I'm trying to reassure.

Ever the calming presence, Ender is patient as he says, "It's not going to work this time, Rose. He's gone."

He's gone.

I hear those words. They replay in my mind repeatedly,

but I don't fully process them. Surely he doesn't mean... "He's not dead! He's just sleeping. Just give me a little longer and I'll wake him up. It will work. It has to work!"

"It will not."

"*Why won't it?!*" I scream, whirling on Ender. "What are you telling me?" Tears sting my eyes. I'm so fucking tired of crying and being in survival mode. I don't want to feel like this anymore. I just want Malix.

Ender sighs, the pitying look he gives me makes me want to claw his eyes out. It doesn't matter that Ender is a giant man that vaguely resembles a boulder with horns. At this moment, I feel like I could destroy him.

"I mean this time; your gift isn't going to free him. Come. I have much to explain and very little time." Ender beckons me forward.

I don't move and stay wrapped up in Malix. "I'm not leaving him."

"Very well." He sighs. "We can talk here."

Talking is the last thing I want to do. Especially with Ender who possesses more secrets than the universe. Still, there are things I want to know. Things that apparently only The Guardian can answer.

"How did I get the ability to wake dragons but can't do it to my own husband? Why did you bring me here, only to take him away from me?" Fat tears are freely rolling down my cheeks now, but I can't find it in me to care.

"Humans possess magic they don't know they are capable of," he starts and I'm ready to yell at him for giving me another nonanswer, but then he continues. "The history of Mescos is not something I can give you in the next five minutes. But know this. Mescos was made to protect magic and magical beings.

"Humans once held their own power. It was given to

them by their creators to live peaceful lives and work together to prosper in these lands among their supernatural counterparts. That peace was short-lived though. A darkness came into Mescos, killing many of the humans in an attempt to steal their magic."

None of it makes sense. This isn't the history of the universe we were taught in schools. But how could I even begin to argue while I stand in the very place he speaks of, breaking curses in ways that I can't explain?

"The founders of Mescos preserved the magic and split off into six different territories, in hope of combating the threat we now know as the Nephilim. These people grew corrupt in their search for power, becoming the Nephilim we know today," Ender continues.

"I don't understand what that has to do with me. Please...just tell me how I can wake Malix." Nothing else mattered right now.

"The magic in Mescos needs new hosts. You have been given the ability to break your people's curses, but Malix is a representation of more, and therefore what you did to the other dragons won't work on the king because Malix is his kingdom. If you want to awaken your husband—"

"—I need to save his kingdom?" I finish, my brain slowly processing everything Ender is telling me.

"Precisely. Malix protects his kingdom by protecting and strengthening the wards. You must strengthen the wards to their former glory if you wish to keep your kingdom safe and have your husband back."

"How do I do that?" I would do anything, but I'm also just one fucking person. How was I supposed to do something Malix or his dragons haven't been able to do? Ender claims it's because I'm human but...there's more to the story that he's not telling me.

I just don't understand why.

Ender glances at something behind me. "I have to go."

"You have to—what?"

Ender begins walking toward me. For a moment I think he's going to try and pry me up, but then he walks right past me. "Ender, wait!"

I can see the slowly shimmering light of what I now know to be a portal. He's leaving.

"Ender!"

"Talk with those you trust. Put your faith in your dragons and lead. You can do this, Rose. No one else but you."

I scream for him again. To give me answers...anything. But Ender walks through the portal and it swallows him whole.

He's gone, leaving me with a cursed mate and far more questions than answers.

CHAPTER 32
ROSE

Grief is tangible. It wraps itself around your heart, slowly and then all at once. The hands of grief squeeze and squeeze until you feel like you can't possibly take it any longer, then and only then, does it loosen. Just to start the process over and over until everything becomes too much. Too heavy.

It's also an emotion I'm intimately familiar with. My first heartache happened when my grandmother passed away. It was the first time I ever experienced death and it scared me. Seven years later, my parents followed, and my world collapsed. I lost those who I loved dearly.

And now Malix is gone.

I don't remember screaming. I don't remember much of anything once Ender left me, but my throat is dry and my ears ring. My body is draped over Malix as if shielding him from the curse.

But it's too late.

Ender says he's gone.

But he can come back, a small voice inside my head reminds me. It just fails to leave out the impossible task that lies ahead of me. A task I now must complete on my own.

The door to my chambers bursts open, followed by a soft curse. I don't have the energy to look up. Instead, I press myself deeper into Malix's side. He's so warm and I can almost delude myself into believing he is giving me a hug.

Soft, but firm hands gently take hold of me. I struggle for only a moment until I catch sight of a familiar face.

Vivia.

"You should be with Mina." I don't know why those are the first words out of my mouth, but my brain is only capable of linear thinking. Mina is sick. Therefore, Vivia should be with Mina.

Not here, prying me away from my husband.

"I had an urgent matter to discuss with you. But..." Vivia glances at my sleeping husband and I watch as understanding dons her face. Confusion turns into dread.

"He's cursed." Vivia is smart. She knows I would try to wake him immediately and that my screams expose my failure. "But you can't wake him up."

I didn't think I was capable of any more tears, but stubborn ones pour down my cheeks anyway. I don't know Vivia that well, but that doesn't stop me from crying into her chest. My words start tumbling out then.

I tell her about Ender and his cryptic words. How Malix is different and wouldn't be able to be awakened like the other dragons. How if I want my husband back, I have to figure out a way to strengthen our wards—whatever the fuck those are—and keep the Nephilim from entering Dragon's Keep.

"Ender claims I have powers, but I don't. I'm just a human woman with very human abilities. I'm not special and I'm terrified that every one of those dragons that I just brought out of cursed sleep will die due to my incompetence." Fears spill out of me; some I didn't even know I had until I said them.

I wait for Vivia to agree with me. To tell me how everything I feel is true and we should prepare for the worst. After all, she has seen the Nephilim's brutish strength and power up close, so she should know more than anyone how fucked we are.

Except she doesn't say any of those things.

Vivia takes my hand and squeezes it gently. Her soft brown eyes hold nothing but comfort and something that looks a lot like respect. "Not special? Tell that to every single family you have reunited by awakening their loved ones. Or Mina who has never had such a wonderful friend like you."

"But—"

"Don't deny it, My Queen. In your short time here, you have changed the lives of so many people. Perhaps it's time you see the impact of what you have done."

I snort. "Yeah, I can see the impact just fine. Mina lies in a healer's room and Malix is cursed."

"Due to things out of your control. Did you capture my wife and slice into her face? Did you curse Malix?"

"No, of course I didn't, but—"

"Exactly. Mina doesn't blame you and I can guarantee you that neither does Malix," Vivia says. Her assurance in me almost makes me want to believe her, but I still can't help but feel like the situation is out of my control.

"What if Ender is wrong?" I whisper. "What if I don't actually belong here and the awakening thing was just a fluke?"

Vivia shakes her head. "No. I've known Ender for a long

time. He doesn't make mistakes. If he brought you here, there was a reason for it. As you know, he's not very forthcoming."

That's putting it lightly. Everything about Ender is a mystery, down to his very existence. I don't know what game he's playing or the stakes he holds in all of this, but something tells me he has just as much to lose.

But I'll let him keep his secrets.

For now.

"Listen, My Queen—"

"You can call me Rose," I interrupt.

"I could, but I'll stick with Queen for now. To remind you who you are." She winks, a knowing smile on her face. "You have two options. You can continue to mourn what is lost or you can fight for your kingdom and your husband."

"That's not much of a choice," I mutter and I hear Vivia laugh. I know why Malix likes her as an advisor though. She says things you need to hear and not just what I want to hear.

I needed the reminder. I'm queen, whether I feel like it or not. Malix would want his people protected and it's the least I can do for him. I'm not going to let all his hard work as king be for naught.

I don't know what the hell I'm doing, but I know I'm not going to stay in my chambers alone with my own thoughts. Malix would want me to fight. He saw my strength even when I didn't, and now Vivia sees it too.

Maybe it's time to believe them.

Vivia notices the change in my demeanor because she smirks at me as if she knows my answer without me even having to say it. "I want to fight for Dragon's Keep."

"Welcome to the fight, My Queen."

A fight I'm not certain I have the power to win, but I

must try. For Malix and for Dragon's Keep. The pressure settles on my shoulders like metal armor, heavy and impossible to ignore.

I wipe at my puffy eyes one last time before I remember Vivia came in here for a reason. "What is it you wanted to tell me?"

The smile on Vivia's lips fades and she's once again the resilient warrior. I brace myself knowing the next words she speaks will be hard to hear.

"My Queen," she starts, and the world around us disappears. "Trusted reports have spotted Gadreel. He's days away from fully escaping his prison. We must start rallying our army."

CHAPTER 33
ROSE

We waste no time getting prepared for Gadreel's escape and the inevitable attack that will follow. Every morning I join Aracelia and Vivia in the meeting room to discuss work and split responsibilities. The most important item on our agenda is making sure all the awakened dragons are receiving the care they need.

All the former council members have been awakened, but with Malix indisposed, I don't know who to trust. Did others follow Aeron's way of thinking? Would they accept a human as their queen? For now, my council is composed of just the two of them.

Today Aracelia and I take on the responsibility of checking in on the awakened dragons so Vivia can stay with Mina and start getting the word out that we are going to need warriors for this upcoming battle. Mina is supposed to be well enough to leave the healers, but I have yet to see her. Vivia says she is doing much better, but I'm anxious to see her myself.

Aracelia and I visit families all day, mostly those who have reached out to her or Vivia in need of help. The reactions are all the same when they see me. Confusion and disbelief morph into curiosity at seeing a human. A fleet of questions follow, and most are good-natured. There are a few who are hesitant and clearly see me as other.

I don't take offense. I *am* a stranger and all of a sudden I'm their queen? If I were in their shoes, I would question the person's character and authority as well. Besides, after I answer their questions, most of the dragons seem reassured.

One of the families we visit, the mood of the home is different from the others we have entered today. The house is dark and seemingly empty. A layer of dust coats everything in sight and the faint smell of mothballs lingers in the air.

There's one faded orange chair in the middle of an otherwise empty living room. An older man rocks back and forth in his chair. I don't recognize him, which isn't surprising. Everyone's faces—dragon or human—had become a blur after a while.

"Good afternoon, Caliban." Aracelia's voice takes up too much space in the quiet room. The man, who looks like he could be my grandfather, looks at Aracelia. His eyes are void of any emotion. I'm not even sure he fully acknowledges our presence in his space.

"We wanted to check on you. See how you are since your awakening," Aracelia's voice remains calm and I'm glad that she's here. The woman is a fierce warrior who could break me apart with just her pinkie finger, but she's also extremely gentle when the time calls for it. Like now.

Caliban's forlorn face droops even more. "My wife,

she's..." but the words never come out. He's overcome with grief as sobs wrack through his body.

Aracelia curses softly next to me, regret written across his features. "What is it?" I whisper, though Caliban is too distraught to pay us any mind.

"When Caliban succumbed to the sleeping curse, his wife was beside herself with grief. She had known her mate since they were hatchlings and experienced almost all her life with him. She declined rapidly. If it were possible to die of a broken heart..." She trails off, but I don't need to hear anymore. My heart hurts enough for Caliban and his deceased mate.

The thing about me is that I can't be around a person in pain and not want to help in some small way. Logically I know I can't take away a person's pain, but I can provide their pain some company. Sometimes just your presence is all a person needs.

"My Queen." Aracelia's words are a warning which I ignore. She cautioned me against approaching a dragon in distress, but I've never been one to ignore pain.

Caliban sees me approach, though he's still in the midst of his despair. I crouch down next to him, placing my hand over his. It's cold to the touch. Actually, the whole room is freezing. It's a cold day outside and the house seems to have soaked in all that chilliness.

"Aracelia, could you light a fire?" There's an old fireplace behind Caliban's chair that looks like it hasn't been touched in ages. Aracelia nods before dusting all the cobwebs and dust away from the fireplace so she can load it with firewood.

I feel the heat of the fire as soon as Aracelia starts it with her dragon fire. Caliban's body eases just a fraction, but it's something.

"What was your wife's name?"

Caliban sniffles, running a finger under his nose. "Salinea."

"Salinea, that's a beautiful name." I smile and for a moment, I swear Caliban returns it. "Do you want to tell me what she was like?"

People don't know how to act if they've never dealt with the death of a loved one. When my parents died it was always the same apologies and the same stories of how much they were loved. It's fine, but it doesn't paint the real picture. It's almost like a caricature of who they really were.

No one ever asked me to describe the parents I knew and loved. They only ever wanted to tell me their stories or simply forget they passed all together. I get it. Death is weird and hard. No one likes talking about their own mortality. But I had wished that one person would ask me about the parents I knew.

Caliban still hasn't pulled away from my touch, which I take as a good sign. The older dragon takes another few minutes to compose himself before he starts talking. "Salinea was a good chef, but a terrible baker."

We both laugh, though his is still full of pain. "She would make all my favorites and never get mad if I asked for the same food multiple times throughout the week. Once in a blue moon she would get a wild hair and think she'd need to make cookies. Always turned out burnt. She even started a small fire in the kitchen once."

"My mom was like that too. Could make the best dinners. So good that you wanted to lick your plate clean, so you didn't miss a single drop. But the moment she attempted to bake a cake or cupcakes..." I shake my head. "Let's just say we had to ban her from ever baking."

"Did you lose your mother?" Caliban asks, noticing the way I spoke about her in past tense.

I nod. "Both. My mother and father." Once I would have been a crying mess on the floor, unable to speak about them. It still hurts, yes, the pain would never go away. But it had become more manageable.

But losing a mate, a person you chose to spend your whole life with, is not something I have experience with yet. Malix isn't lost to me in the way Salinea is to Caliban. If the pain and hurt I feel over my cursed husband is even a fraction of what Caliban feels, then I'm amazed he even had the effort to get out of bed this morning.

Caliban goes on to tell me that Salinea and he had two children, but unfortunately both ended up passing away at a very young age. He speaks of her love for singing and knitting. The way they would dance to music only they could hear in the evenings.

He also speaks of their childhood and their dreams. The day they shared their first kiss and how they were inseparable ever since. I cry when Caliban does and join in for his laughter.

I spend most of my day with Caliban. Aracelia finally had to leave to continue checking on the other families, but I assured her I would be fine alone.

I'm not sure how many hours I spent talking with Caliban, but soon both of our stomachs are growling. The poor man doesn't have much for food, so I make a mental note to stock him up tomorrow, but for now I work with what I have.

I make a potato and beef—or what I hope is beef—soup and dish it up into two bowls. I grab two wooden spoons before bringing the food back to Caliban.

"You didn't have to do this," he says and graciously

takes the bowl from me. I kick the small footrest up next to him before taking a seat.

"It's the least I can do." I wave away his protest and we fall into a companionable silence. Caliban isn't crying anymore and he's eating. Baby steps but all in the right direction.

Another silent minute goes by, and Caliban says, "You were the one to wake me up. I remember your face and then I remember being rushed away by another man."

"Probably Otis." I sigh. "He kept me prisoner until I awoke everyone. He wasn't a good man, but Malix—"

"The king?"

"Yeah, my husband—"

"Your what?!" Caliban jolts out of his chair, nearly knocking his bowl over in the process. It takes me a moment to understand what he's doing. He awkwardly bends forward and says, "I didn't realize you were a queen."

"Oh." I shake my head, standing up and gesturing back to his seat. "I am, but don't feel the need to worry about titles. I would rather we just continue to talk as friends."

Caliban purses his lips together, unsure. After a tense few seconds, he finally nods. "Very well, but I'm certain you have more important duties to attend to than sitting with a grieving old man. The king will be worried."

It is my turn to hold back my tears and share with Caliban what happened to Malix. "So you see," I say, once I finish explaining to him about Malix's curse, "Aracelia, Vivia, and I are checking on all the households and looking for fighters. That's why she left, but I felt like my duty called me here."

"I don't know you well, but I can already tell you are a fair and just queen. I trust the kingdom in your hands, and if there is any way I can help, I will." Caliban reaches for my hand and squeezes it like I did to his earlier.

I hope I can live up to that expectation.

After that we finish dinner without any further hiccups, and he tells me more about Salinea. The sun has long ago disappeared from the sky by the time I leave with the promise to check on him soon.

I walk back to the castle, taking the longer route that will weave through my gardens so I can have a moment just to think.

Tomorrow I will attempt to strengthen the wards around the kingdom, a feat I'm not sure I'm capable of. Ender sure seems to think I am, and I have to hope that The Guardian is correct. I don't want Dragon's Keep to fall, nor do I want any harm to come to those under my care.

I'm not going to force any dragon to fight for our kingdom, but I have asked. Between me, Aracelia, and Vivia, I hope to amass a small group to help ward off attacks. Aracelia and Vivia are familiar faces to the dragons, so I hope they manage to get some support.

By the time I make it back to my room, exhaustion sets in. I pull off my clothes and get into bed without bathing or brushing my hair. I know I'll regret it in the morning, but right now I just want to be with Malix.

Aracelia and Vivia helped me move him to our bed earlier. He's lying above the covers, arms at his side. If I close my eyes I can pretend he's sleeping and that when I wake tomorrow, it will be to his sweet kisses.

I cuddle up to Malix's side, pressing up against him. "I wish you were here," I murmur, letting a single tear roll down my cheeks. It's odd to talk about someone as if they were dead, when they are clearly alive but unreachable.

"I'm not going to give up, Malix. I'll protect your...our

home. Until my dying breath." I imagine his arms around me and his sweet words of reassurance, reminding me that everything will be okay.

I soon drift off to sleep, escaping to my dreams where I know Malix awaits me.

CHAPTER 34

ROSE

Whoever left a tunic and pants for me to find when I woke up should get a promotion. I have enough to worry about that I don't need to add accidentally exposing myself in a dress to the list. It is also a testament to how deeply I slept last night when I didn't even realize someone had slipped in and out of the room without so much as stirring me.

I hesitate about leaving the bed. Malix hasn't moved since last night, of course he hasn't, why would he? But a small part of me wished for a miracle. I want him with me when I try to strengthen the wards today.

Easy enough...except not, since Nephilim are closing in on our borders. Vivia and Aracelia do a good job of putting on a brave facade, but I can see the worry and doubt creep in when they think I'm not looking. I can't even blame them. Those are the same doubts and insecurities running through my mind.

Sighing, I lean over and place a gentle kiss on Malix's cheek. "I'll be back soon." And how I pray that's true. Even the soft chirping of the early morning birds seem to be singing a forlorn song.

With great effort, I extract myself from the bed and change into the outfit one of the maids probably left. When I pull the tunic over my head, there's a knock on the door, which I assume is Vivia or Aracelia. The maids simply walk in.

"Come in!" I call, straightening the tunic. It's a little big on me, but still preferable over a dress. The door opens and I look up...only to stop dead in my tracks.

"Mina?" My voice is barely above a whisper. Vivia had said Mina was getting better, but the scar on her face will most likely be permanent now. A harsh pink cut runs from her left eyebrow horizontally down to her neck. Most of the skin has knit itself back together, but some of the cuts had been so deep it would take longer for them to heal completely.

I'm not sure who moves first, but soon we stand only inches apart. I throw my hands around her neck, pulling our bodies close. Mina's arms come around me and tighten, as if she too can't quite believe she's here.

"You're okay. Oh fuck, Mina, I'm so damn sorry. I've wanted to come and see you, but Vivia said you were still recovering, and I didn't want to intrude. But I couldn't stop thinking about you and...and..."

"Goddess, Rose, I need you to breathe." Mina laughs, the sound nothing but joy. I don't know what I expected. For her to hate me? To yell at me for leaving? "I'm okay. I promise."

"But you're hurt."

"You mean this?" She pulls away to point out the new scar across her face. "Listen, did it hurt? So much. But it doesn't anymore, and I don't blame you, so stop blaming yourself. I chose to help you and I told you to run when things got dangerous. And you want to know something else? I would do it again. Not because you're my queen, but because you're my friend."

"I'm sure I'm your most high-maintenance friend," I attempt to joke and it causes Mina to smile. The scar doesn't diminish the light in her eyes when she smiles. If anything, it makes Mina appear fierce and that holds its own type of beauty.

Her smile soon fades, and I notice what causes the abrupt change. Mina isn't looking at me anymore but behind me to the sleeping Malix on my bed. "Vivia said the king fell victim to the curse, but I didn't want to believe it."

That makes two of us.

"I've tried to wake him up. Every night since this happened," I explain. He's only been asleep for a few days, but it feels like a lifetime has passed. "I don't want to leave him in case…"

In case I fail, and the Nephilim invade Dragon's Keep. Saying it out loud feels like a bad omen. Still, Mina nods like she understands. Maybe she does, since her own wife will be at my side, leaving her wondering if she is okay or not.

"I know the fight you have ahead of you, and I don't want you to worry about Malix…as impossible of a request that is." I wonder if she's thinking of Vivia and if she is capable of not worrying about her wife. I feel like I already know the answer.

"I'm going to stay with him," she continues. "Me and my son, once he wakes up. I figure since you'll be watching over my wife, I can watch over your husband."

Despite wanting to both cry and scream over the situation, a laugh bursts out of me. "Deal. Then let's promise to never have any more scary adventures."

"Honestly, I'm too old for this." She laughs, despite hardly being older than me. Mina reaches out and squeezes my hand. "I'll protect him while you protect the rest of us. Just come back to us in one piece, okay?"

"No promises." We share one last hug, neither of us wanting to be the one that lets go first. In the back of my mind a dark thought appears, making me question if this is the last time I'll see Malix and Mina. I don't let it take form though. I can't afford to think like that.

When we finally break apart, Mina's eyes are glistening with unshed tears. "Good luck, My Queen. I can't wait to hear all about it when you get back."

When. Not if.

Casting one last look at Malix, I squeeze Mina's hand before leaving to find Vivia.

I find Vivia waiting for me in the meeting room, alone. I frown, wondering if I missed something. "Where is Aracelia? Were you not able to get any of the dragons to help?"

Vivia doesn't answer me. Instead, the dragoness takes my hand and starts pulling me forward. "You're going to want to see this, My Queen."

My stomach drops. "I swear if this is another bad thing, I'm going to explode." Vivia laughs, but still says nothing about what she wants me to see. I'm helpless to do anything but follow.

We go straight out the door and down the hallway.

Vivia makes a right to a different hallway that leads us straight out to the castle grounds, closer to the gardens. I have to jog to keep up with her. She may look human right now, but her strides and swiftness are pure dragon.

I squint against the sun the moment we walk outside. It takes my vision a moment to adjust and another to comprehend what I'm seeing.

Aracelia walks up to us, a smirk on her face at my dumbfounded expression. "Morning, My Queen. We have a few dragons that will be assisting us today."

"A few?" I choke out. There's nothing "a few" about the number of dragons waiting out here for...me? And these are full-fledged dragons, large and fierce. The only ones who wear their human skin are Vivia and Aracelia and I'm sure that's for my benefit.

"Well, more than a few. I would say a hundred or so, give or take. I lost count," Aracelia shrugs flippantly, as if she were commenting on the weather rather than the small army she procured.

My head swivels between her and Vivia like a defective bobblehead. "How did you get all these dragons?" More importantly, what did they promise, and do we have the ability to deliver it?

"I told them their queen needed warriors. These are the dragons that came," Aracelia says.

I hear her words, but my brain is still ten steps behind everyone else. "I don't get it. They don't even know me. Why would they come?"

Vivia chuckles. "Because every single one of these dragons were awakened by you and have come here today to show their gratitude."

Every single dragon here was awakened by me. I let

those words sink in. For the days I was down in the cellar, I lost count of how many dragons I awakened, but I guess that number to be pretty steep. The proof of that theory is now laid out before me. Dragons of all colors and sizes take up space around the castle, farther than my eyes can see.

But one catches my eye. A small dragon, nuzzling against two larger ones. When the hatchling turns my way, I immediately recognize him. Even in dragon form. You don't forget your first and Cyrus was the first dragon I awakened. He dips his head, his parents following his lead, and appreciation radiates from their family. He's home with his parents, saying goodbye before they follow me into battle.

This is so surreal.

Not as surreal as the dragon approaching me, leaning down, their snout only inches away from my face. I don't recognize this dragon, not until he speaks, that is. *"You sat with me and allowed me to grieve and talk about the love of my life. Let me help save yours."*

Caliban. He came. Because of me.

My eyes sting with tears, and I only manage to say, "Thank you." The words don't convey my full gratitude, but they'll have to do for now.

Aracelia leans over, slinging her arm over my shoulders. "You'll come to learn that dragons are very protective of their own. You are one of us, our queen. That's the title none of these dragons take lightly."

Well damn. "I'm just...wow."

"You didn't think you'd go into battle alone, did you?" Aracelia raises her brow, a knowing smirk on her face.

"Uh...actually, yes?" Logically, I know strengthening the wards isn't going to be as simple as me going to our borders and snapping my fingers to make everything better, but I still kind of hoped it would be like that.

Not a full-on battle.

Fucking hell.

"So, this isn't overkill," I mutter.

"No, definitely not. The dragons know their job. Keep Nephilim away from their queen so you can repair the wards," Vivia says.

"And how do I do that exactly?" I try to whisper, but the dragons closest to us cock their head to the side. Already I feel like I'm letting the dragons down. Ender said I would know what to do. That in Mescos, I possess power, but it still doesn't feel like it.

Aracelia brings a hand up to my shoulder and gives it a squeeze. "You'll know what to do when you feel it. All the kings and queens of the past didn't grow up knowing, they simply knew when the time came. Don't worry though, we will help you strengthen it. You will lead us."

I open my mouth to protest before a flock of black birds springs up in the distance, spooked by something I can't hear, but can imagine.

"We are out of time, we need to go. Now." Aracelia turns her back to us. She shifts and a mighty growl reverberates around us, only to be picked up by the other dragons. A battle cry.

"It's time to go, My Queen. Hope you aren't afraid of heights," Vivia says before shifting. Seconds later, a plum-colored dragon stands before me. *Hop on, Your Highness,* she says through our link.

Everything in me screams to turn back. To stay with Malix until this is all over. But the dragons are looking at me, ready to follow my lead. Their belief in me is the only reason I climb on the back of Vivia's dragon, holding on to her for dear life.

"*Ready?*" Vivia's voice is loud in my head. I hear the chants from the other dragons too, following Aracelia's battle cry.

"Ready," I lie.

Then, we take to the skies.

CHAPTER 35

ROSE

The wind bites at my skin relentlessly, as my body flattens against Vivia's even more. I've never considered myself afraid of heights before, but I also have never been atop a dragon's back, flying countless feet above the ground. I cling to Vivia with all the strength I can muster, afraid if I loosen my grip for even a second, I'll fall to my gruesome death.

Any naive hopes of a simple mission is quickly shattered the moment Vivia says we are close to the wards. Something feels wrong. I feel like a ball of yarn slowly being unwound, waiting for the moment I completely come apart. It's not my own feelings; I'm picking up someone...or something else.

A loud crack comes from somewhere below and the next moment an entire tree trunk spirals through the sky, hitting a small red dragon. A roar of pain follows, and the injured dragon drops from formation. I hear their cry for help growing more desperate until suddenly I can't hear or feel the dragon anymore.

Gone.

Just like that.

"Nephilim!" Aracelia shrieks, warning the dragons who are farther back and didn't just see the loss of one of our own. They felt it though. The pure terror as the dragon dropped from the sky.

"Fuck..." Vivia gasps and I don't think she meant for me to hear it, but I do. Despite my better judgment, I lift my head in hope of getting a better look at what made the dragoness panic.

Immediately I wish I hadn't.

On the horizon, just past a thicket of trees, stand creatures who appear to have walked out of the darkest nightmares. Some stand as tall as the trees while others are high above. They are human-like, but all their features are elongated. Arms. Legs. Torso. Their skin looks as if it has been charred and is stretched taut around their bones. They also have wings, or rather what may have once been wings. Black feathers on their back, heavy at the top, but the feathers are nearly nonexistent the lower it goes. Just ripped or bruised skin.

They are nightmares come to life, sent to destroy everything in their wake.

Unfortunately, their sights are set on us.

Aracelia starts barking out orders to dragons, giving them places to go and defend. By the looks of it, she's no stranger to war, so I'm happy to let her direct the dragons. Vivia and I have our own goal, which seems more impossible by the second.

A Nephilim ventures closer, breaking away from their group. Their high-pitched groans are nails on a chalkboard, making me shudder uncomfortably. The Nephilim come closer, far too close for comfort, before they run into an invisible shield.

It flickers, only momentarily, but I see it. The wards. This is why we are here. The Nephilim screeches. The sound is so loud and my ears ring with the sound of the creature's displeasure. Stick-like fingers curl into a fist before banging down on the wards.

The air around the wards ripples, a faint light flickering into existence and out again. The magic keeping up the wards is breaking down in front of us.

"Vivia, hurry!" Sheer panic engulfs me. It's so unexpected and raw, and I feel like crying out for help. But it's not my emotions I'm feeling. It's almost as if the wards are begging to be restored.

What did Vivia say about the royals from the past? That strengthening their kingdom wasn't a learned trait, but something that came instinctually. Ender, in his own roundabout way, taught me I possess some sort of magic within Mescos. He also assured me that I'm exactly where I need to be. Did he see this happening?

I have no time to think about the mind of Ender because Vivia is flying faster and heading toward the ground. The closer we get to the wards, the more I feel a budding connection with them. It's energy, coursing through one entity into another. Except the energy around the wards feel wrong. All wrong. Like the power is flickering and any moment will leave completely.

Vivia lands and all the air whooshes out of me. Landing fucking sucks, but the whole experience has been terrifying. I'm in no rush to ride on the back of dragons again, anytime soon.

"We need to go, My Queen." Vivia's words get my ass in gear and I carefully climb off her back. My feet hit the ground with a sound of relief. Yes, I'm definitely meant to be firmly on the ground. Less chances of falling to my death.

However, from my new vantage point on two legs, the enormity of the nightmarish Nephilim are overwhelming. Their feet alone are as big as me. One carefully placed step and I would be little more than dust beneath them.

Focus, Rose. Stop thinking about being crushed to death.

More Nephilim have joined the first one, hitting their fists against the wall. Each fist to the wards jostles something deep within me. The integrity of the kingdom's protection is waning quickly, giving me very little time to figure out how to restore them.

Vivia steps up next to me, human and completely naked. I try not to stare, since nudity isn't a big deal among the dragons, but it's still shocking each time a naked dragon strolls by.

"Do you feel the wards?" There's a tightness to her voice that hadn't been there before, as if she's afraid of my answer.

"I do. They are failing quickly though." As I say that, a rip rumbles the foundation. Vivia reaches out to steady me and a loud screech has us both jerking our heads to the side. "Holy fuck," I gasp.

It shouldn't be possible, but two Nephilim have broken through our invisible barrier, and have stepped foot into Dragon's Keep. A few dragons are on them in an instant, but more will follow.

The Nephilim are lethal in battle, cutting down dragons with makeshift weapons or their bare hands. Two more break through, with an entire army behind them. If the majority of the Nephilim are able to break through, Dragon's Keep will fall.

"Vivia, what am I supposed to do?" There's a panic in

my voice I can't hide, desperate for any answers or solutions she can provide.

Vivia's attention swivels between me and the intruding Nephilim, body braced and ready for action when the time calls for it. "Open yourself up to the magic. Malix says it feels like opening a door, letting the magic of the wards enter your body. Once he has the door open, I'm able to help him strengthen the wards. It feels like you are stitching a protective blanket tightly together, making sure not to leave any loose threads."

The first half, at least, is something I'm a little familiar with from waking the dragons. I dig deep inside me, searching for the magic behind the door. It's a faint call, but it's there all the same.

"I feel it," I gasp. A sigh of relief leaves Vivia's lips, proving my suspicion from earlier is correct. She is just as nervous as I am about my connection with the wards.

I picture myself opening a door, letting the cool air meet me. Energy and unclaimed power wash over me, but not in a way that overwhelms me. It's subtle, a stranger, but a friendly one in need of help.

"Yes! I feel it now too. That's perfect, My Queen." I preen at Vivia's praise, gaining more confidence. "We should be able to—"

Before I can process what's happening, Vivia dives for me and we go rolling to the ground. A long axe-like weapon lodges itself into a tree only a few feet away from where I'd been. Not far behind it, the scream from a Nephilim follows and it's approaching fast.

"Go!" I scream at her. The plan had been that Vivia would stay with me to help me strengthen the wards so the process would go faster. That shit isn't happening now though. Not when Nephilim are out here trying to decapitate me.

Vivia's a warrior. I know she's itching to join Aracelia in the battle and honestly, I need her to watch my back. Not stand with me during the process.

To her credit, Vivia doesn't argue, even though uncertainty races across her features. She pulls off of me and soon her deep purple dragon is standing above me. A second later she flies out, heading straight toward the Nephilim heading this way.

Before I can see the blood bath that will surely follow, I scramble to my feet and fix my attention back on the wards. Vivia said it would feel like threads being knit together and I search for that. To my horror I feel it, but these strands are frayed, held together by a single thread.

This is completely different from awakening dragons. My mind has to work in ways it has never had to before, pulling at invisible threads and accepting the magic of Mescos to help me in my task.

The world around me heats up as dragon fire burns around me. Sweat pools on my scrunched-up brow and drips down my back. It is growing increasingly uncomfortable, but I ignore it. I have to in order to keep my attention on my job. I ignore the shrieks and screams of fallen enemies and friends.

It's a slow process, stitching up each unraveled strand of thread, knotting them tightly together until they are secure. Over and over, I do this, panting from the mental exertion, but it's working. I feel the wards pulse with a newfound strength. It's still extremely fragile, but there's a difference in the energy. It's stronger...almost more excited.

I just need more time though. Always more time.

The cries from the battle are only getting louder. It

takes everything in me not to turn around and watch the chaos unfold firsthand. Sheer stubbornness keeps me rooted in place along with the need to save Malix and Dragon's Keep.

My eyes are closed, and my attention is on restoring the wards, so I don't see or hear the creature approaching me until it's too late. "Mortal."

The voice isn't one I have ever heard before and doesn't sound normal. It's scratchy and speaks as if multiple people are talking at once, all saying the same thing but in different registers.

My eyes snap open as cold fear washes over my body. Only a few feet away, standing just outside our borders, is a Nephilim. But there's something different about him. He's taller than the rest, by at least half a foot. He wears an eyepatch over his left eye and I see a faint jagged scars peeking out from underneath. He also speaks, something that I haven't heard from the others.

Is this Gadreel?

I'm torn between fleeing or staying, but somehow, my feet stay rooted to the spot. If I can just knot the threads together faster then maybe it'll be enough to keep this deadly creature away from me.

"Mortal," he speaks again, but steps forward. His movements rattle the ground and I brace myself, so I don't fall over. "So small. So frail." The Nephilim laughs, sounding like thunder during a particularly nasty storm.

Vivia is no longer near me. She's off in her own battle, keeping the Nephilim behind me away. I'm on my own.

Faster. Concentrate. You can do this.

I repeat the mantra over and over in my head, hoping if I believe it enough, it will come true. The wards stitch themselves back together only marginally faster and I try to keep the panic building low in my belly at bay. I can't give up. Not with so much to lose.

The ground beneath me shakes again and the Nephilim approaches me. Hysteria builds in my chest, but I shove it down, only just. "Death is here, mortal."

This time I can't help it. I scream, breaking my hold on the wards as I stumble back in my desperate attempt to get away.

The Nephilim laughs again and keeps walking. I pray that enough of the wards have been restored to keep the giant out. The Nephilim stops just outside our invisible walls and I hold my breath, praying to any god, goddess, or deity that will listen.

Everything hangs by a thread...literally, and my sense of safety shatters the moment the creature crouches down and extends his arm out. Without so much as the slightest hesitation, he pushes through my half-formed wards with his sight on me.

I open my mouth again to scream, but no sound comes out. My survival instincts finally kick in and I run. I make it only a few feet before a large hand comes down and cages me inside. It grows darker and darker until all the light from outside is gone.

"Mine." Is the last word I hear before his hand prison begins to close in on itself, becoming tighter and tighter until I'm pressed against the Nephilim's fingers and palm.

He applies pressure as his fingers clench around my body, and I scream. I scream for Malix and I hope he knows how hard I tried. I scream for Vivia and Mina, apologizing that I couldn't create a safe kingdom to raise their boy.

And I scream for myself, knowing I'm about to take my last breath before my bones and body are crushed.

MALIX

I'm alone in my dreams. Void of companionship, color, and sound. It's just me in a dark room, impatiently pacing back and forth. I'm tired, but I'm also restless. Angry, but strangely at peace. These conflicting emotions make no sense to me, just like the vast emptiness before me.

I should be somewhere, but no matter how hard I try to wrack my brain, nothing of importance comes to me. Nothing other than the whispers of someone needing me. Someone desperately wanting me to wake up.

But who?

Perhaps it doesn't matter. I'm confined to the darkness with no chance of getting out. Or am I? The feeling grows stronger, paired with a sense of urgency. The need to be by this person's side. It's not just one either, though one voice reigns above all others, I hear cries from several voices, calling out not a name, but a title.

King.

Over and over again. King. That word gets overshadowed by another one though. One more powerful than that of a ruler. Mate.

The voice sounds female and so far away. Tendrils of fear snake around my body, but not ones that belong to me, at least not entirely. I think they belong to her.

Images of deep-auburn hair, silky-smooth skin, and the warmest of eyes assault my brain in rapid succession, changing from a happy woman to one bent and broken. A deafening roar rings out around me, but no one else is here. Just me. The sound came from me...but why?

More fear winds tighter and tighter around me until I'm suffocating, choking on fear that doesn't belong to me. It belongs to her. A floral name. Daisy? No, that doesn't sound right. Maybe...Rose.

Rose. The sweet smell of summer. A red wine so rare it is meant to be savored. Something that is *mine*.

Rose is mine.

The cold fear that washes over my body is my own. Rose needs me. Rose needs help. But where the fuck am I? A melodic sound calls my name, sounding like chimes on a windy day.

I take a step into the dark. And then another until I'm walking toward the voice. I'm directionless in this darkness, but my ears guide me. Closer and closer to the voice until it's a loud ringing sensation in my ear. No longer pleasant, but rather an ominous ring hinting at an unfavorable outcome.

Take me to Rose, I think repeatedly. My voice doesn't work here, but my thoughts do, and they are loud. Demanding to take me to Rose. To the people who need me before it's too late. Before I lose myself.

"*Rose!*" I roar and for the first time, light filters in. I squint against the harsh lights, panting as if I just flew miles with no breaks in between. My heart threatens to burst out of my chest.

"My King!" A familiar voice gasps. It takes me a moment to gather my bearings, but soon my eyes focus in the bright room. Mina stares at me with wide eyes as if I have just startled her. There's a nasty-looking scar sliced across her face that hasn't been there before. I don't ask her about it though, because my mind immediately zones in on the one person I want to see that is missing from my bed.

"Rose. Where's Rose?" My voice cracks, dry from disuse. I would be embarrassed if I weren't so fucking confused. I went to sleep and now everything is different. Wrong.

I don't appreciate the look of pity Mina gives me. Not one bit. "Mina. Where is Rose?"

My words come out harsher than I anticipated and I immediately feel bad when she flinches. I go to apologize, but Mina is already speaking rapidly. "You've been cursed, My King. For a few days now. Rose tried everything she could to wake you, but she couldn't and today they went to strengthen the wards and—wait! We don't know if it's safe for you to leave!"

The moment she said Rose is at the wards, I shift. My dragon erupts from me, painfully, after days of keeping him locked out due to the curse. Mina screams at me to stay, but that's the last thing I plan on doing when my damn wife is in danger.

And she is in danger. I feel it. Her fear and desperation. It's a rancid taste in my mouth that I can't get rid of. It threatens to poison me unless I find her. I pump my wings faster and faster, closing the distance between us rapidly, but still too long for my liking.

Tracking her down isn't hard. She's screaming in our bond, though I'm not sure she realizes she's doing it. Even while I was cursed, there was always something—no, someone—speaking in the back of my mind, begging me to come back. She doesn't know it yet, but she's the reason I woke up. I'm certain of it.

Even if she wasn't screaming out for me, I smell the blood and smoke from dragon's fire. I hear the shrieks of the dying and wounded, as well as the victory calls of those who have slain their enemy.

More importantly, I see the Nephilim; their twisted soulless bodies wreaking havoc on my people and decimating my wards. And among the chaos somewhere is Rose. One small mortal in a sea of dragons and Nephilim.

Anger consumes me and fire erupts from my throat, raining down on the group of Nephilim attempting to break their way through the wards. Their screams should satisfy me, but they don't.

Murmurs go through my head of the other dragons realizing I'm here. Most are relieved, thinking my presence will bring an end to this battle. If they believe simply showing up will be enough, they're sadly mistaken.

More and more Nephilim break through my wards, I feel the invisible barrier deteriorating rapidly. I also feel Rose's work wrapped up in the wards and pride swells through me. My wife tried and I plan on helping her see this through.

I'm frantic in my attempts to find her. Rose's terror is still evident, but this close to so many dragons makes picking her out a near-impossible task.

In my frenzy I almost miss him. The crouching Nephilim with his hand extended into a fist. He's large, even for his kind. I fly lower and that's when I see the eye patch covering his burnt side. My blood runs cold at the recognition of Gadreel, the Nephilim king.

Another scream fills the air, this one closer and familiar. I recognize her instantly, though it's a scream of terror I never wanted to hear coming from her.

Gadreel has my wife.

I see red. I'm no longer a man, but a beast intent on eliminating the enemy. I dive for him, talons ready to dig into flesh, and rip. I'll rip each limb off if I have to. Gadreel sees me diving for him at the last minute and hisses. He moves, but not enough, and my talons dig into the side of his head, just shy of his good eye.

Gadreel roars, jerking his giant body off the ground. In the process, he opens his palm, and a limp body falls from his grasp. I catch a glimpse of auburn hair. "Rose!" I roar. She's falling to the ground faster than I can get to her. The drop will break her body if Gadreel hasn't already.

I pump my wings faster, willing myself to get to her. But I'm too far away. Too much distance between us.

Just when I think I'm about to fail my wife and watch her die, a dragon swoops in just in time, catching Rose on her back. I hear the breath leave her lungs, and a small groan of pain. The small sound fills me with palpable relief.

Vivia drops to the ground, and I follow suit. I shift the moment my feet touch the ground and sprint the remaining distance. *"Rose!"* I'm only capable of saying her name. Nothing else. She has to be okay. She must. There's no other alternative.

Rose lifts her head from Vivia's back. Eyes puffy with dark circles underneath. She stares at me as if I were a ghost. I take advantage of her shock to look over her body for any obvious signs of injuries. There's a bruise forming on her cheek and she winces when she tries to put weight on her left side, but otherwise she appears fine.

"Malix?" She sounds so unsure, and my heart fucking

breaks for her. I hate that she's been going through all of this without me.

"I'm here, little dragon," I assure her, but I know we aren't out of danger yet. Not even close. Gadreel laughs behind me, and I know my time is up.

"Vivia, stay with Rose. Don't leave her side!" I order and my second nods. I give Rose one last lingering look. I want to hold her, to reassure her that I'm fine and that I'll keep her safe. But to keep her safe, I have to make sure Gadreel doesn't fully enter Dragon's Keep.

"Go," Rose says, as if sensing my spiraling thoughts. "I'll work on the wards." She doesn't look to be in any physical condition to give more of herself to Dragon's Keep, but we have no other options.

So, I unleash my dragon once again.

I love you. The words are on the tip of my tongue, begging to be unleashed before I leave Rose. She needs to know. Needs to know that in the few short weeks she has stormed into my life and changed its entire foundation. I can never go back to how things were.

Rose smiles at me like she knows my thoughts, which she probably does through the bond, and it's so damn good to see her smile. "Go," she whispers again, giving me the final kick I need and take to the air. I spare one last glance behind me to make sure she's okay, before bringing my attention back to Gadreel.

The Nephilim king smiles. "Your father was a lot stronger than you, Dragon King. You'll be reacquainted with him in no time." Seemingly out of nowhere, Gadreel pulls out a deadly axe, probably weighing more than the average mortal.

Dragon's Keep didn't fall then, and it won't fall now. I

have too much to live for. More memories I plan on making with my wife.

Like mirror images of one another, we lunge. Metal against fire. Dragon against Nephilim. Evenly matched in all the ways that count.

Gadreel's axe flies through the sky, missing me by mere centimeters. His miss provides me the opening I need, and I lunge for his neck. Gadreel isn't an easy appointment though and my teeth snap in midair as he dodges my attack.

We continue this dance, two kings battling for land. I tire more quickly than normal since I'm still overcoming the lingering effects of the curse. My fatigue doesn't matter though. Gadreel simply needs to be distracted so Rose can work without delay.

She's who Dragon's Keep needs right now.

Their queen.

CHAPTER 37

ROSE

"**D**on't look behind you. Focus, My Queen," Vivia says for the umpteenth time, which is easier said than done.

"If your spouse was fighting the biggest Nephilim after waking up from a curse, I think you'd be interested as well," I snap and immediately feel bad. I'm not upset with Vivia, she's just unfortunate enough to be the recipient of my ire. Far too many emotions are rampant through my body. Fear, anger, confusion, and panic.

"I'm sorry. I don't mean to snap at you." Vivia has gone out of her way for me. Protecting me and coming to my rescue when I thought for sure my body would hit the ground. I'm running on pure adrenaline, ignoring the pain that will surely follow once it wears off.

"No apologies necessary. I understand the need to check on your mate and I don't fault you for it. But now is your chance to help him." Vivia's hands rest on my shoulder, keeping me steady. "I will help as much as I can. You've opened the door for me; I feel the threads."

Another burst of fire roars to life behind me, the heat dancing across my skin. I breathe in the smoky ash, coughing as it fills my lungs. My concentration is waning quickly, even as I force myself to reach for the ties and thread them back together. It's a tedious process, especially with the extent of damage our wards have taken.

A battle rages behind me, my mate fights for not only my life, but the lives of the entire kingdom. Pain lashes through our bond and despite Vivia's earlier warnings, I tear my focus away from the wards and frantically search the skies for Malix.

Except he's not in the skies.

Malix is on the ground, one wing curled in. Blood oozes from a deep gash on his wing, keeping him bound to the ground. The Nephilim king approaches him with what might pass as a twisted smile. He thinks he's already won.

Malix is a deadly foe. Taking the advantage of the sky away from him is a setback, but his fight isn't over. I desperately want to call out for him, but I can't risk distracting him. Despite his injuries, he's holding his own and I need to be doing the same.

"Sorry, I'm back. I'm focused," I murmur and turn back around. My eyes close and I work at drowning out the distractions around me. The pounding in my ears subsides to a muffled ring. The heat licking at my skin fades to only a mild annoyance.

Vivia works beside me tirelessly. It's strange to feel connected to her in this way, both working on restoring our wards, but the help is appreciated. Still, our work is slow. Our time is ticking away quickly, each passing second the wards struggle and allow more Nephilim to come through.

The more I work, the more something becomes increasingly clear.

I need Malix. Vivia isn't my husband and although working with her is faster than working alone, it's still a far cry from what I believe Malix and I could accomplish.

Vivia seems to come to this conclusion the moment I do. Our eyes open and we stare at each other. Her struggles are easy to read. She doesn't want to leave me alone again, but she needs to get Malix. Her king gave her an order and she is bound to obey it, but her queen is about to go against his words.

"I need Malix, Vivia. I know you feel it too. Take his place and let him come to me." Malix isn't far away, and no other Nephilim are coming my way besides the ones attempting to break through. I can keep them out though, but I need Malix.

Vivia considers this for only a second before nodding. "I'll keep Gadreel from fully crossing over. If he breaks through, his power will strengthen the rest of his people. Our wards will be rendered useless. You're going to have to work fast."

"Such a great inspirational speech. Thank you for that, Vivia," I deadpan. She grunts in reply and shifts into her dragon.

"Be careful," she says to me, as if I needed that reminder. Then she's gone.

I'm alone again, but this time I'm not scared. There's a certain selfish pleasure in doing something that is bigger than just myself. The hefty weight of responsibility isn't lost on me though. However, I'm not allowing the fear that comes with the responsibility to consume me. Instead, I relish the task.

Before Dragon's Keep, back at Grym Hollow, my life felt very much out of my control. I lost my parents and couldn't do anything to save them. They died on impact. What I thought I had under control had been my love life, but even that was stripped from me by the two people closest to me.

I have control now though. My body vibrates with it. Power courses through my veins and only gets stronger when warm, sweaty arms wrap around me. He leans into me, more hurt than he's allowing himself to show.

Doesn't matter. I can be strong enough for the both of us. Malix doesn't have to do this alone. The realization that I don't have to do this alone either hits me like a ton of bricks. It's almost painful to realize that I have love and a purpose. Something I pretended I didn't need for the longest time. Deep down though, it was always the one thing I craved above all others.

My energy connects with Malix's and erupts so beautifully that tears come to my eyes. It's new and still growing, but it's strong and vibrant. I feel him everywhere on my body, inside and out. I feel his fear and determination. But most importantly, I feel his love. His love for me. It's overwhelming and everything I have always deserved but have never allowed myself to have.

We weave together vibrant colors, laying out our fears, desires, wants, and needs. There are no secrets between us, no hesitations keeping us apart. Something snaps into place, and I *feel* him. His emotions, his fear, and his love for me. An unbreakable bond takes root.

Strength soars through my body and I'm unable to contain it. Too much, too fast.

So I push it out to the only thing that needs it more than me.

Before my eyes, I watch the shimmer of the wards spark, appearing for all to see before sending a light into the land. It flickers once more before becoming invisible to the eye. It's not gone though. No, it's back, strong, and ready to defend Dragon's Keep.

The wards pulse with the strength of Malix and me combined, working in tandem. A scream, followed by a curse, rings out and I turn just in time to see Gadreel jerk his body back. His chest is flushed a pinkish color, and he pounds on his chest as if he's putting out a fire.

More high-pitched screams erupt and I follow the noises until I'm turned in Malix's arms, looking out at the result playing out in front of me. A few dragons lie on the floor, unmoving, and my heart hurts for our fallen, though they are few.

The remaining Nephilim inside our borders burn. Not from dragon's fire, but the protection the wards grant us. This was why Gadreel was desperate to shatter our wards and why Malix strove to strengthen them as often as he could. Alone, that burden must have been hard to carry, but neither of us is alone anymore.

The Nephilim burn as they try to leave, but none of the ones trapped within get out. They fall to the ground with a resounding thud before turning to ash in front of our very eyes.

Silence follows. Neither dragon nor Nephilim speak. Slowly, and then all at once, the dragons roar in triumph and solidarity. Joy spreads fast among the dragons and it's hard not to get caught up in their contagious excitement.

"We did it!" I jump into Malix's arms. He grunts but catches me, and a second later he's kissing me. It's hard, passionate, and completely dominating. Everything I missed while he was cursed. My body arches to him, and if we weren't in the middle of a forest with half of our kingdom watching, I'd demand him to take me.

Reluctantly we break apart, gasping to catch our breath. "It was all you, little dragon. You awakened our people and rallied them. You restored the wards. We are standing as victors because of you."

I beam at his praise. So many people helped. Mina. Vivia. Aracelia. Malix. And of course, all the dragons who came to fight today. Every one of them should be recognized for their bravery and loyalty to Dragon's Keep.

My pride diminishes somewhat when I realize that not everyone who came into this battle will be going home. Their family and friends will never have the chance to rejoice in this victory with the fallen, but they can rejoice in the fact they died as heroes. I make a vow right here and now to memorialize all that we lost.

From the corner of my eye I see Nephilim shuffle away from the wards, though Gadreel doesn't move. Malix pulls me closer, a low growl leaving his lips. Gadreel hisses in response. "Mescos will fall to the Nephilim, and I'll see to it that you die with it." He lets the threat linger before he turns and walks with his people. For now, we are safe.

Malix doesn't let me go and I'm not inclined to move out of his embrace. "What now?" I ask, hardly believing this is over. That the immediate threat is gone. I'm not naive to think they won't be a problem again because Nephilim will always pose a threat for as long as they live, but we can celebrate our win for now.

"Now, wife? Now, we mourn and bury our dead, thank our people, and we head home." Malix wraps a loose strand of my hair around his finger and tucks it behind my ear.

"Home. That sounds nice." I smile and pull out of his embrace. The best part is knowing I can run into his arms whenever I need it. "You ready, My King?"

Ready to face our people. Ready for the future. Ready for anything that comes our way.

Malix threads our fingers together and nods. "Lead the way, My Queen."

Hand in hand, we walk to our people. To celebrate. To mourn. To love.

MALIX

Two weeks later

Rose's cheeks hollow as she takes me deeper into her mouth. She may be the one on her knees, but there is no question who holds the power here. My vixen of a wife looks up at me with sultry eyes, as she expertly sucks down my cock. She's too fucking good at this and she knows it.

"Fuck." It's the only word I'm capable of. I've been stripped down to my most primal needs and nothing else matters besides our combined pleasure. I'm dangerously close. If she keeps sucking me so vigorously, I'm going to explode in that sinful mouth of hers.

We can't have that. My queen needs her pleasure first.

I pull back abruptly and Rose gasps. "What the fuck?" she whines, grabbing for me. My mind short-circuits when her teasing tongue licks my cock from tip to balls.

"Fuck." Again, she renders me incapable of eloquent speech.

I groan and dig deep within myself for the willpower to pull back. When I do, I pick Rose up and toss her onto our bed. She bounces once before scrambling to right herself. The seductress spreads her legs, her wet pussy glistening for me. I'll never tire of the sight.

"Malix." This time her tone is a demand. She reaches down between her legs to rub small circles on her clit. Rose throws her head back, small moans leave her lips. Her body is flushed with arousal, nipples peaked and demanding my attention.

So, I give it to them.

I'm on her in seconds, my body presses her down into the mattress. "What do you need, little dragon?"

Rose doesn't answer. Instead, she reaches between us and grabs my cock. She runs it through her sweet cream, coating me in her arousal. She then leads me inside of her and we groan together.

"You're so fucking big," she whimpers, tightening around me. I want her to choke my cock, squeeze until I come undone.

We move in tandem, meeting each other thrust for thrust and bite for bite. I pepper her neck with kisses, sucking on the spots I know will drive her crazy and will leave my mark on her. The sounds she makes, loud and soft, drive me wild.

"Malix, I'm close. So damn close." Rose wraps her legs around my torso, pulling me deeper into her. I reach between us, taking over rubbing her sensitive clit.

Seconds later she screams out for me, and I love it. I follow her over the edge, and we ride out our orgasms until we are nothing more than a sweaty mess on the bed. No matter how many times I take my wife, it will never be enough. I have a sneaking suspicion she feels the same.

When we catch our breath, I carry Rose into the bath I had prepared for us. I've quickly come to realize my favorite time with Rose is after we fuck. She gets cuddly and nuzzles into my side. I never took myself as a man who enjoyed holding his partner after intimacy, but Rose brings out parts of me I didn't know existed.

And to think this marvelous woman is my queen, it truly astounds me.

I gently place Rose in the warm water and follow her in, wrapping my arms around her. It's been two weeks since we've restored our wards and banished the Nephilim from our kingdom, but I haven't fully embraced our safety yet.

So much has changed in a few short weeks. I'm no longer the sole head of my council; Rose is by my side each meeting and has invited Mina and Caliban to replace the openings Aeron and Otis left behind with their deaths. The other council members are slow to accept the newcomers, but they've been warming up to the idea. All of them seem to trust my mate.

Since the battle, no dragons have fallen into a death-like sleep. Our borders are not only strong but thriving, and I no longer have to go out daily to restore them. All because of Rose.

She still refuses to see the monumental part she played in saving our kingdom, but I remind her any chance I get. But I'm not the only one. My people have accepted her as queen and embraced her fully. According to Vivia, she is more popular than me. Each evening when I retrieve Rose from her garden, I also have to chase away a few hatchlings that have started to follow her everywhere.

Secretly, I think she likes the attention.

Rose can sense my thoughts and feelings and fills our bond with love. "Do you ever stop thinking?"

"About your safety? Never."

She laughs and shakes her head. Then her mood sobers. "Do you think they'll be back?"

I don't have to ask who *they* are. It's the same question I grapple with daily. "I think the other kingdoms will feel their wrath before we do. It is a possibility that we will be called to fight again."

Rose nods. "We sent word to the other kingdoms. They should be preparing."

They should be. Knowing the rulers of the other kingdoms, I imagine they are doing nothing but preparing for an upcoming attack. The scariest thing is that no one has reported Nephilim sightings since the battle. They're out there, but not making their presence known.

"But for now, we are safe." The words feel strange, especially because I think they are mostly true. "What should we do with all this free time we have?"

"You mean between restoration, meetings, building a new council, and day-to-day tasks?"

"See? So much time," I deadpan.

Rose mulls over this idea. I feel hesitancy through our bond, and I don't care for that shit. "Speak your mind, wife. What is it?"

"It's about our wedding."

Those were not the words I expected, and my body tenses. Rose and I haven't said out loud that we love each other. But I have felt it through our bond. It's stronger than it's ever been. It took restoring the wards for it to fully snap into place, but now we are tied together, our souls one.

Sensing my obvious confusion, Rose turns in my arms so that we are facing each other. She cups my face between her fingers. "This is not me saying I don't love you or want to be married to you. I do love you, Malix."

The words are out. I didn't expect the swell of emotions that they bring with them. I knew how she felt but hearing the words...it makes it more. More real. More true.

"I love you too, Rose." I've never spoken those words to anyone else, other than my mother. My father was not an affectionate man. The most I got from him was a pat on the back when he was feeling extra sentimental. I know he loved my mother fiercely, but never publicly. I want everyone to see how much I love Rose.

Rose's body visibly relaxes, a smile brightens her features. "Then I would like to make a demand."

My brow arches in question. "And what is that, little dragon?"

Rose bites her lip, a movement that shouldn't be seductive, but hardens me anyway. If she notices, she doesn't comment.

"Maybe it's silly, but I always had a vision of my wedding day. Nothing big or fancy, but..."

"It didn't involve getting married in private and me leaving directly after?" I finish.

"Well, yeah." She blushes. "And I know we have a billion other things to do and even though the Nephilim aren't an immediate threat right now, we still need to stay vigilant, but I was hoping...maybe..."

One day, my wife won't hesitate to advocate her wants and needs to me. She'll grow into the fierce queen I know she is.

"Rose, would you like a proper wedding? One that isn't in private. Where you can wear the dress of your dreams, surrounded by the friends you've made here?"

"Yes. More than anything." She gathers my hands in

hers, bringing them up to her lips. She places soft kisses on both. "I want to marry you again."

"And what of children?" The words topple out before I can stop them. It's not something we've talked about at great length, but there's no putting it off anymore. Confusion and fear color our bond and I hold Rose a little tighter.

I want children. As many as Rose will allow, but if she allows none, I've also made peace with that. As long as I have my queen.

"I didn't think I would ever want to be a mother. Or maybe I was afraid because those I love tend to leave me." My heart breaks for her and I want to assure her that I'm here. I won't ever leave her. She's my mate.

"But," she continues, running her hand up my chest in a distracting manner. "With you? I think motherhood could be a beautiful adventure."

Those words have never sounded sweeter. I gather her in my arms, pulling her closer. "I think after all we've been through; our kingdom deserves something to look forward to. What better event to start with than the wedding of their king and queen?"

The look of pure joy on my wife's face makes everything up to this moment worth it. I know then I would do it all over again. "A party of love, laughter, and tons of food."

"And then we can nest to get started on producing our heirs." I haven't forgotten that Rose and I were deprived of our nesting time. Days, even weeks, where we are consumed by each other without any interruptions.

"What's nesting?"

I smile wickedly. "I'll tell you all about it later." I don't feel like talking anymore. I want to get lost in Rose, so I kiss her.

My queen is home at last.

EPILOGUE

The Guardian

The first match proves fruitful, just as I expected it to be. Rose and Malix are what the mortals call star-crossed lovers. I sensed it immediately after meeting with them both, and although I hadn't been sure their love and devotion to one another would be enough to stop the Nephilim, I held on to hope.

Which paid off.

However, one match doesn't win wars, nor does it forgive me for the sins of my past. Maybe nothing will, but I'll chase the feeling of redemption for as long as it takes.

This is my fault after all.

I plagued my home, hurt people who trusted me, and sacrificed things that were never mine to begin with.

Immortality is truly a curse that allows endless possibilities for corruption and greed to take over. I had thought

I would be the exception, but my arrogance couldn't be contained until it was too late.

Now I am destined to fix the mistakes of my past, or risk losing the one being whom I love above all else. If I want her back, I need to succeed. If I don't, I will lose everything that I have ever held dear. Mescos and my mate.

Guardians can't survive without their mate.

Funny how I once relished in the title of Guardian. Yes, people still call me that, but they don't know what I did. They don't know that I'm no longer worthy of such an honorable title.

But she was. She's always been. This prestigious position was what she dreamed of doing ever since she was a little girl. We took the trials together, fought together, and became the fiercest guardians the academy produced.

I had everything. My mate. Immortality. A family.

But it hadn't been enough for me and now I'm paying the ultimate price.

My body aches, growing weaker by the day. My powers and abilities will continue to wane until I fix what I broke.

To add insult to injury, I can't fight these creatures. No, it would be too easy that way. The Divine Beings never make anything easy. I have to find mortals to do the work that I cannot. If more die because of me, well, that's just another name to add to the never-ending list.

The last few matches haven't worked. Maybe I'm losing my touch, but I remain positive that I found the right one this time. Tortured souls call out for other tortured souls.

Right on cue, as if summoned by my melancholic thoughts, a door slams, followed by hurried footsteps. They grow closer and closer until they reach my door. I wait.

This is typically the time where most of my matches leave because they no longer want to go through with it.

Who could blame them? I know firsthand what it feels like being ripped away from your family, even if it was your doing. The feeling is haunting and all-consuming.

I wait with bated breath. I don't know what I will do if this woman walks away. From everything I have observed after our first interaction, she's the perfect match for the alpha wolf.

Just when I think the match will turn and leave my porch, she knocks.

I let out a sigh, body sagging in relief. With one last glance around the room, I answer my door and meet the future Luna of the Alpha pack.

WANT MORE?

Want the "nesting" scene Malix so desperately wants with Rose? Make sure to join my newsletter to read all about their night together.

Sign up for my newsletter here!

ALSO BY TATI B. ALVAREZ

<u>Dawn Of Dasos</u>

1. The Ambrosia Throne

2. The Ambrosia Deception

3. The Ambrosia War - *Coming Soon*

<u>Grym Hollow</u>

1. The Dragon's Rose

2. *The Wolf's Mate - Coming Soon*

THANK YOU FOR READING!

I can't thank you enough for picking up my book. I hope you enjoyed it as much as I enjoyed writing it! If you did and are willing please consider leaving a review on your favorite book sites. This helps out small authors like me so much. Thank you for your continued support!

About the Author

Tati B. Alvarez lives in Austin, Texas with her family. She spends most days lost in her own head, creating stories. When she is not writing, you can find her vacationing at Disney World.